MAD

WOMAN

ROCKING

MAD WOMAN ROCKING

FARRAH B. MANDALA

the kind press

Cover Design: Nada Backovic
Internal design: Nicola Matthews, Nikki Jane Design
Edited by Georgia Jordan
Photos by iStock and Steve Johnson, eberhard grossgasteiger & George Rosema on Unsplash

Cataloguing-in-Publication entry is available from the National Library Australia.

NATIONAL
LIBRARY
OF AUSTRALIA

ISBN: 978-0-6452626-5-0
ISBN: 978-0-6452626-6-7 ebook

For Stacey Jayne

CONTENTS

PART ONE

PART TWO

PART THREE

PART FOUR

To all of it I have given my effort and my love.
In imagination I can feel the feather touch of snow flakes on
my face, feel the freezing water of the lagoon enfolding me,
on a hot summer day, and I would celebrate it all.

— Elyne Mitchell, *Towong Hill: Fifty Years on
an Upper Murray Cattle Station*

PART ONE

It's best to start at the beginning.
And all you do is follow the Yellow
Brick Road.

— Glinda the Good Witch, *The Wizard of Oz*

Enfolded by the Valley

The wild wind, dancing through the old elm trees, spoke of her bravery; it whispered signs of success. A woman who had always bitten off more than she could chew. Striving for brilliance.

SEASONS OF LIFE

Rosie drives along the road. A plane creates a long white streak across the sky. The radio plays.

I love this song.

Rosie turns up the volume.

Anne loves this song. My daughter has always introduced me to such great music and literature. Mumma always told her to turn it down. I guess she was an old lady. Anne's great-grandmother, my grandmother. She was old my whole life. All I knew as a mother.

The music plays loudly. Filling the car with sound.

Looking out the window, Rosie notices a willie wagtail dancing on the wire of a fence.

This song always reminds me of MJ. 'You Were Meant For Me'. Is it Jewel?

The words, it's like I wrote it about her.

Rosie looks across the paddock. A fox darts across the road.

Holy shit. I nearly hit the poor thing.

It runs with speed across the paddock and over the bank, out of sight. The sun shines through the window. Rosie dodges a pothole on the home road.

I should go for a walk up the hill. I need to write. Get something on the paper.

Tears fall down her face.

Rosie greets her faithful dog at the gate. They walk inside together.

Sitting at her desk, she opens the journal, finding her pen.

So much I've forgotten. So much I remember so clearly. I'll get it down before I lose it all. Just get it down on the paper.

Rosie picks up her pen and begins to write.

It was an ordinary July day. The middle of winter. I can't remember what I was wearing. I must have been cold. The afternoon. I can hear the clang of the gate. I just thought it was Polly coming to join us in the van. Ainsley and I were playing cards. Polly's face. Her face. I remember her face. Polly told me. She was crying. Then those words. A crack in time. There is before those words. Then there is after. A crack that tore my life apart. I need to tell you something, she said. We stepped out of the caravan. MJ has been killed in a plane accident. Were they the words? Were those the exact words? I don't know now.

Rosie's hands tremble. The words bleed onto the paper.

I fell to the ground. No. I should have. I should have. No. Disbelief washed over me. A sick feeling. I wanted to vomit. I couldn't cry. I couldn't cry. The world was washed in grey. The colour drained from the world. I can't remember what happened next. All I wanted was her. All I wanted was to say sorry. To rewind. To stop her stepping on that plane.

Rosie cries. Rosie cries the tears that wouldn't come that day. Rosie puts down the pen.

That's enough. I'll get some gardening done.

Rosie walks along the slate path. The leaves of the grand gingko tree in her garden are changing, turning a vibrant yellow and falling slowly from the branches; creating a carpet, wet underfoot. Bending down, she begins pulling out weeds. She thinks of many autumns before. They often merge but seem distinctly different, especially as she reads through the pages of her journals.

'What are you doing, Nanny?' Rosie hears as she stands up. Glancing around, she sees Billy walking down the path towards her, his golden hair illuminated in the sunlight. A large, dusty box nestled in his arms.

'Hello, darling. I'm just mucking around, pulling a few of these mongrel weeds out. What have you got there?'

'I found this old box in the shed at home. I can't get it open.'

'Didn't you ask Dad?'

'Nah, he tells me not to go in there, to stay out of the junk, but I was looking for a new nesting box for the chook pen. But look at it, I snuck it over in my bag. Can you help me get it open?'

'Sure, darling.' Wiping her hands on her trousers and rolling her eyes, Rosie knows she can't say no to Billy, as much as she tries.

'Bring it into the laundry. We don't want dust and shit everywhere inside.'

Pulling an old, rusty box down from the shelf, she finds a strong, blunt knife to jam under the lid and prise it open. Billy holds on to the end of the box.

'It's a tough old bugger.'

The box finally gives way, and dust spills into the air.

'Wow, look at that.' Billy jumps with excitement. 'It might have treasure, money maybe.'

'I wouldn't get too excited, sweetheart. Just hold, hold your horses.'

'Open it—I bet ya it's like a million dollars,' Billy says as he jumps on the spot.

As the box opens, a lining of faded tissue paper sits snuggly on the top. Rosie lifts it gently to reveal its contents. String firmly holds a bunch of letters. Rosie carefully lifts them out, so gently, like handling a newborn kitten. Handing the letters to Billy, Rosie picks up the brooch underneath. She rolls it in her hand momentarily, then slips it in her pocket.

'Let's open them,' Billy says.

'Slow down, sweetheart. No rush, untie it gently.'

Rosie gets a cloth and wipes the bottom of the box. Carved into the bottom is a name.

'What does it say, Nanny?'

'It says Daisy, my mother's name. This must be my mother's box. What do the letters say?' Rosie glances over at Billy.

They begin to open them. Dogs barking at the dairy breaks their concentration.

'Oh no, I can hear Dad's ute. I better go. I don't want him to kick my arse. Let's hide them, I'll be back tomorrow. Don't open them, Nanny, wait for me.'

Billy puts the pile back in the box. Racing down the veranda, ducking under the wisteria draping down from the archway, Billy glances back and gives her the thumbs up. Grinning, Rosie winks. Sneaking a glance, she notices the name on the back of the pile: Tina. She opens the cupboard, puts the box on the top shelf, then closes it.

We will look at it tomorrow. Bloody Billy—he'll be the death of me. Digging out junk from the shed. Probably some pen pal Daisy had. I'll wait for Billy to come back to look at them. Better get that walk in before it gets too late.

Setting off on her walk, she reflects how each year, each season is unique—in rainfall, events, farm work—but always surrounded by her mountains. Enfolded by her valley. The autumn her daughter was born was cold and wet, and winter winds seemed to arrive early that year, with the snow on the mountains.

How the years have quickly slipped away.

Rosie ruminates while remembering those first weeks of motherhood, still fresh in her mind.

It has never left me, the feeling of uncertainty, vulnerability and overwhelming joy, of discovering a new love never experienced before.

This year is dry, with bright, warm, sunny days. The nights are cold and the entire valley sleeps soundly, seeking warmth.

Rosie opens the old, heavy gate by lifting it slightly and pushing it with the weight of her hip. She knows each gate on the farm and each necessary trick. She thinks about the time she was racing down the hill in the old land rover.

Unable to stop it. The breaks had failed. MJ screaming. I tried to keep my cool. Smashing into the gate. One of the good gates on the farm. It swinging right around, nearly even with the fence. They were the early days. That gate has long been replaced.

It has been a long time since she ventured beyond her garden and took this walk, but today, the sun has inviting warmth.

It will be good for my poor old knees to get out and exercise.

Picking up a stick, she pulls some small branches from it and holds it tightly.

This little fella will serve as a pretty good walking stick, I reckon.

Each step she takes is slow and purposeful as she walks up the gradual incline; they call this the 'Hill Paddock'. Each paddock has a name, a purpose, a routine; ploughing, planting, harvesting and harrowing. Her intimate knowledge of this land is as though the paddocks are a patchwork quilt she has made by hand; she knows each intricate stitch. This is the tapestry of her life. This land holds her stories, her memories, regrets, sorrows, tears, laughter, her hopes and her dreams. This valley enfolds her, in good times and in bad.

When she arrives at the dry gully, she decides to sit for a moment on a big, mossy rock under the shade of a stringy bark tree. Watching a flock of cockies feeding under the trees lining the home road, she ponders how quiet they are as they busily feast.

I remember that day the four of us went shooting cockies. Pa had had a gutful of them destroying the crop. He gave us a quick practice at the dairy. Rattled over the creek in the land rover. MJ clinging to the gun like it was about to explode any minute. We all took it in turns. Polly and Ainsley, they got sick of it after a while and went and threw rocks in the creek. MJ was good, a great shot. She didn't let a single one rest on that paddock. That loud gunshot would scare them off. Different times. They get a nice feast these days.

A newly born foal prances and nudges her mother. The sight is reminiscent of the playfulness of her own children as toddlers, her grandchildren, whom she wishes could visit more. Before she allows loneliness to enfold her, the mountain calls. Grabbing her stick, she keeps slowly moving.

Walking at a steady pace down the track, dry and dusty, clearly worn from countless cows' hooves over many years, she breathes in the cool, quenching freshness of the mountain air. Through another gate. Untwisting the thick wire, she notices the worn and weathered gatepost, reminding her of her reflection in the mirror. Its varying shades of grey are like her aging hair. She ponders how all things, with time, show age.

I guess there's beauty in conveying what we have endured. I could only imagine all this gatepost has been beaten by: the harsh Australian summer sun, the unrelenting fog and frosts in the depths of winter, pelting rain and all the unavoidable brutalities of the seasons.

Walking on, Rosie admires the big red gums.

I love all the different colours, textures; how big and grand they are.

I know them all so well, like old friends. Beautiful things. Permanent. Enduring. How slowly and strongly they grow.

As she moves on, the bush becomes thicker and the track narrows. It gets steep and Rosie leans on her stick, steading herself.

I could sprint up this hill once upon a time. MJ and I had a race once. I'm sure she'd won. Or better still, ride up over the ridge on Trixie. But that was a lifetime ago now.

Wiping the sweat from her brow, Rosie stops momentarily and has a drink from her water bottle.

I'm pleased I decided to bring this bloody thing with me now. This bastard climb seems harder than I remember. As with most things these days, it is a little harder and slower.

Following the single track that goes along the edge of the ridge, she pushes aside the branches that overhang the path like a crocheted blanket. Walking down through a dried-up gully, she watches each step taken and makes sure she is stable before taking another.

That's all I need, a broken leg at my age. Slow down, you old fool. We've had our fair share of broken bones over the years. This track has become quite overgrown since I was here last.

Disappointed there is no water running, Rosie remembers times when the fresh water trickled down over the rocks.

I would get off Trixie and drink the fresh water, straight from the mountain. Untouched. Pure.

Climbing carefully over the bank, she sighs with relief.

There it is, what I've been longing to see.

The gully shows signs of water, carving a path, digging and moulding the land like a sculptor.

I still remember the night this gully got washed out with a big landslide. God, it only feels like yesterday. Humble gully. Sand, rock, trees, all succumbing to the force of nature. Water rushing down the hill.

Unstoppable. Filled with ferocity. Several inches of rain had fallen in one night. We could hear the roar of the water. The kids pestered us to see it. What a spectacular sight, when we first saw it. We were awe-struck by nature's great power and force—how it had excavated a big gully that once contained only a trickle.

She looks up and sees that bare ground is now covered. With the inevitable passing of time, the grass, trees and moss found a home and the landslide is a distant memory. Eyes filled with tears, Rosie presses on.

She strolls gratefully downhill into a lush, grassy clearing.

I have always loved this natural opening.

A section between the trees frames a picture of the valley and town. Taking the scene in with a deep breath, she proceeds along the track—a worn track where four-wheel drives have been, on their way to spray blackberries or round up cattle. Rosie is filled with a deep sense of pride.

Tom still works this land, the land my grandparents and great-grandparents had worked. Hopefully one day Billy. Maybe my life has had some purpose. I have a special relationship with this land. It has nurtured us and we have nurtured it.

The texture of the dry grass beneath her feet is firm and familiar. The call of magpies, smell of eucalypt, crickets humming, a song of sorrow, distant caw of crows, searching to feed on misfortune. She is momentarily lost in the song of the bush. Reminded of death, an important part of the cycle of life. She instinctively knows this, but Rosie still feels no comfort in that simple knowledge, no comfort for her beloved, taken too soon. Despite the grief and tragedy threaded through the many blessings of her life, she knows only survival. The cycles and seasons of the valley are intricately interconnected and continue to go on; like the rising and falling of the sun, life must simply go on.

The familiar track brings forth memories of a time when life was chaotic, with children, farming and trying to keep on top of the endless work.

I had dreamt of, envisaged, yearned for this precious time in my life. Time to rest. How ironic. Now I miss those days. When there was a messy, busy house filled with laughter, excitement, tears, chatter and warmth.

Admiring the brown butterflies that move about the trees, she thinks of how profoundly the butterfly transforms itself and how she too has transformed several times in her humble life. Each change and season has brought her strength and wisdom; an understanding not to fight against the currents of life but to float with the flow of the water. Like the life-giving water from the mountains, she learnt long ago to simply surrender to time, change and seasons. Each season brings its own joys, its own blessings, like the beauty of the snow-covered mountains in winter, the colour palette of the deciduous trees in autumn, the warmth of the sun in summer and spring's flowers in her garden.

After slowly walking down the track, lost in her thoughts, she makes it back to the gate.

I'm glad I came out today. What do they say? If you don't use it, ya lose it.

Embracing the beauty surrounding her, in the corner of her eye she notices the most amazing sight. Turning around and casting her eyes up, she is engrossed by two wedge-tailed eagles flying above the ridges of the mountain, circling and floating with wondrous grace. Taking the spectacle in, she drinks in the moment as if it's thirst-quenching water from the mountain.

I love these big birds of prey. I'm always impressed by their beauty every time I see them elegantly fly. I wish I could rest all day and just watch them.

Mesmerised. The call to light the fire beckons her as the sun sits low on the horizon. A cold autumn night lies ahead.

Rosie curiously peers near the track to check if the old wombat still uses his burrow, and the fresh dirt gives her a welcomed answer. Calm and peace dance around her as she walks home, counting the sheep with their lambs. Passing the big red gums, Rosie ventures down the paddock to the mare and her foal. She puts her hand slowly through the fence, and the filly—clothed in patches of chestnut and white—inquisitively comes closer to smell her hand. The filly's big bright eyes, framed with her long lashes, are vibrant and curious. Joy washes over Rosie as she feels hope for the future in the foal's gentle touch.

Reaching the bottom of the Hill Paddock, Rosie unties the remaining gate. Nearly home, she sees the silhouette of her loyal old dog, waiting for her patiently at the front gate. The sight of a flock of galahs flying overhead permeates her thoughts; her attention is drawn to the flood of grey and pink cast across the pale sky.

They are majestic. I love this land. This valley. These simple pleasures touch me so deeply, even after all these years.

Placing carefully chosen feet, she crosses the ramp, walks past the dairy as the sweet smell of manure comforts her. She passes the familiar image of the rust-stained shed leaning. Chained dogs bark. Chickens freely roam, pecking purposefully as they go. She admires the solid meat house built by hand, still standing strong.

As Rosie waltzes up the track to the house, she hears the creek flowing beyond the hum of the dairy. The kookaburra perched on the fence post swivels its head as she notices a bright-orange fox dart down over the ridge, into the valley. It races across the paddock, disappearing into a sea of tussocks.

Passing her front garden, she notices many weeds to be pulled out but admires the myriad of flowers blooming. She considers the amount of mulching and pruning to be done before the imminent winter arrives.

Reaching the front gate, she affectionately greets her old dog. They pass the woodshed, where she has killed several snakes, found some buried newly-born kittens and spent hours filling and emptying a boundless woodpile. It slants a little these days but still keeps the wood dry. With her old dog's tail wagging, they waddle inside together.

As she pours the boiling water into her stained teacup, through lace curtains she sees the sun setting outside her kitchen window. She carefully carries her full cup outside and sits on her old wooden chair, which is covered in the fox fur that she had tanned so long ago. It is still so thick, rich in vibrant orange and red colours. The image of Tom's face when he so proudly gave it to her, his prized kill, is in the centre of her mind. An image of youth and innocence.

He has no time for shooting these days—there's always work to be done.

She sighs as she sits on her old chair on the side of the hill, and the old dog tenderly kisses her hand with his wet nose. Her legs are tired from the walk; she is happy to sit and rest. In that moment, she is content and grateful for her faithful companion. Grateful for the brilliant colours painted across the evening sky.

Thank you, God, for all the seasons of my life.

The cool evening breeze whispers through the old elm trees. As she sips the warm, soothing tea, she soaks in the last remnants of light from the setting sun, sparkling like fairy lights across the paddocks, illuminating the weeds and dry grass.

I'm pleased with all I have achieved in my humble life. Is that it? I wonder if there's more. Is there more for me to do before my time is up?

Thinking of all the happiness life in this valley has brought her, along with the tragedy she has endured, she is thankful for it all.

Watching the light dance as it begins fading into night, Rosie lets herself be enfolded by the beauty of the valley she so deeply loves.

Home Amongst the Woods

Every time
I've fallen apart
I've had to start
Building
Building a new castle
A home amongst the woods

Every time
I build
A grander castle I build

Every time
I fall
I rise
A little higher
Leads me down
A path
To my home amongst the woods

Every time
I'm lost
I find a treasure buried
In the rubble
On the long road home
Home amongst the woods

Every time
I spin out of control
I find the strength to dance
In sunshine
In rain
On my way home
Home amongst the woods

Every time
I lose
I find
A gift
Amongst the trees
That leads me home
Home amongst the woods

THUNDER AND LIGHTNING

The brooch catches the sunlight, resting on Rosie's desk. She picks it up and admires its colour, the different shades of purple, as she moves it rhythmically in her hand. She places it on top of a doily and makes her way out to the garage. Packing the back of the ute, Rosie arranges it like a puzzle, tightly packing everything to avoid movement or damage.

It has been a while since she has visited them. It is a large delivery: a painting, plants, fresh fruit and vegetables, clean empty jars and bags of dry cow manure. Reversing out of the driveway, she smiles as her faithful dog makes himself comfortable in a sunny position to wait patiently for her return. The silhouette of the magnolia tree catches her eye.

Indicating, she checks for cars before turning onto the back road.

I'm looking forward to getting out for the day. Tilly and Ash always provide some entertainment. I wonder if they'll be at each other. Such a volatile relationship, lots of blues over the years. It's a wonder they've stayed together all these years. As Mumma would say, 'Saves two other poor bastards.' God, I miss Mumma and her way with words. I really should start writing them down, so they're not lost forever.

I wonder if Billy will be over later to look through those letters. I was so tempted last night to have a look through them, but I will keep my word. The boy, the sweet boy looks straight through me if I try to lie. Just like Lottie used to.

Slowing down at the intersection, she puts on her indicator, and looks both ways. An old ute drives past, and she lifts one finger to wave. He returns the gesture, an older man with a floppy hat.

I wonder who that old fella was. I didn't recognise him, which is surprising. I thought I knew most people in the valley. I guess I don't get out much these days.

Rosie drives at a steady pace so she can inspect the farms and houses as she goes. Searching for change. Reaching another intersection, she turns left and heads towards the mountains. The road bends and coils like the undulating hills. The paddocks have a green tinge. She passes dairy farms with black-and-white cows scattered through the pastures. A rattle in the back makes her check in her rear-view mirror.

Oh shit, I hope I packed that stuff properly; it really should have rope on it. She'll be right. Shouldn't be any coppers out this way.

The valley narrows as she gets closer to the hills; the bush encroaches as the cleared land decreases. Driving past Wally's place, slowing down, dropping into a lower gear, she strains her neck to look back to catch sight of him, but she can't see any sign of him.

I should call in and see how he is. The old bugger is nearly bloody a hundred. He really shouldn't be living there on his own still. If only those useless sons of his gave a shit.

She feels an obligation to check on him and promises herself she will pay a visit soon, especially after all the years he had worked for her grandparents, breaking in horses, moving stock, fencing, whatever needed to be done. She thinks of Wally, when he was younger, running Trixie around the yard.

I watched in awe. His skill to tame and teach a strong beast to obey. Running an empty hessian bag over her. Patting and talking to her. He had an unspoken bond with and understanding of horses. Mutual admiration. Love. I'll never forget the respect he displayed to the animals. I guess

I always tried to take a leaf out of his book when I cared for animals. Rearing calves. Milking cows.

Rosie drives around a tight bend and over an old, narrow bridge, then turns up a dirt track. Trying to avoid the strewn potholes, she hits one and bounces in her seat.

Oh, shit. The old ute's suspension is buggered.

The trees are thick along the side of the road. Small patches reveal clearings. A few houses are hidden away. She turns onto the track, over the ramp that leads to Tilly and Ash's place. Driving over a slight incline, Rosie sees their small farm, hidden beneath the huge mountains. Their own slice of paradise. She sees the goats feeding in their paddock, then spots Tilly's short blonde hair in the garden as she parks at the front gate. Tilly walks over to her while wiping her dirty hands on her bright pink overalls. She has a wide smile, her sparkling green eyes shine as she squints and puts a hand on her brow to block the sun. Her singlet reveals her skinny arms, tanned from the sun and covered in a tapestry of tattoos; Rosie looks at the line of birds that reach up along her neck and behind her ear.

'G'day, my girl,' Rosie says as she climbs out of the ute. Warmth fills her, feeling Tilly's presence.

'Look at this big load,' Tilly says as she inspects all the gifts. Her golden hair glistens. 'Aw, thanks, darl.' Tilly's warmth and enthusiasm is apparent as she wipes her forehead with the back of her dirty arm.

Kissing Tilly on the cheek, Rosie responds, 'You're welcome, darling. It's been a while, so I thought I better not come empty handed.' She gives her a wink.

They begin unloading the ute. 'Where's Ash?' Rosie queries.

Tilly flashes Rosie her typical cheeky, big grin. 'She's down at the yards, fuckin' round with that bloody stallion—ya know that wild thoroughbred we got off Stapleton's last winter?'

'Aw yeah, he must have grown since I've seen 'im,' Rosie responds.

'He has. A big, strong bastard—bloody dangerous if you ask me. But you know what Ash is like, fucking bull-headed 'bout everything. She's determined to get on the big mongrel.' Tilly continues to unload.

'She hasn't got on him yet?' Rosie says with surprise.

'Nah, he's as mad as a cut snake, but she reckons she's makin' progress. If I had my way, he would've been in a truck and down the road long ago. But ya know, whatever keeps her happy and off my case.'

'Anything for a quiet life, lovey, is the way to go.' Rosie strains to lift the large bag of cow manure off the back of the ute and places it against the fence. Admiring the garden—a maze of garden beds, constructed with a plethora of materials, from corrugated iron to old bed frames— Rosie recognises a section of an old picket fence. She's fascinated by the bits of string, poly pipe, netting and decorations hanging everywhere— how they keep it intact like a tangled spider web.

It's our Tilly to a T.

'Let's go in and have a cuppa,' Tilly says, motioning her head towards the house. 'We'll get this beauty inside.' She admires the painting in her hands. 'We'll go down and see Ash, after we have a cuppa first.'

They walk up the wooden steps onto the veranda and through the wooden door; Rosie notices the dark-green paint is peeling. The light shimmers as it comes through the orange-stained glass. She takes her boots off and pulls her socks up before taking a seat at the table. Lavender and patchouli fill the room as a candle burns in the corner. Tilly fills up the kettle and turns it on to boil. She sets out two cups and places tea bags in them. 'Do you have sugar?' Tilly asks.

'Nah, I'm sweet enough,' Rosie replies. A white cat moves around her feet, caressing her legs and swishing its tail in a slow and rhythmic dance. Affectionately patting her, Rosie says in a sweet voice, like talking to a child, 'Hello, Georgie girl, you always know you'll get a pat out of me, don't ya?'

Tilly opens her pouch of tobacco and pulls out her papers; she fills the paper with tobacco and begins to roll a smoke while she waits for the kettle to boil.

Looking around the room, Rosie appreciates the eclectic mix of furniture, an upholstered chair draped with bright, colourful clothing. She notices the shape and colour of the large, sprawling houseplant in the corner. Large lamps hang from the ceiling.

They must use those oil lamps at night, being off the grid and reliant on that solar power they have.

Piles of books are stacked sporadically throughout the room. A wooden cabinet is covered in dried flowers in vases, jewellery and seashells—a beautiful chaotic order to it all. The light is caught by a crystal hanging in the window. Rosie notices a wind chime beside it; everywhere she looks there is more to see. Observing several of her paintings on the wall, she remembers Tilly as a young girl, coming into her studio, admiring her paintings.

She has been collecting them ever since. I remember her always keeping up with the boys. Will and his mates, partying hard. Will telling me that time, 'Tilly isn't into dudes, Mum, ya know, like some chicks are like that.' I've always admired her for knowing who she is. So bloody strong in her convictions. Always living life true to herself.

'Have you seen Wally lately?' Rosie asks as she reaches down to caress the cat's elongated back.

'We saw him last week.' Tilly puts some clean cups on the shelf. 'He came up to give Ash a hand with Eckie; he reckons he's coming along nicely. Despite the fact he's still a fucking mad stallion. A bloody wild spirit. Wally reckons Ash can tame him, so I guess, if anyone knows, it's our Wally.' Tilly fills the cups with boiling water and adds a dash of cold water from the tap. 'Let's go out the back into the sun, so I can have a smoke.'

'Sounds good, lovey.' Rosie rises from her seat.

They walk down the hallway; it is filled with colour and photos. Walking through the laundry, Rosie admires the old cement wash tub. A bar of their organic handmade soap rests comfortably on the side. Rosie watches her step as they walk down the ramp into a gravelled area. In the centre, a long table made from large logs stacked together is bathed in warm sunshine. Sitting opposite Tilly, she studies the toilet wall behind her, covered in rusted metals arranged like an art gallery display. Looking through the archway, she sees a small garden bed with a large sculpture in the centre. 'Is that one of Stella's artworks?' Rosie asks as she points towards it.

Tilly turns around. 'Yeah, she gave it to us in exchange for some skin products. Isn't it fucking amazing! She's so talented, that girl. She calls it *Call of the Lovers*,' she says, singing the name.

Looking closer, Rosie sees the metals intertwined at the top; the strands of metal curve over and greet each other. At the base, they are a mass of tangle, they are one. It evokes memories of Tilly during the time after Rosie lost her son.

Tilly coming to our house. Caring for me. Cleaning the house. Cooking. Helping Blake on the farm.

Waves of emotion, a mix of sadness and gratitude, crash on top of her. Rosie sips her tea, trying to shake off these intense feelings.

'She is a unique talent, how she does it. It amazes me. So clever.' Thirsty, Rosie sips from her teacup as her skin soaks the sun in.

Tilly drags on her cigarette. 'I saw Bobby is havin' another kid.'

'Really? How many will that be now?'

'I think number four. She just keeps spittin' 'em out.'

'What about Max? Any news on him?'

'Last I heard, he was in jail. Too many drugs, I think. Getting into the hard gear. Remember he went up the coast, he was in that accident? I think it fucked him up a fair bit. He's never really been the same since.' Tilly drags deeply on her cigarette.

Rosie shakes her head in response. 'You were all such a good group of kids, back in the day.' She gets up, drinks the last of her tea and says, 'Let's go down and check out this horse.'

Tilly puts her cigarette out in the black, round ashtray.

'Righto. Leave ya cup 'ere,' Tilly instructs. They begin to follow the path down the hill. Seeing the round yards, Rosie can hear the rhythmic pounding of the stallion's hooves as he runs around the perimeter. Ash is in the centre of the yards, holding a thin rope. As they get closer, Rosie can see Ash's dark, long plaited hair; her tight jeans reveal her muscular legs. The horse canters around the yard, his nostrils moving in and out as the air is forced through his lungs.

As they approach the yards, Ash glances at them with her dark brown eyes, whilst remaining fixated on the horse. Moving towards them, Ash lets the stallion break its circuit. She swings the rope over her broad, sun-soaked shoulders. Her walk is distinctive. Proud.

Ash is like no other woman I've ever met. Quiet, yet charismatic. Not like Tilly, in her own unique, unassuming way.

'Hey, Ash,' Rosie says. 'He's looking good. Grown a lot since I saw him last.'

'Yeah, he's coming along nicely. He's a bit of a wild spirit. Taking my time with him. He is still a bit hesitant to trust me, but we'll get there.'

Tilly passes Ash some water through the fence. They look at each other. Their connection palpable.

'I might let him out now. That's enough for one day.' Ash unlatches the gate.

They watch Ash open the gate and the stallion, rich chestnut colour glazed by perspiration, races through it.

Look at his strong legs. His speed. He moves with such determination.

Running out into the paddock, he lowers his head and kicks out. They watch, mesmerised by his beauty as he canters down the paddock.

'Such power and beauty,' Rosie says out aloud to no one in particular. She pauses for a while, watching him. 'What do you call him, again?'

'Eckhart is his name,' Tilly replies. 'I call him Eckie and Ash calls him Hart.'

A strong woman. Tenaciously trying to tame the wild.

Rosie watches Ash climb the fence with energy and ease; her strong arms pull her up, and she leaps down with agility. Ash throws her arm around Tilly's shoulder as they begin to walk back to the house. Rosie admires the rows of herbs in the long, raised garden beds lining the path as the three of them walk. She turns to catch one last glimpse of the stallion. Looking across the paddock to his figure in the distance, she feels his spirit, strong and wild like thunder and lighting.

TREASURE

Leaping Soul

My soul leaps
Bursts, bounds
Filled with words
Creativity
Soul seeks connection

How did they take you?
Drifting, floating
Swirling out of this world
Into the next

Hot wind sweeping
Towards my loves
Too far to touch
Run for safety

Leave books, possessions
Behind to burn

Keep my babies safe
Where do you reside?
Floating amid clouds
Transported to another
Place and time

How my heart has settled
Since that cold July day
Embraced my craziness
The fruits of my insanity

When will the stars, moon align
Be at peace
With my leaping soul

Daylight creeps softly into her bedroom. Rosie rests her tired eyes, trying to delay the arrival of the morning. She stretches, daydreaming a day without plans lies ahead of her. The kookaburras sing their morning song, breaking her thoughts and filling her with abundant energy. A burning desire to explore. Hearing her dog shuffling from his bed, she gets up and lets him out.

'There you go, sweetheart. Go out to the toilet.' Rosie props the door open and watches him waddle out.

Loading the washing machine, Rosie considers different places to visit and see; then a perfect place comes to mind.

The gate makes its familiar sound as it slams shut. Rosie adds detergent and presses start on the washing machine. Taking a deep breath, she looks up at the old hooks hanging from the ceiling of the old laundry.

That'd be Billy boy now, ready to check this box out.

'Nanny, I'm back. Sorry I couldn't come over yesterday. Jimmy was over.'

'Yeah, no worries, darling. I forgot about that. I did know he was coming over, anyway.'

'Do you always have to run everywhere? For heaven sake, just slow down. What's your father doing?'

'He's straining a fence up in the Hill Paddock. A branch fell on it. He won't be long, so we better have a look.'

'Alright, let's have a quick squiz.'

Rosie lifts the box out. She carefully takes out the letters and hands them to Billy.

'Be gentle, remember, they are very old and fragile, like me. I don't want them ruined.'

'Alright, alright. Stop stressin', Nanny.' A cheeky grin is plastered on Billy's face. Rosie feels his excitement.

Rosie soaks an old towel in the water of the large cement wash trough in the laundry. The cloth cleans the layer of dust from the box, revealing a varnished wood grain. Admiring the craftsmanship, she rinses the cloth and gives it a further wash.

'What do they say?' Rosie asks Billy, watching him with the letters out the corner of her eye.

'They are from someone called Tina, Tina Butler. I can't really read the writing—it's like all squiggly and old fashioned. Her address says London. Did Daisy have a friend from London?'

'Yeah, I guess so, I don't know. I might have to ask Aunt Phoebe or someone.'

The barking dogs interrupt their inspection.

'That'll be Dad. Quick, Nanny, give it here.'

Taking the box from her, Billy slips the letters inside and returns them to the safety of the cupboard.

'Alright, darling, give me a quick hug,' Rosie says.

They embrace quickly, before Billy runs along the veranda and out the gate, yelling, 'Love ya!'

'Love ya, sweetheart!' Rosie responds, her hands firmly on her hips. She squeezes out the cloth and hangs it on the edge of the trough. She dries her hands on a towel before she moves inside.

Stoking up the fire, she makes sure her old dog will be comfortable for a few hours. Fluffing up his bed and stroking his fur, she instructs him to stay, as he lays his head down with acknowledgement.

Still so obedient and intelligent, after all these years. You poor old fella.

A warm smile wraps across her face as she places her camera and sketchpad in her cane basket. Carrying the basket through the front door, Rosie grabs the brass handle of the door, worn smooth from touch, and closes it gently behind her. She admires the spreading pansies lining the path from the veranda to the front gate. She pulls out a few weeds from the wheelbarrow planted with bulbs as she walks through the gate, stopping for a moment to breathe in the fresh air and the scene of the mountain before her.

Its grandeur still amazes me. When I take the time to stop and appreciate it.

As Rosie drives, she remembers the many times she has been to this spot before. She thinks about a time she went there with the kids.

We had a picnic and the kids explored. Anne must have been about ten … that would have made Tom seven, and Will three.

The memories of the day fill her mind; images of Will climbing a tree, Tom patiently and protectively watching him. Anne collecting flowers and practising handstands. Rosie tries to remember whether it was school holidays or just the weekend, but the details evade her.

How time has slipped away from me. It still takes a lot for me to accept. When I was younger, I thought the kids would never grow up. I would never grow old. Those days would last forever.

Storing her precious memories like valuable treasure, she says a quiet prayer.

Please don't let my mind fade, my memories be lost.

Driving through the section lined with thick, tall pine trees, she turns off the main road up a dirt track. Rosie puts the ute into a lower gear, and the engine groans. It has been years since she was here; she turns down another dirt road, hoping it's the right one from memory. As she continues, she knows it is the right track because she sees the group of large trees in the distance. The lush grass is cleared and mowed. She parks her ute under the shade of the trees. A strong memory comes flooding back to her.

The first time I came here, I must have been young. Just Mumma and me. We came with bags and small spades to dig up daffodil bulbs.

Rosie smiles. The golden glow of the sunlight through the window warms her face.

Mumma had clever and often resourceful ways of collecting plants. She would happily take cuttings of things she liked. Mumma was also generous with her own plants, giving friends and family many plants from her garden. It was a fun day, the two of us selecting bulbs and filling the bags. Daffodils that still flower in my garden each year. They fill the front garden.

Climbing out of the ute, Rosie puts her camera around her neck. Looking up at the tall trees, she notices some are changing colour.

As she begins wandering around the garden and taking photos, she discovers mushrooms, treasures hidden within the thick mulch from fallen leaves. As she kneels down to capture their unique red-and-white clothing, moisture dampens the knee of her trousers. The smell of rotting leaves wafts through the air. Dappled light weaves its way through the trees' canopy. An old tank stand, still standing tall, provides a contrast to the trees. Placing the remains of a brick chimney in the corner of the photograph, she tries to capture the colour and delicate sprawl of a lone Japanese maple. Escaping the shade, she stands in the small section of sun, searching for ideas. Rosie makes her way around the garden.

It is a lost world. Imagine a family living here. Imagine what the old house must have looked like. Children playing. A family planting these trees. These trees still flourishing, though now abandoned.

Rosie looks up, admiring them.

Sitting in the shade, she begins drawing. Trying to replicate the shape of the trees; old oaks with circular wounds from lost limbs. Admiring a gum tree, she studies it intently; its thick, dark, sap-drenched bark—a mixture of red, brown and black—like strong armour. The sun announces itself as it bursts through the clouds. It makes the trees look weathered and textured, and creates distinctive shadows on the ground.

Rosie sits and marvels at the birds eating acorns, scattered across the ground like a bumpy carpet. The feeding king parrots are green with orange breasts. The crackling sound of their chewing is the soundtrack to her thoughts. Rosie tries to be as quiet as possible so she can watch them, undisturbed, feeding and foraging. Rosellas, painted rich red and striking blue, fly down to the ground to get their fair share of seeds. A pair of kookaburras, sitting sternly in a tree, attentively watch the activity.

Rosie listens intently to the sweet chirping song of the birds; it's soothing to her soul. Admiring the ground littered, covered in discarded acorn shells from the oak trees, she casts her gaze up to rosellas walking on a branch, it swaying under their weight. She's drawn to a kookaburra flying up into the shelter of the tree carrying a worm or lizard—it's hard to decipher. A leaf gracefully falls from a tree. The parrots come closer, not noticing her. A king parrot is perched on an old, dilapidated fence, balancing on the remnants. What remains. What has survived the weather. What time has not rotted away, or destroyed. What has not decayed.

The parrots pick up the seeds with their feet and eat them like a baby with clumsy fingers. Mess falling all around them, they remain unperturbed and content, feeding in the warmth of the sunshine. A large group gathers as Rosie tries to remain invisible and take some photos. She notices some multicoloured parrots with the same shape as a rosella.

But these have spotted feathers. I wonder what they are.

Rosie feels a chill in the air and the call of dusk.

I better get going.

She dusts herself off, her sudden movement sending the foraging birds into the trees for shelter.

Driving the back road on the way home, Rosie stops on the way. She climbs out with her camera and begins to take photos of an old shed standing lonely in the paddock.

I love the rust. The colour. The signs of age and survival. The way they were designed and built. Countless times, I've driven past it. Always noticing it and appreciating its beauty. I'm glad today I finally decided to stop and take some photos.

Ideas for a painting start forming in her mind. Surging inspiration pulsates through her.

Rosie parks the ute in its cleared spot in the garage and climbs out; she slams the old door. She walks around the back via the veranda, collecting a large piece of red gum from the wheelbarrow before going inside. Taking her boots off, she closes the door behind her with her elbow. She places her basket on the end of the long kitchen table. She carries the wood to the fire and gently places it on the red bricks in front of the golden glow. Sitting in her armchair with a groan of relief, Rosie lovingly greets her old dog. She feels the kiss of his wet nose from the place she left him. His tail wagging, he is always so happy to see her. It fills her with warmth.

My most valuable companion, my friend. Delight. My treasure.

Leaning into the chair, she stretches her back, then leans over and picks up one of the journals from the cardboard box.

I really need to start getting all this sorted.

The journal is old, falling apart; the cover is filled with a mixture of pastel flowers.

This is my very first journal, I think. This must have been the one I started when I broke my leg.

Skimming through some poems, she admires the illustrations and decorations.

God, I've been writing poetry for a long time.

Rosie goes back to the start, reading the date below the poem.

Twenty-sixth of January 1961; this must be my very first poem.

The poem is handwritten in her juvenile text; there is a drawing of water, trees and a bridge. Surrounding the poem are colourful pictures of butterflies and birds. As she reads it, an image of her sitting on her bed, leaning against the wall, writing, comes to mind.

Thank You, Lord

I sit under a lush palm tree
And watch the fish swim with glee

I see the reflection in the glassy blue waters of the gentle aqua sky
And the tower that stretches up so high

As I look at nature I say to the Lord
Thank you for things great and small
Thank you Lord, for things short and tall

'Cause I like the way you've created Earth, Lord
Thank you for letting me come aboard.

Looking at the poem, the drawings and the box full of journals, she pulls them out and spreads them out over the floor. Rosie ponders how poetry and art have threaded their way through her life. A deep yearning burns inside her.

I wish I could share this with the world. Instead of hiding it away in boxes to collect dust and probably one day rot. What will become of it all when I go?

Ruminating, Rosie takes a deep breath and rubs her face. She digs dirt from under her nails.

I've got to get my arse into gear and sort it out. I should clean out under that bed. Get rid of some of that junk while I'm at it. I should make a start now.

Rosie lifts herself with her hand pushing her up. There's a knock at the door.

That's weird. It's not often someone comes to the front door. I hope there isn't a cow on the road. That's all Tom needs.

Moving to the door, she steps over the piles of scattered journals and walks through the dark hallway. The pronounced silhouette of a man reveals itself in the doorway, behind the screen door. As she gets closer, the figure comes to life as the light exposes his facial features. Opening the door, her heart drops for a few moments, and she holds her breath. Rosie can't believe who she is seeing. A ghost. His red, curly hair sticks out from under his cap and, peering back at her, his dark brown eyes are mesmerising. Her lost son has returned and she is faced with a haunting sight. He appears to sense her shock and distress and begins to speak. A British accent emerges.

'Oh, hello there.' He puts out his freckled hand to shake hers. Rosie hesitantly takes hold of his sweaty hand and shakes it gently.

'Um, I'm Phillip, Phillip Butler. I'm looking for …' He looks down at his paper. 'Um, Mrs Pearl Lane.'

As she realises this is a young man who is not her son, but a spitting image of him, Rosie regains some composure and manages to finally speak.

'She is not here, but I'm her granddaughter, Rosie Lane,' she says, taking a deep breath. 'I think you better come inside, darling, and we will have a cup of tea.' Her Australian accent fills the air in stark contrast to the smooth edges of his English accent.

'That would be lovely. Thank you. I didn't mean to startle you.'

'No, dear, you just look very much like my son. My son passed away fourteen years ago.'

They walk through the hallway and lounge room into the kitchen; Phillip's eyes scan the walls like a curious child.

'I'm so sorry to hear that,' he says as he takes a seat at the long white table. Looking around, his eyes fixate on the large painting above the fridge and freezer, a harvesting scene, lush like the English countryside. He seems to be absorbing everything around him with intrigue. Putting the kettle on, Rosie feels her heart racing and sweat running down her back. Her mind speeds through a myriad of possibilities this young man presents.

Who the fuck is this? How can he look identical to Will? Have I finally lost my fucking mind?

As though he reads her mind, Phillip begins to explain who he is. 'It makes sense that I may look like your son, as I think we might be related.'

'Well, let me get the tea ready. Lucky I don't drink, as I'd be having a scotch right now.' A nervous laugh is all she can manage as she pours the hot water into the cups.

'Do you have milk or sugar, lovey?'

'Just one sugar, no milk, thank you.'

She places the cups on the table. The sound of Phillip's teaspoon stirring the tea breaks the silence. She cannot believe the sight before her as Phillip takes his hat off.

He pulls a piece of paper out from his pocket. It is crinkled, the colour faded. He flattens it out on the table. 'My father passed away recently. We have only just moved to Australia. Both my parents are Australian, but I grew up in London. We always knew my father was adopted. My grandparents moved to the UK when he was only young. We had assumed that he had never planned to find his birth parents but when we were packing up to move, we found his birth certificate and this piece of paper with the name Pearl Lane and this address on it.' Phillip rushes through the words, his explanation apparently well rehearsed. He slides the pieces of paper across the table as she takes a sip and then places her cup of tea down. Placing her glasses on, Rosie begins to read the words and dates.

None of it makes sense.

With hesitation, Rosie speaks. 'It says here that your father was born here in 1947, a year before me, and that his mother was Daisy Lane. That is my mother.' She points to her chest and a frown forms on her forehead. As the information sinks in, after a long pause, Rosie continues. Rosie notices Phillip gripping his cup tightly, dipping his tea bag with steady concentration. She wonders if he's nervous. 'This doesn't make sense. My mother never had any other children.' There is a crack in her voice, tears well at the base of her eyes. 'Well, no one told me she did.'

'Well, I actually don't know,' Phillip says. 'My father never spoke to me about any of this. We have only really discovered this since his passing.'

'This is a birth certificate, so it must be right.' Rosie looks at the paper as if the words are going to all of a sudden change. 'So this would make your father my brother, so you'd be my nephew.' Rosie pauses and looks across at him as she takes her glasses off. 'But, darling, what I'm trying to understand is, you have my red hair and brown eyes. You look just like Will and me.' She smiles. 'My mother, Daisy, she had brown hair and green eyes.'

Phillip asks, 'So where does the red hair and brown eyes come from?'

'From what I understand, it comes from my father. I never knew my father.' Breathing deeply, Rosie looks out the window, letting the news coalesce. Putting her glasses back on, she focuses on the page. 'It says here, *Father unknown*. I wonder if your father,' she reads again, 'Robert, was actually my full brother.' Pausing, she looks directly at Phillip. 'Maybe, we had the same father?' Rosie continues to read, searching for clues or answers. Her words fall upon the table as she tries to make sense of it.

'Well, that would make sense,' Phillip says. 'Do you have red hair on your mother's side?'

'No, darling, nowhere in the family. Just Will and me, and from what I have been told, my father.

'It has to be. Well, I'm glad you came, Phillip. It's just a lot to try and take in, you know.' Rosie's face softens.

'Well, I didn't want to come here and upset you. I just feel like my father would want, would want me, to find his family. You know, his biological family. I think he had plans to find you before he died but he was too ill in the end to travel back to Australia.'

'You said your mother is Australian too?'

'Yes, they met in London. She was travelling and then moved there but she grew up in Australia. We have moved back here. Actually, my wife and two children have moved with us. My wife is Australian. It's a bit weird, I know. Everyone says, "What are the chances?"' Phillip talks fast.

'I never thought there would be a chance I'd have a brother, a nephew. Oh my God, my head is spinning.' Rosie places her hands on her forehead.

'I must admit, I was hesitant to find you, but I think my father would want me to.'

'I'm glad you did, I'm just feeling overwhelmed.' Rosie wipes a single tear that manages to escape her eye.

Before they can fall into a barrage of sharing stories of their separate lives, now connected, Phillip says, 'I better get going, my wife will be waiting.'

'Oh, that's fine, dear.' Rosie feels relieved that he needs to leave.

As she walks Phillip out, she points out the photos of her family. The resemblance is uncanny. Rosie watches from the doorway as Phillip walks up the garden path. Many questions hang in the air as she closes the front door.

CONNECTION

Rosie moves the curtains, looking out to see the dim-faced dawn.

I have a brother; my mother had another child. Possibly a pen pal. Some girl called Tina. The brooch. Who knows what secrets it keeps?

The news keeps swimming around her head as she tries to make sense of it.

If they had two children, why didn't he marry my mother? Why was Robert adopted? Why did they keep me? It's all too much. I'm too old for this. It's all too much. I better get into town today and check the mail and buy some supplies.

She puts on her nice clothes. A skirt, a singlet and a cardigan. No boots and overalls today. She brushes her red curls and pins them back with golden clips. Looking into the mirror, she studies her reflection.

I wonder what my father looks like. Is he alive? Dead? Married? With more children?

For the first time in her life, she has a yearning to know. To search. To find him. Mumma's voice rings in her ears.

'Let sleeping dogs lie. Don't go looking for ghosts. Dragging up the past. Every bastard's got skeletons in the cupboard.' I know she'd say that. She'd definitely say that. Why did she hide it? Bloody hell, I had a right to know. Mumma and her funny ways. Maybe I'll ask Phoebe. Why didn't Jassie tell me? She would always tell me everything.

Brushing her teeth, Rosie makes a mental note of all the things she needs in town. Rinsing her mouth, she spits the toothpaste into the sink and washes it down the drain. Lost in her to-do list running through her mind.

Buttering her toast, the creamy, soft butter spreads with ease over the hard surface. A random memory of being beside a creek in a small Irish town comes into her head.

Ainsley's future husband's home town. I loved that time together. Driving along narrow roads, eager to discover coastal gems. Being hungover, wild and free. It seems like such a long time ago now. Well, I guess it is. It's nearly fifty years ago. I often wonder whether I had really experienced it or if it was just a dream.

After placing the butter back in the fridge, she scribbles a shopping list, not confident in her memory. Packing her wallet and shopping bags, she double checks everything. She places a big log on the fire, then affectionately strokes the fur of her old dog, saying sweet goodbyes; comforted he will be sleeping soundly by the fire when she returns.

Walking out to the ute, Rosie feels a chill in the air, forcing her to lift her shoulders and brace her body. Glancing over the valley, she sees the sun is gradually peeking through the dancing clouds. Starting the ute, she turns the heater on, checks her bags for her wallet and list as she waits for the ute to warm up. As she backs out of the garage, the sun streams through the back window, illuminating the cobwebs in the corners. Driving past the dairy, she admires Billy's chooks, feeding, scratching and searching.

They are healthy and happy. Loved by our precious boy.

Whilst filled with warmth, she gets lost in reflection.

Tom was the same as a boy. Always had a love for animals. Always caring for his siblings. The first one to stand up to a bully picking on a small kid at school. I think it comes from Blake, not me, that calm tenderness.

Rosie remembers Blake, sitting on an old drum, playing with a litter of pups.

He was soft. Caring, and took great delight in animals. How I miss him. The comfort of his arms. His slow, rhythmic walk. I'd give anything to see him waltz through the front gate again.

Before she allows herself to feel grief or self-pity, she reminds herself of all she has to be grateful for, like Tom and Billy. Driving into town, she looks across the paddocks, admiring Tom's limousin bulls near his house.

Large beasts. They are muscular. Strong. Displaying a palette of different shades of red and rich orange in the paddock. Look at the motorbike track Billy has carved on the side of the hill. I can only imagine the hours he has spent weaving his way around it. Him and Jimmy I suspect. Two little ratbags.

Smiling, she pushes the clutch in to change gears. Rosie inspects the neighbour's paddocks on the way to town. A flock of birds fly overhead.

She pulls up near the post office and parks the ute. Getting out, she makes sure she has everything she needs. The post office, an old building, one of the first built in town, is a reminder of a different time. Built to last, thick walls; a grand structure, preserved by the white painted exterior.

Opening up the postbox, she grabs the pile of mail and takes it back to the car and throws it on the front seat. The sun shines brightly, reflected on the glass. Slamming the door, she makes her way to the supermarket, going over the list as she walks.

Walking along the main street of her quiet town, she greets the people she passes; she secretly hopes she doesn't run into anyone wanting a long chat.

Focused, she selects a trolley from the bay and begins pushing it along the first aisle, collecting everything on the list, grabbing extras as she goes, placing them neatly in the small trolley. Her simple local supermarket has four short aisles. Rosie remembers the years when Anne worked here, as her part-time job, while she was at high school. Rosie visualises her.

So young, friendly in her work uniform. I was so proud of her then, even in a humble job as a check-out chick. I knew she would always aspire to more. She always desired to spread her wings, to study and travel.

She smiles and acknowledges the other customers as she goes, enjoying the moment to think of her beautiful girl. A mother ahead of her argues with a tantrum-throwing toddler as she carries a newborn strapped to her chest. As Rosie approaches, she grins at the frustrated and overwhelmed mother. The mother looks at her apologetically, embarrassed her child is making so much noise and disruption.

I remember those days. Will was the worst for throwing a tantrum. The wild one.

'What a challenging age. You are doing such a great job juggling these two,' Rosie says warmly as she places her hand gently on her shoulder. As she peers at the newborn, nesting against the mother's chest, the sweet smell transports her to a precious place. Memories of motherhood. The mother's face softens. Rosie notices visible bags under her eyes, telling the story of many sleepless nights. Rosie talks to the toddler, who appreciates the attention. She admires the newborn, sleeping soundly. Rosie gives her time, asking her questions, forgetting she is in a hurry.

I remember how difficult those years were. Raising young children. I remember it as though it was yesterday. How did I ever survive it?

The young mother continues shopping. Rosie happily waves goodbye to the toddler. The little boy's face is filled with a grin, spread from ear to ear. He mimics her action.

Returning to the car, she is sure she has forgotten something but is eager to get home.

Rosie arrives home, happy she has that job done for today. She carries the pile of letters and bags of groceries inside. Dumping them on the end of the long white table, Rosie flicks through the pile of letters. Recognising many as bills.

I'll look at all those later. What's this one? I recognise the handwriting.

Rosie pulls it from the pile. Flips it over and begins opening it.

It looks like a letter from Ainsley. I've been thinking of her quite a lot lately. Time and many seas separate us. We have a bond from that year together. I came home and Ainsley stayed. We have written a lot over the years. Ainsley was there when MJ died. When I went to hospital. When my world fell apart and then she dragged me overseas. Over the years, I've had the desire to cut her out completely. Not a simple, easy friend to have. But there is this unbreakable bond that keeps drawing me back. I always wish I could feel that close connection I felt during that year.

Opening the envelope, she hesitates.

I wonder what Ainsley has to say. I'm always excited and a little nervous when a letter arrives.

Rosie reads with intrigue.

Dear Laney,

I hope this finds you well. I know I should write more. The summer is on its way. I am planning on visiting in October. It will be so good to be home. To see you all, to be back in the valley. Surrounded by our mountains. I have been thinking of you a lot lately. I cherish our time together, the wonderful, amazing year travelling. I can't believe so much time has passed. Remember that time in Amsterdam? Rocking out on the dance floor. We were mad. Crazy. I still remember you spinning around like a mad woman rocking. I miss those days. I feel so old. I hate getting old, it just doesn't suit me.

Rory is back in Ireland with his mother, she is unwell again. My son I barely see these days, except when he wants something. It has been a long, dreadful winter here. The worst I think I've ever seen. The sun never shines and I long to be home in the Australian sun. Remember those beautiful summer days, hours spent floating, playing, swimming in the creek? The four of us. If only we could all be together again. I feel so old now. My arthritis is getting worse. I'm trying a new, natural remedy. I have a cruise planned next month; I can't wait to get away with the girls. I can't wait to see you during the glorious Australian spring.

I hope you're well. Love to all the family darling.

Love from Ainsley B. Porter.

It seems short for Ainsley, like there is a lot she is not saying.
Thinking nothing else of it, Rosie places the letter in the drawer with all the others from her.
Despite the frustrating way she can be, I'm still grateful for our connection.
Walking into the study, Rosie thinks about all the letters she and

Ainsley have sent over the years. Their shared love for writing poetry. Pulling out a box from beside the fireplace, she looks through a yellow folder, and pulls out a poem.

This is one. This must be from when we were around sixteen. Ainsley was always so tortured. The one to be with all the boys. She so desperately wanted to be loved. To fill that void.

Shaking her head, Rosie is transported to a different time. Feeling Ainsley's pain, feeling the grip of despair.

I'm Wanted

> *All my innocence has been wasted on the sexually driven,*
> *intoxicated and heartless flings that have passed by my door*
>
> *I was waiting for my knight in shining armour*
> *I was waiting for the telephone to tell me, I'm wanted*
> *Well, I heard someone got their fingers into you*
>
> *I was waiting for your waves of love to sweep over me*
> *I was waiting for the commitment to tell me, I'm wanted*
> *Well, I heard you let someone take advantage of you*
>
> *I was waiting for the meaning in my life*
> *I was waiting for someone to tell me everything's alright; I'm wanted*
> *Well, I heard you let someone take the fire from within your eyes*
>
> *I was waiting for someone to tell me, I'm wanted*

NOTHING GOLD CAN STAY

Looking across the valley, Rosie feels the damp grass on her feet. The sky is dark; there is a distant glow on the horizon, clouds painted shades of grey, tinged with pale pink.

The break of day shows a sign of promise, of possibility; the blessing and curse of change. New beginnings and unfortunate endings; the passing of time. Unstoppable. Like the flow of water, running constantly. The predictability brings me comfort; day breaking, the birds chirping with the rising of the sun. The creek flowing. My mountain standing strong. Many things in life are unpredictable, fragile; a blooming flower, only a moment to enjoy its beauty before it dies. It reminds me of Robert Frost's poem in the The Outsiders *I read when Anne was a baby. I'll read that again when I go back inside.*

Casting her eyes over the horizon, she sees a dark streak of pink spread in the sky. As she walks, she watches the sky become a mass of colour, a spectacle of brilliance. Rosie marvels at God's painting.

I would love to be able to capture it on canvas.

The illuminated clouds become yellow and orange as the sun rises further over the horizon. Walking around the garden, enjoying the plants, the flowers—barefooted, feet feeling the cold, damp ground—Rosie breathes in the cold air and wraps her dressing-gown tightly around her for warmth. The sun creeps further over the mountain range, lighting up the valley. Slowly the darkness is fading and the morning light awakens the garden. The birds rise and whistle. Hearing the familiar hum of the dairy, calves bellowing and barking dogs in the distance, she watches the clouds drift from the horizon as the sun is revealed. The bright ball of fire, giant ball of energy, floating in the sky. Rosie contemplates God making the sun, appreciating each new day as a blessing.

Making her way to the edge of the hill, she looks across the valley, the sun shedding light on the green paddocks, the town in the distance. Poplar trees, tall and grand. Giants. Lining the creek. Golden statues shining in the morning sun. Dew on the grass drying. The fresh air warming. The garden awaking as the sun rises. The glory of the season captures her senses and imagination. Reminded of inevitable change and transformation.

Rosie strolls back through the front gate, along the cement paths, paths that were made by her great-grandfather; he was a great lover of cement, of building. Rosie remembers the time a snake died in the water tank at the side of the house, when she was a kid.

We had to empty it and clean out the rotten stench. I remember seeing my great-grandfather's signature marked on the inside of the tank. Carved into the cement, Thomas W. Lane *in the most beautiful handwriting you have ever seen. I can just imagine him, cementing the tank by hand, carving his name as he finished.*

Sadness stirs inside her as she considers her own mortality.

What will be my lasting legacy? What will be left?

The pebbled path leading along the side of the house is filled with white, rough stones. They are hard on her bare feet. Strolling through the fernery, she bends down to feel the delicate texture of the maidenhair ferns. They are fine and intricate. Checking the soil to see if it's moist, she feels the dry earth. Rosie goes to the edge of the house and turns on the watering system. Bending down, she begins weeding around the hellebores under the dogwood, spreading the remaining mulch in the garden as she goes. As the water soaks the pebbled path and drenches the ferns, she takes the secateurs hanging on a post and begins trimming the ivy covering the water tank.

Like giving a mop of hair a haircut. Give this old fella some form and shape.

After noticing the azaleas and rhododendrons in the adjacent garden bed, she removes dead branches, adding to a pile on the lawn.

When Rosie exhausts the possibilities of pruning, she returns the secateurs to their spot and turns the sprinklers off. Walking back along the fernery, she admires the bird's nest fern in the corner, its long, green leaves reaching out. She removes some brown and shrivelled ones at its base. Slowly pacing, Rosie appreciates the tall bromeliads collecting water, their grey, speckled foliage and bursting pale-pink flowers.

Her eye is caught by the beauty of the row of daisies with white petite petals, yellow centre. She remembers when she planted them.

They were nearly dead. Bought them on sale. They were pot bound and dry. Look at them now. Since placing them in some soil—a bit of water and a good dose of manure—look how they have flourished.

Running her hands along the diosma hedges as she walks past, she lovingly feels their texture. As she reaches the corner of the inside garden, she sits and relaxes on a seat. Rosie runs her hand over the wood, feeling its grain, the smooth weatherworn texture.

These beautiful table and chairs Blake made for me so I could enjoy this spot in my garden. What a noble, generous man he was. I still feel like I was not worthy of such a blessing. I love this place. This spot in the garden. To drink tea. Draw. Write poetry or read. It makes me think of Virginia Woolf's A Room of One's Own *when she wrote, 'a woman must have money and a room of her own if she is to write fiction.' It resonates with me. In this moment. In my garden. Free to write. Paint. Express my ideas. So many women of other times were denied the right. Were silenced. I should write. For women. For all women. As power. As freedom. I need to pass this on to my granddaughter as a gift. I do not want her wings to be clipped. I do not want her creative expression to be stultified. I must lead by example. What was it I read the other day by Elizabeth Gilbert? The essential ingredients, courage, enchantment, permission, persistence and trust. It's not always easy but always possible. Fall in love with creativity. Let go of the fantasy of perfection; nothing is ever beyond criticism. I think that's what she said in* Big Magic. *All I really want to do is start something and bloody finish it; I'd love to prove to myself that I can do it. No one else has lived this life. No one else has this story to tell. No one else but me.*

Getting up from the seat, afraid to sit for too long, Rosie goes inside and changes into her work clothes, something practical and warm.

She moves towards the dairy, to the vegie patch. She looks at the cleared bed. Rosie moves bags of compost and manure to its edge. Leaning down, she spreads it along the rows of dirt. Spreading it, mixing it, she filters it through her hands, digging and rotating the golden brown, rich earth. Rosie imagines all the nourishment the soil is receiving, working hard, with vigour and vitality. Hands dirty, brow sweaty, feeling connected to the cycle of the earth, one with the soil. Mixing the manure and compost through the vegie patch, she loves that her waste, the garden's waste, can be reborn.

It decays, decomposes, then goes into the ground to feed new plants, bloom into flowers or fruit. I love the cycle. Birth and death. Have I done enough to justify my life? My children? My farm? My garden? My art?

There is a deep longing in her.

I know I must write that book before I die. To be happy. To be satisfied with my life. I want them to know the wisdom, the lessons I've learnt. The lessons from this beautiful, messy life.

Moving inside, she finds the book amongst the chaos of her large bookcase. She runs her hands through the thin layer of dust, then takes off her socks before sitting down. Her old dog warms her feet as he rests his head affectionately, just happy to be in her presence. Rosie skims through it and reads the section she loves.

Here it is, this is it. The sunrise scene. The Robert Frost poem. 'Nothing Gold Can Stay'.

The section fills her with sadness. She thinks about the pain of time, its inevitable destruction and decay. Engrossed in the memories of golden moments that could not stay, she cherishes them and simultaneously grieves their loss. Not letting herself sit with that pain for too long, she gets up from her chair, her old dog following her movement. She goes into the kitchen and makes herself a cup of tea, then turns on the television. Rosie feels she needs the company of the noise floating in the air. She sits down in her chair. Her old dog is beside her; she leans down and strokes his fur, admiring the tenderness in his eyes. She picks up her crocheting; the fine white reminds her of the doilies Anne used at her wedding, covering the tables. Her mind casts back to that magical day *When everyone was there, all together and happy. Moments treasured all of one's life. Cemented in time. Etched in my memory. I am very fortunate and blessed. The bright blue sky devoid of a single cloud. The sun was bright and warm. The perfect temperature. There were nerves and excitement. Placing my grandmother's pearls around her neck. Anne looked radiant. The stereotypical little girl about to marry her prince. Also filled with doubt and anxiety that it wouldn't all come together. The wedding preparation and anticipation was the best. The weeding, mulching and planting. Lots of pruning and cleaning everything. Fixing things left undone for many years. Blake making the arbour. Anne collecting and giving instructions.*

Closing her eyes for a moment, she remembers dancing with Anne late into the night.

I told her I was proud of her. How much I loved her. We were drinking.

Laughing. Dancing. Oh God did we dance. In my arms we rocked together, to the beat of the music, two women, mad with happiness. Mad women rocking.

Rosie looks at the family photo from that day sitting in the middle of the mantelpiece.

Our smiling faces. The boys looking so smart in their suits. We were all so unaware that tragedy would soon creep, fall, bleed into our perfect lives. Like a sunrise fading, this perfect moment in my life did not stay. The fragility of life. The ever-present promise of change; that nothing gold can stay.

A Precious Soul

Filled with jewels and gold
You were vibrant and bold
We pray for your dear soul
To return to God to make you whole
We can't help but question and ask why
May you shine brightly in our night's sky
Your memory be strong in our mind's eye
Your cheeky grin
Masking your pain within
An old soul filled with jewels and gold
Beyond your years
Leaving your legacy forever here
Your friendly manner
Sometimes the good die young
May we all send you love
To take you into God's arms
Where pain evaporates and there is no harm

May all our tears fill a river
To deliver you home
Where you will no longer be alone
A beautiful soul
Filled with jewels and gold
Forever young
Now bathing in God's light and love
You have walked the earth, many times before
May you make it to where you're going
To walk your journey once more

WOMAN AT THE WELL

Run with Wolves

She is a wild spirit
Wild like the wind
Free
Eager to explore
She is a wild spirit
Who wants to soar
To epic heights
She is as bold and brave as the waves
A wild spirit
Who will grow to be a wild woman
Like many wild women you know
With heart and courage
A wild woman who will run with wolves

Looking through the wardrobe, Rosie moves through the clothes methodically, sliding them along the rail.

Bloody hell, all these fucking clothes and still nothing to wear.

Tall, dark, wooden panels stand above her. The old handles are loose. Pushing the door shut, she opens the other side. She selects a long skirt and a warm cardigan. She runs her hands through the scarves hanging, then unravels one whose colour complements her outfit and wraps it around her neck. She puts on her black and practical boots.

It feels like it's too cold for sandals. A part of me wants to stay within the warmth of my old farmhouse but I better go to mass. To worship. To honour the sacrifice of my saviour. I'm disappointed Anne and the kids are staying in the city, to be with Tim's family. I just need to be patient, as always. They will come up after Easter.

Feeling very petty and selfish, Rosie thinks about the sacrifice of Jesus. Looking at the cross on the wall in her study, Rosie is reminded of rebirth, salvation and transformation.

As she walks up the steps and into the chapel, she notices familiar faces. After dipping her fingers into the holy water, she makes the sign of the cross. Reaching her normal pew, on the right-hand side of the chapel, she genuflects. She looks to the large figure of Jesus. Crucified. Nailed. Crown of thorns. She takes a seat, by herself, on the long pew.

As the mass proceeds, her mind drifts. Through her prayers. Fears. Her desires. Her appreciation. Recurring thoughts plague her.

Who is my father? Who was this brother of mine? Do I even want to know? After all these years. Does it really change anything? I guess there's Phillip and the kids to think of. What if he's still alive? What if I could meet my father? He'd have to be in his nineties now.

She tries to push the thoughts away, but they continue circling her, like a merry-go-round.

Rosie speaks the words, feeling them in the depths of her soul. 'Lord,

I am not worthy, but only say the word and my soul shall be healed.' As she kisses the feet through the veneration of the cross, an image of Jesus comes to her. Kneeling, washing the feet of his disciples.

Leaving the church, Rosie feels a chill in the air. But she also feels the promising warmth in the sunshine making its way through the clouds. The colour of the autumn leaves lining the street catches her eye. With a spring in her step, Rosie is reminded of the story of the woman at the well.

Arriving home, she searches the dusty shelf for her Bible. Finding it, she runs her hand over it. The black leather is worn and well loved. Rosie opens it instinctively to the right passage.

This is the one. It's in John. I thought it was called 'Woman at the Well' but it's 'Jesus Talks With a Samaritan Woman'.

Rosie sits with this for a long time; the word truth reverberates in her mind.

I'm only seeking the truth, nothing more. What if he is my brother, my full biological brother? Who has children and grandchildren? What if I have the chance to gain another family? But maybe they don't want that. I should just forget about it.

She slams the Bible shut and places it back on the shelf.

Walking through her garden, she ponders the ideas and symbols of Easter.

The egg. The rabbit. Salvation. A chance for rebirth.

Her heart pines.

Hopefully salvation is for everyone.

Rosie considers different women she knows.

They've all made different choices. Paths they have taken; to get married, or not. To have children or not. Their addictions. The things that fill their lives. Family. Work. Art. Food. Some lonely. Some happy. Jesus spoke to this woman. Unmarried woman, at the well. Surely this God of mercy, forgiveness, of compassion, saves us all, despite our sin.

She reflects on her poor choices in her life.

What about all my mistakes? My myriad of regrets.

A deep well of shame bubbles to the surface.

In the depths of my heart, despite a life riddled with sin, I am saved. I have been transformed through the mercy of God's grace. Oh please, God, may we all be saved, despite our choices.

Rosie senses the desperate hunger of the poddy calf, a mother's intuition; smelling it, sensing it like a fox smelling fresh chickens. She ventures inside, through the front door, to fill the bottle. She checks the warmth, remembering feeding Anne's children with a bottle.

How poor Anne had agonised over not being able to breastfeed. Like I had. Like my grandmother had. Trying to comfort Anne that I had been fed by another woman. A stranger, a local woman who'd had a baby at the same time as my mother. My mother who didn't survive childbirth. Look at these feathers at the back door. I wonder what the stray cat has caught.

Placing the bottle down, she picks up the straw broom and sweeps them away.

Lottie fed Billy, a natural mother, adoring her child. Then she fucking left. Left him. I remember what Mumma would say. 'Not even a mongrel dog would abandon her pups.' Mumma saw the world in a very black-and-white way; she could never understand that life isn't always that simple.

Rosie walks down the hill as the calf cries. The chill in the air makes her shiver slightly. She opens the gate to the old chook shed. The calf is snuggled in the corner, in a bed of hay. Under the tin roof, protected from the weather. The calf leaps towards her. Rosie strokes her soft black-and-white coat. The calf nuzzles her and sucks on her clothes. Rosie places the bottle in her mouth and begins feeding her.

You beautiful thing, you look just like your mother. Look at you, all black with a white head, just like her. What a shame, dead from mastitis.

'Good girl, Bella, my beautiful little girl,' she says to her affectionately. The calf drinks enthusiastically. She looks at her hollow side, and hopes she is not hunched over forever. Rosie begins thinking about Mumma raising her. Her surrogate mother, Aunty Jassie.

One of my earliest memories is climbing into Aunty Jassie's bed. I must have only been about three ... well it was when she had leukaemia, so she would have been around thirteen. I think she was around thirteen when she was diagnosed. Jassie was always the quiet, calm, loving one. I loved climbing into her bed, snuggling in and she'd stroke my red curls, kiss my forehead. Mumma was the practical one, always made sure I was clothed and fed. Aunty Jassie was the one I went to for comfort. She'd pick me up when I was upset or hurt. I guess, in a way, it's no surprise she found God. I think she is probably a saint, or an angel sent from God. She was always so wise beyond her years, beyond this world, as though she could feel the love of heaven calling her. I remember her telling me about making a promise that if she survived, she'd dedicate her life to God. Such a sacrifice, I couldn't have done it. I imagine that nurse, reading the Bible to her when she was on her deathbed. A child, praying, preparing for death. I wonder if she ever crossed paths with that nurse again. I remember she came here once, years later. I'll have to ask her.

The calf begins to slurp the last remnants of the bottle. 'You've had a good drink, haven't you, Bella girl? You hungry thing,' Rosie says while stroking her back. The calf shakes its head up and down, trying to get more milk. 'It's all gone, bubba.' The calf wags its tail and jumps towards the gate to try to stop her from escaping. Rosie closes the gate and latches it. Walking back to the house, swinging the bottle, she notices a kookaburra resting on the fence post, inspecting the paddocks like a diligent watchman. Rosie thinks of all the poddy calves she has raised over the years.

I've been a mother to many. I've been a surrogate mother to many children and teenagers and even adults over the years too; Billy, Stella, Tilly and Lottie. Motherhood extends past the conventional. Sometimes abandoned pups need a mother. Not by blood but just by love. Why did my own mother not keep my brother? She survived the birth; there was no reason to abandon him. I guess there was a reason. I guess, I can't make assumptions. The box. I wonder what the letters are about. I'll wait for Billy, won't spoil it for him. I'm surprised Jassie or Phoebe never mentioned a pen pal from London. Phillip grew up in London, didn't he?

Her chest aches with sadness as she thinks of her mother giving up her child. She thinks of all the injured animals she'd bring home as a child to save and raise. She hears Mumma's voice.

Oh by God, Rosie, we could send you to Antarctica and you'd find some poor injured penguin to save. You're unbelievable, you are.

As she glances back down to the old chook shed, to where her little Bella is resting happily, she smiles.

SUNRISE

Slowly sitting down, Rosie looks at the canvas. Bare and untouched. Visualising colour, shape and texture, she picks up a brush and swirls it in the fresh paint. Beginning to paint the large canvas, instead of splashing paint everywhere, she is meticulous, taking her time. Rosie considers the colours she wants to capture.

The feeling. The moment when the world is still, filled with anticipation. I want shades of pink, purple and light blues. A golden trimming of yellow.

Beginning to create the scene in her mind, she paints rolling hills, dark and silhouetted. Then carefully places each brushstroke across the horizon. Colours mixing. A melody. Moving. Dancing on the canvas. Looking at a photo she has taken, she studies the shape of the clouds. She transfers each shape methodically from the photo to the canvas.

As she keeps painting, a rhythm takes over. She gets lost; her thoughts wander in a meditative state. Magic swirls around her in a dance. Dabbing the thick paint, she gives the clouds depth, texture, making it feel as though you could reach out and touch their soft, fluffy surface.

Rosie is reminded of a poem she wrote when she was working in London. How she would cling to any sign of the landscape or the wildlife within the city—feeling desperately homesick, yearning for gum trees and her mountain.

Rosie wipes her hands, feeling satisfied with the first layer. She looks and considers what it needs. Tilting her head to one side, her red curls slowly block her eyes before she sweeps them aside.

Looking through some piles of paper for the poem, she is frustrated at never being able to find anything.

I really need to organise all of this, create some kind of bloody order. Oh, here it is. It's a wonder I can find anything.

Reading it, she is transported back to that time and place.

Salvation

> *Sun rising*
> *Golden hue illuminating the horizon*
> *Looking beyond*
> *Birds perched on a light pole, watching the traffic*
> *Cars scurrying like frantic ants collecting food*
> *Beyond the power lines*
> *Traffic lights*
> *A bird flies in front of a peach-soaked sky*
> *Driving*
> *Looking beyond*
> *Road building, excavation, flashing lights*
> *Mesmerising sunrise, speckled colour ever evolving*
> *Painting a masterpiece*
> *Beyond the silhouetted tree, resting on the hill*
> *Looking beyond*
> *The city lights sparkling in an endless sea*
> *Signs of salvation*

The loud children pushing
Playing
Feel the warmth of sunshine
The train rattling past
The ever-present strong mountain, standing tall
Looking beyond
Feeling salvation

Haze over distant mountains
Driving
Cusp of night and day
Street lights, pedestrians crossing
Setting sun
Clouds painted in pastels whisper across the sky, like freshly
scooped ice cream
Vibrant effervescent moon
Sweet smell of daphne, flooding the front door
Dancing wildly in the wilderness of potential and brilliance
Bright young eyes, lovingly looking
Warm arms greeting
Looking beyond
Seeing graceful signs of salvation

She thinks about how some things have never changed in her
life.

*My powerful relationship with the earth. Our fauna and flora. I
can't remember a time when the beauty of colour didn't make me feel
alive. The soft fur of a newly born calf. The sweet smell of daphne at
the corner of my veranda; it has always made my heart leap. I can really
appreciate now how courageous it was to travel at such a young age. How*

I missed the gum trees. Craved the comfort and protection of my valley. The mountains surrounding me like a life-giving embrace. Laying back, floating in the water of the Greek islands, wishing MJ was with me. Still heartbroken and lost. I healed. The wounds did heal, but I remained forever scarred.

The tears sting her eyes; she lets them fall, tasting their salty bodies. As she sits in the moment of despair, her strength evaporates. She knows it will always return, but for now, she will be broken. She lets the tears wash her face. Her heart sink.

How cruel love can be, the torture and yearning. How did Daisy endure it? Being separated from her child.

As she walks outside, the kookaburra nesting in the willow tree sings its song. Rosie glances away and then looks back and it's gone. Feeling an emptiness, she craves a certain connection. A loneliness plagues her. She glances at the meat house, and a memory comes to her of her and MJ sitting up there, talking, singing songs together.

We shared everything, talking for hours late into the night. Climbing trees. We knew each other's fears, hopes, dreams, pain and trauma. I miss that connection. I miss someone knowing me and understanding me like that. I crave that kind of intimacy. Watching The Wizard of Oz *together. Aunty Jassie putting it on for us. Making us warm milos. Aunty Jassie introducing me to the art of Frida Kahlo. Sitting in her bed, looking at her paintings. Jassie explaining Frida's interesting life story and the messages in her artwork. We dreamt of going to Mexico to visit Frida's house. Imagine taking Jassie now. The old, devout nun.*

The idea excites her and scares her simultaneously. Looking across the valley, she sees the light is soft and warm. Rosie dreams of wild adventures. A poem comes to mind, one she wrote while overseas with Ainsley. When they were finding each other's company unbearable.

Sink

Water and romance

A muddle of putrid water, below the surface
What is left unsaid
Cuts deep
Rusty bottles
Broken
Deep below
The murky water

If only we were honest
Say what we think
Then this leaking boat would most likely sink

The gate into the garden creaks. After glancing around, Rosie watches as Billy comes running, skipping across the lawn.

'What's happening, my love?'

Out of breath, Billy says, 'Let's check the box. Have you opened it?'

'No, darling, I've been waiting for you. I keep my promises, you know.' Rosie wraps her arm around Billy's shoulder as they move inside.

'We have a bit of time while Dad milks the cows.'

Rosie pulls the box out from the laundry cupboard and takes it to a table under the window. The morning light streams in, illuminating the worn wood of the box's surface. Billy watches eagerly as Rosie carefully opens it and takes out the letters.

'You open one and I'll open one,' Billy instructs with authority in his voice.

'Ok, just be careful.'

Rosie hands Billy a letter from the pile. She takes an envelope, and slowly opens it. Inside is one piece of paper. She glides it out of the envelope. It is thicker than a letter. It's a black-and-white photo. A little boy.

I wonder who this is? He must be about four or five. It's old.

Turning it over, Rosie inspects the back for clues but it is blank.

'What is it, Nanny?'

'Mine just has an old photo of a boy. What about yours?'

'It's a very short letter. It's a bit weird.'

'What does it say?'

'Alright, I'll read it. *Dearest Daisy, I hope this finds you well. We are very happy and cared for here. My husband has started his new job as a general practitioner in a small village. Our boy, he starts school in a week. I hope to send photos. Many blessings to you. Tina.*'

'It's not that weird. Why do you think it's weird?'

'Like it's a very short letter to send all the way from England. Like that's over oceans and all those countries.'

'You are right. Yeah, it is strange.' Rosie frowns.

'How many more are there?' Billy stretches his neck to peer inside.

Rosie quickly counts them. 'There's four more.'

'I better go. I've got to get down and feed the calves. We can look at the others tomorrow.'

'No worries, sweetheart. Let's do that.' Rosie puts the photo back in the envelope and places the pile back in the box. Closing the box, a thought comes to her mind. She sees Phillip's face.

'See ya, Nanny!' Billy calls from the gate.

'Love you, honey! Will you ever slow down?' Rosie shakes her head.

Rosie moves inside and puts on the kettle. Staring through the window, she watches the leaves move gently as she considers the contents of the box.

DECAY

'What are you doing, Nanny?'

'I'm looking through this box.'

'What's this, Nanny?'

Billy picks up a newspaper clipping and studies it.

'That's Mary Jayne, we called her MJ. My best friend.'

'Why was she in the newspaper?'

'That plane accident. See the photo of the plane? She was in it. That's how she died.'

Rosie searches through the letters and notes.

'What are you looking for?'

'I'm trying to write something and I can't remember what happened. I thought I had written something years ago and put it in this box. I can't bloody find it though.'

Billy places the newspaper article on the desk.

'It mustn't be in here,' Rosie says. 'I'll have to keep reading through my journals.'

'Dad wants to know have you seen the friesian bull? He can't find him anywhere.'

'No, sweetheart, not in my travels.'

Rosie packs up the box and puts it back under the bed. They hear the toot of a horn.

'Sounds like Dad, honey.'

'See ya, Nanny.'

'Love ya, darling.'

Rosie is riddled with anxiety. A flock of cockatoos fly above. She stretches her neck to watch the majestic sight from underneath. They weave, dart in formation, singing, floating. The breeze blows through the trees; she is calmed by the spirit, reminding her she has no control. Kneeling down, Rosie pulls the weeds from the garden bed.

I remember the funeral. The cold wind blowing. The rest is a blur. Is that enough to start a book? I feel guilt. Intense guilt. The tears don't flow. The memories floating in murky water. I remember Mumma showing me the newspaper. I don't remember Mary Jayne's mum giving me that box. When did that happen?

Relaxing, she surrenders to God as her hands are submerged beneath the ground.

What about my old friend, Wally? He'd tell me about his childhood. He'd say, 'The only toy I ever had was a mongrel old rock, you know. I'd drive it around the dirt, none of those fancy bloody toys your kids have now.'

She chuckles to herself as her hands flatten the earth from where a weed has been removed.

I laughed so much that time he came home after being on a plane for the first time. I can still hear him saying it. 'Oh, by geez, I was all that way up there, just sitting there, drinking a cup of tea, for Christ sake.' The changes that man has seen in his lifetime. I must get over and check on him soon.

The sound of a car travelling around the road captures her attention; the sound travels easily down the hill, breaking through the still, quiet air.

Decay and transformation. I love running my hands through the compost, uncovering worms, filtering the dirt through my hands. Dark. Rich. Fertile. It reminds me of taking Billy fishing and searching for worms

in the piles of cow shit. Digging through the ground with a pitchfork.
Mixing the compost with the dirt. Removing weeds. The weeds go in the
compost pile. A harmonious cycle. Digging up the garden bed.

Planting a big, round bed of bulbs, freesias, ranunculus, tulips
and daffodils, Rosie makes sure she has them up the right way before
submerging them in the black dirt. She lays mulch to cover them like a
warm, protective blanket. Rosie feels satisfied.

Rosie rakes up the flowers fallen on the path from the camellias,
making piles. She picks them up and places them in the wheelbarrow.
Rosie delivers them to the compost.

Feeding it with good organic matter. Considering the state of the
earth, I don't like to think about the world outside my garden and
valley too often. I'm concerned about the world my grandchildren are
inheriting. I know I have raised my children well, to love and respect
the earth. The mother and provider. I'm proud of Tom for turning the
farm organic. Removing the use of pesticides and finding creative ways to
work with nature. My garden, like a child, a friend. The love of my life.
Mutual care and respect. It cares for me spiritually, physically, emotionally
and mentally. I care for it in return. Maintenance, nurturing, planting,
pruning, admiring. Constant love. Like the love of God. God's garden. It
scares me to think I will die, leave my garden, one day. Hopefully not too
soon. I hope I die in my garden. Resting, immersed, enfolded by it.

Rosie prunes, cuts the dead fronds from the fern, then lays them on
the ground like carpet. As she cuts them up, an image of her mother in
a photo on the mantelpiece comes to her mind.

I wonder what kind of mother Daisy would have been. What if I had
grown up with a brother? The other four letters. What will they reveal?
I wonder how that box got over to Tom's place. The photo. Who is that
boy? Is it who I think it is?

Bending down, she begins pulling weeds out, shaking the dirt from the roots.

Well, there's no point going down the road of what ifs. What has happened can't be changed. When I get rid of this mess I've created, I better go along the veranda and collect those plants to be re-potted. Some of them are so bloody pot bound, it's a wonder they can get any water. Everything needs water. Oh the droughts we have endured. The stress. The constant fear that water will never return. I remember Mumma describing the cows: 'They are that poor, you could hang your hat on their hips.'

Having piled the weeds in the wheelbarrow, she wheels them to the compost pile. Rosie thinks about life on the land, her family's endurance, their ability to deal with failure as well as success. She stirs the decaying food of the compost with the pitchfork. A poem she loves, 'Cold Anniversary' by Jennifer Strauss, comes to her mind.

The line, 'nature rots' … this poem I have read and thought of many times. 'Time, I say steals …' Time does steal. I imagine all the endless possibilities my boy's life held. Marriage and children. My best friend. A child, taken. A future stolen.

Rosie cannot hold on to those thoughts of loss too long. She digs with strength and determination.

I must accept the blessing and curse of nature. Time must pass and all things decay.

Rosie watches the fire and considers cooking dinner.

I've thawed sausages from the freezer; I guess I better cook them up.

She watches a group of galahs fly into the tree. A cow bellows. A plane casts a line across the sky. The sun is setting; the clouds are lined with pinks and grey. A cockatoo screeches. A calf calls for its mother. The coals are red, glowing with heat. The flames flicker, dancing around the edges of the logs of red gum. Rosie is filled with contentment. Feeling blessed. Mesmerised by the colours of the flames, she is captivated by the fire. She listens to birds singing as they prepare to nest for the night. The light begins to fade as night descends.

Cooking her sausages on the barbecue outside, she arranges the bread and cheese on the plate. She picks up a knife, pricks the sausages and watches the fat ooze out, remembering summer evenings of barbecues and backyard cricket.

The kids were teenagers. Drinking beer and socialising like adults. The laughter, the fun; one of my favourite times.

In the final remnant of light, the memory makes Rosie smile.

HAZELWOOD

Warrior of the Bush

The gum tree
a tapestry
bold, strong
patient
shedding skin
dead branches fall
transformation
letting go of what is no longer needed

Warrior of the elements
leaves grow, dry
drop
continuous cycle
drought and floods
scarred by bushfires
marred by time

The old gum tree
relentless, resilient
wise
standing tall

The warrior of the bush
a home, shelter
refuge

The gum tree
a beautiful creation

The old gum tree
the warrior of the bush

The brushstrokes are strong and deliberate, sliding over the paper. She paints in a chaotic yet purposeful way. The tree begins to form. Rosie admires the colours, textures and form in the photo she has taken. A tree she has admired beside the track leading around the back of the hill. She tries to convey the courage, strength and endurance she describes in her poem. The admirable warrior of the bush. Rhythmically layering the paint, she lets her mind drift. An image of riding past the beautiful old gum fills her mind.

MJ riding a horse, such grace and beauty. Riding up to the bush to make cubbies or pick blackberries before they were sprayed.

The image of them as kids riding their horses in the creek bareback comes to the forefront of her thoughts.

My white, stocky pony, Trixie. MJ's big, strong chestnut, Dagger.

As the paint swirls on the palette, her thoughts drift.

We shared everything; I thought we'd be together forever. When do you ever know that it's going to be your last goodbye?

There's a pang of pain and regret in her chest as she thinks about their last goodbye. When she saw MJ walk out her gate for the last time.

I can still hear that sound, the clang of the gate, a simple 'See ya'. I bloody hate that expression now. Always say to the kids, 'Love ya'. You never know when it's the last time. No hug, or tears. I was such a fucking selfish teenager then. Closed off to the world. Self-righteous. Cloaked in ignorance. We shared our deepest, darkest secrets. We shared our dreams and plans for the future. So many futile plans, lost. Forever.

Waking early—birds chirping quietly outside—she still feels weary but her strong thoughts are keeping her from going back to sleep. Lying in her warm bed, enclosed in the blankets, thinking about her dreams, she is dreary. The picture in her mind confuses her. The image of an old lady under a tree. The thick green leaves forming a mass, a cover, like an umbrella.

It was like a hazelwood tree. It was like the one in the park in London I used to admire.

Trying to recall all the things in the dream, her head swirls. She closes her eyes. The images are powerful in her mind.

A stone hedge, a hill; it was bathed in warm light. I remember her kneeling down. The old lady handing me a box. I go to open it but then I must have woken up.

The dream has rattled her. It is too early to get up, so she reaches over to grab her book. After turning the touch lamp on, Rosie reads for a while. Her mind keeps transporting her back to the images in her dream. The warm orange glow.

Frustrated she can't focus enough to read her book, she decides to get up.

Wrapping herself in layers, peering outside, she sees it is still dark and tranquil. Rosie feels the quiet and stillness of the early morning.

Walking through the house, she turns some lamps on; she has always hated the dark. She stops in the lounge room and stokes up the fire, strategically placing some kindling on the few coals burning from the night before. Entering the kitchen, she begins to make a cup of tea. She peers out the window as she patiently waits for the kettle to boil; there is darkness and quiet. With her hot cup of tea, she sits in her rocking chair next to the fire.

She rocks in her chair, sipping her tea. Pondering the meaning of her dream.

Rosie closes her eyes and a memory comes floating back to her. She is driving down to the creek; a kookaburra sits on the fence, waiting patiently, then follows her along the road like a messenger. Sitting under the bridge in the car. Considering the end. An end to the misery. Considering walking into the water and disappearing forever. Rosie visualises herself in this memory so vividly; she remembers it as if she were floating above, hovering outside her body. Scattered rain on the windscreen captures her attention as she sits there rocking, arms wrapped around herself. Watching the water flow over the rocks, she knows she must go on. She can't run and hide; she must deal with this tragedy.

Rocking in her chair, Rosie is pained by the memory but she reflects on her strength. She thinks of all the winters she has endured. Contemplates the inevitable end of autumn and the long, bitter winter ahead.

Closing her eyes again, she visualises her younger self in the car by the creek. Tears soaking her face, she imagines herself opening the door and holding her hand and looking into her eyes, telling her: 'You are so strong. You will survive this. Be brave. The sun will rise tomorrow.'

Rocking in her chair, she looks out the window to the sun dancing through the trees.

Hold on to the sunshine. The winters can be long; the sun will always shine again. Cherish these precious times because you never know when tragedy may arrive.

Absorbed in grace. Warmth and gratitude flood over her as she closes her eyes. Clutching the warm tea in her hands, she rocks in her chair.

A mad woman rocking.

"True belonging is not something we achieve, accomplish or negotiate with others—it's something we carry in our hearts. Our wild, messy hearts."

— Brené Brown

PART TWO

You are capable of more
than you know.

— Glinda the Good Witch, *The Wizard of Oz*

Cold Resolve

The fresh water flowed gently over the rocks, dancing rhythmically; it was resilient and cleansing. It spoke of her power. A mother, nurturer and creator of life.

BITTER COLD

Dear MJ,

I have let so much slip from my memory. I wish I could go back and record it all. I wish I had done it all differently. Told you how much I loved you. Told you that you were my world. Why did I shut you out? Why didn't I stop you? Pick up the phone. I want to tell our story. I remember the moment you told me. I had just come out of hospital. On crutches with a broken leg. We were outside the library and you said, 'you will write a book one day.' You saw something in me I couldn't see in myself. Have you cursed me? All these years. Have you been proud of me? I have been holding on to this book like a caged bird. It is time to release this caged bird. Let it sing. Let it fly out into the world and all I need to do is begin. I need to take each part of this tapestry and write each square, thread it together to form a quilt. I am constantly trying to convince myself of the value. The message of this novel. I'm going to write it to you because you always loved my writing. Wild teenagers. You saw the brilliance in my creativity and expression. You always brought out the best in me. You were a shining light in my humble life.

My old body aches, carrying this unfulfilled potential. I'm searching incessantly for the time. The words. The inspiration. I toss and turn with doubt.

Love ya,
Laney

Gently placing a piece of red-gum wood in the old stove, Rosie thinks of the scones her grandmother had cooked in this same stove. The smell. The warmth. Jam and cream flood her thoughts. She can taste it, feel its texture. Rosie glances at the dust and cobwebs she should clear away. For now, she will enjoy the heat and being transported back to her childhood. She places her striped beanie over her greying, red, curly hair. Thick gloves on her wrinkled hands. Ragged gumboots over her thick socks. She ventures outside into the cold. She looks out the back gate and down the hill; it is a mass of white. Everything in sight is frozen. Covered with a dusting. Painted with a thin layer of frost. Her breath creates fog in front of her face. The screech of the old back gate as she passes through it reminds her of nights waiting for her husband, daughter and boys to return. Nights out shooting or when they were being picked up from a party. The sound of the gate meant she could finally get to sleep soundly, knowing they had returned safely.

Rosie treads carefully through the wet, boggy ground, past the brick wall. The grand gingko tree is bare. A silhouette against the fog. She hears the dogs barking, roar of the motorbike chasing the cows in for the morning milking. Tom's whistle travels across the paddock. A chorus of her life.

Pa whistled the same. I clearly remember it as a young child.

She steps with trepidation down the steep hill. Following the narrow path, she makes her way through the fence.

It's hard for this old body to bend down, especially in this bitter cold.

She passes the remnants of the old stone wall. Avoiding the slippery grass, she sticks to the path. Turning around, she sees her old dog waiting at the gate.

He knows that these days, he's too old to follow.

Rosie smiles, remembering when Tom brought her beloved dog home.

'Six dollars at the clearance sale,' he said with pride as he placed the little black-and-white fluff ball in my arms. He had a cheeky grin, his blonde hair glistening. Tom never said much with words but sometimes his blue eyes would sparkle. You could see a glimpse of what he might be thinking and feeling. He said, 'He's a ripper, ain't he?' I'll never forget it.

She laughs to herself as she recalls how the pup had vomited in the ute on the way home and pissed all over her kitchen floor.

From that day on, we were inseparable. God, all the time I spent training him. What a brilliant cattle dog he was, in his heyday. I could send him over the paddock to round up the cows on his own. You only get a dog like that once in a lifetime.

Rosie looks across the valley as she reaches the bottom of the hill. She pauses to catch her breath and take in the scene. It is a sea of white, beautiful, quiet; she loves the breaking of day. Birds begin to wake and sing as she crosses the rocky gully over the culvert on the gravel track. Hearing the water rushing past, she breathes into her gloves to warm her hands. Picking up a stick, she walks towards the clearing, feeling the sting of the bitterly cold air in her lungs. Looking at the willow trees, she remembers driving the car around this old track as kids. In their old paddock bomb. They spent many hours doing this until they rolled it and her leg was broken. She feels her scar and remembers all the risks they took.

What a beautiful, messy blessing my childhood was.

She walks down into the wet patch. Cautious, she tries not to get stuck. Her gumboots manoeuvre their way through the thick mud. Rosie marches into the grassy clearing. A callous, bitter wind sweeps past her neck. It reminds her of that July day when the plane crashed. The chill in the air that surrounded her while she watched her get buried. How she stood in the crowd amongst the crying. Frozen with disbelief. She ponders how she still misses her vibrant childhood friend. Her best friend. After all these years. Among the broken dreams of Rosie's life. This pain has never left her.

So many moments throughout my life, I've missed her and wished she was there. Like the time I was lying back, floating in the sea, in the Greek islands. I kept thinking, She should be here; oh, she'd love this. *I know now MJ was definitely with me, in spirit.*

At the time, it was little comfort. We were meant to grow old together. How I wish she was here now.

The cold wind is ferocious and blows right through her as she feels a pang of regret still. Even with the passing of time, she can't help but question.

What if I had a chance to change things and do it all again?

I know it all had a purpose. The humility I learnt. The strength I gained. Discovering my spirituality. Appreciating the fragility of life. The true measure of time. My healed wounds make me strong but forever scarred.

Trekking past a small willow tree, she sees a cocoon tightly clinging to a branch. Stopping, she admires it.

It is so perfectly formed.

Rosie marvels at the wonders of nature and considers how things change; the body's ability, profound power to transform and heal. Reminded of her many transformations and the twists and turns of life.

Reaching the fence, before the sadness and cold can completely engulf her, she moves on with resolve. She locates the loose section of the fence and climbs through onto the gravel, avoiding the sharp barbed wire. Rosie feels eager to continue as she hears the creek flowing with intensity. As she walks down to the bank, she sees white foam collecting against the edges. The rain from the last few days is making its way from the mountains. Bending down, she takes off her gloves and, despite the cold, she cups some water in her hands and tastes the pure, fresh water. It quenches her thirst. Placing her freezing hands back in her gloves, she finds her comfortable log and sits down on her jacket, using it to protect her from the ice and damp. Enthralled in the rhythm and persistence of the water, she sees the glow of the rising sun permeating the thick fog. Rosie sits there for a while. Lost in the moment. Listening to the water and enjoying the peaceful valley.

I love how quiet the mornings are. The stillness and peace; like a prayer.

Taking a deep breath, she grabs her stick and gets up and keeps walking along the edge of the creek.

Plodding along, past the old swimming hole, she hears a splash and catches a glimpse of something. She wonders if it is the old platypus.

Will had always claimed it stole his worms.

Rosie passes the barely-standing pump shed, lost in her thoughts. Rosie remembers his red hair. His beautiful brown eyes. Beneath the poplar trees that circle the base of the hill, Rosie walks onto the wide track with purpose. The water glistens off the mossy rocks. An empty bird nest is exposed in the naked tree swaying in the light breeze. The ground has a protective layer of mulch made from the elm leaves of autumn.

Rosie ambles up the cow's track to the dairy. The acacia trees are stark and bare. Deep grooves where the cows have trampled create a difficult maze to negotiate with her feet. Paying attention to every small stride, she places each foot with careful consideration. The recognisable hum of the dairy in the background gives her comfort.

All the hours I spent in the dairy. Every day. Twice a day.

As she makes her way towards the front gate, she casts her eye across the valley. She looks to the paddocks on the hill; yellow lines of fed out hay run through them like veins. Noticing Billy feeding the calves in the distance, she hears them bellowing. The fog is rising; the persistent sun is fighting its way through it. Breaking across the horizon.

Maybe we'll get some sunshine today and I'll get some gardening done. Or like most winter days, I might stay close to the fire.

Rosie strolls past the vegetable gardens covered in straw, looking to the welcome smoke billowing from the chimney of the house. She sees her old faithful dog patiently waiting at the front gate. Smiling, she lovingly greets him with a pat. His tail wags as they shuffle inside into the warmth together.

She picks up the old kettle from the stove and pours hot water into her cup, drowning the tea bag. While the tea brews, she begins to find the ingredients for scones and places them on the table. The long white table she loves. It reminds her of her grandmother. It was given to her grandmother as a wedding gift from her grandfather. Leaving her old dog by the fire, she takes her full cup and goes to sit at her old wooden desk.

Rosie places the cup on a coaster and sits down in the big, comfortable chair to write. Out the window, soft rain begins to fall. She sips her tea. The cup warms her hands.

Maybe it will be too wet for gardening today.

The rain falls lightly, cleansing corrugated iron, painting it like a glaze. Tall elm trees sway as a wild wind blows. Rosie is warmed by the wood fire and pleased to be back inside. In the distance, ominous clouds dance a soothing waltz. In the east, there's a small section of blue sky, with golden clouds brightened by the sun trying to break through. In the west, there are dark storm clouds forming a thick blanket over the mountain range. Affectionately, she looks to the mountain she knows as home. She notices the grass in her lawn soaking in the fresh droplets of rain like a thirsty sponge. Droplets of water cling to the spouting on the veranda.

The weather is turning. I doubt I'll get any gardening done today. Best I get some writing done.

Reading her journals, Rosie tries desperately to find a place to start and some inspiration. She hears the footsteps coming around the veranda. Welcomes a distraction.

Perfect, Billy can help me make some scones.

She places her hands on the armrest to lift herself from the chair. She moves into the kitchen. Billy opens the back door, tears streaming down his face. Tom is carrying a bundle of limp black-and-white fluff. Her heart sinks. Tom's forlorn face drops, with tears in his blue eyes. Speechless. Rosie rushes to pat her old dog as she wraps an arm around Billy, putting on a brave face for his sake. Tears begin rolling down her cheeks. Confusion swirls in her mind. A deep sinking pain rests in her chest.

How did this happen? He was just beside the fire.

As if he had read her mind, Tom explains, 'The milk tanker got him.'

'What was the silly old dog doing on the road?' Rosie whispers in disbelief through a stream of tears. Billy wails. Embracing him, Rosie gives him words of comfort and explanation. 'He had a good life, poor old boy; it must have been his time. God must need a good dog in heaven.' Billy drenches her jumper in snot and tears.

Before they can rest in this moment of intense grief, she suggests they find a special place in her garden. Billy leads the way. Rosie grabs a shovel leaning against the shed on their way. Her face drenched with tears. Billy picks a spot under the paulownia tree in the front garden. Tom places the limp and lifeless body on the wet ground. He clears a place amongst the roses and bearded irises and begins to dig the hole. Billy runs inside and fetches the old dog's beloved crocheted blanket from his spot in front of the fire. Her heart aches and breaks as she realises she will never feel his loving touch again.

On Billy's return, Rosie reassures him this will keep the old dog warm. Tom digs the hole, the shovel slicing the soft ground. Tom moves methodically, wiping his nose on his shirt. Speechless. His pain is palpable. He silently digs.

How would I have ever survived without him all these years?

Tom gently lays the old dog in his final resting place. Rosie takes one last glimpse of his white collar before Billy carefully places the crocheted blanket over him. She quietly prays as the dirt fills the hole. The wind rustles the leaves remaining on the trees. A light rain falls. The fog has lifted. The snow on the mountains is revealed in the east. In the west, dark, formidable clouds are growing. Tom moves a big rock on top of the fresh dirt so they know where he is.

As they head back inside, Billy innocently asks, 'Where is heaven?'

Rosie replies, 'Heaven is beyond the sky and stars. It is a magical place where there is no pain. Or cold. Or suffering. It's always summer holidays there and all you do is have fun.' Through her tears, she looks down at Billy, managing a smile.

'Is that where Uncle Will is?' Billy asks, intrigue and wonderment plastered across his face.

'Yes, that's where he is. Now, he'll have a good dog to keep him company.' The image of them together comforts her.

With her arm around Billy, she glances over her shoulder. The bright orange tail of the fox catches the corner of her eye. It stops. Their eyes meet momentarily, then it races along the edge of the hill and over the ridge, down to the creek. They walk inside and she talks to Billy about scone making.

Sitting on her old wooden chair, Rosie sips her strong black tea. It doesn't have as much warmth as she would like.

I miss the kiss of my old dog's nose.

Sadness and loneliness wash over her. The intense pain of losing her old dog transports her to the memory of the grief of losing her loved ones. It comes rushing. Cascading. Swirling around her like the water flowing over rocks.

This world can be so bloody cruel.

Feeling the chill of July when her best friend was buried. The image of her son taking his last breath. Suddenly, Rosie is overwhelmed with grief. In that moment, without her faithful companion, she feels that the sun will never shine again. Beaten. It all feels futile. Rosie breathes in deeply, then blows across the top of her cup of tea. She watches the steam rise against the backdrop of the tall elm trees.

I accept that this is the price of love; we must accept the pain of loss. I know this all too well. I know this wound will heal too. For now, I will allow myself this moment of sadness. To miss my beloved old dog.

Her aging body aches. Sleep evades her, so she lights a candle and sits at her desk. Her head is spinning. Her heart is aching. Loneliness creeps through her house like the bitter cold sneaking through the cracks. Rosie is searching for a place to start. The right words. For inspiration to lead her by the hand. She picks up her pen and tries to describe how she feels. The words seem to fail.

EAST OF EDEN

Relieved the train is not too packed, she settles in for the four-hour trip. She checks her bag to ensure she has everything she needs.

I'm excited about visiting Anne and looking after the kids. Travelling on the train reminds me of my time in London. Looking out across the houses. The grey skies. Waiting on the platform, as snow drifted and fell softly on my head. Islands of memory, floating in a sea of consciousness. It fascinates me what we hold on to and what disintegrates. My journals are precious now, as my memory slowly fades. They can reignite a flame, breathe oxygen into it.

She opens to the page she is on, placing the bookmark carefully on her lap.

My favourite book, East of Eden. *This must be the third time I've read it. The first was in London. I bought it on a holiday in the Greek islands, with the family I was a nanny for. I still remember it. I found a wonderful little second-hand bookshop. It was cluttered and filled me with wonder. I searched the dusty shelves. Trying to find something in English. Then I found this beauty. I was so young then. Filled with so much excitement. It is tattered now. I read it the second time after Tom was born. Now I've decided to read it for the third time. Hopefully it'll give me inspiration to write. Well, that's not really going to plan. I haven't even started. Written a single thing. Oh well, it will come, it has to. I love Steinbeck. His descriptions. He is so clever and observant. I could never possibly write as well as this.*

Rosie listens in on a conversation between two young girls behind her. They are laughing and giggling.

Oh God, they remind me of Ainsley, Polly, MJ and I travelling on the train. We must have been going on a school excursion. I wish they were here now. Oh us girls, we were clueless. We had no idea what lay ahead of us.

As Rosie reads, her mind drifts away. She prays that Tom and Billy are fine without her.

It's only a week. They are both big boys now. It will be good to get away.

As Rosie arrives at the station, Anne's tender face greets her. Rosie admires her perfectly straight, dark-brown bob as Anne collects her bags.

Anne looks so relieved to see me. She seems very tired and emotional. Many years of seeing her in a state. When she has overdone it. It has made it easy to read that face.

On the car trip home, Rosie tries to probe Anne, find out what's going on. This proves futile, so she takes a Mumma tactic and is as subtle as a sledgehammer. 'What's really going on, Anne? It's not like you to want me to come down.'

Anne appears to hold in welling tears. She holds her breath. Her hands tensely grip the steering wheel. She tries to speak but as she opens her mouth, she begins to cry, like a dam wall breaking. Tears stream down her face. 'I just need a break. I'm exhausted. I'm working.

Looking after the kids. Doing housework. Tim and I are fighting. All the fucking time. He's stressed with work and getting this fucking promotion. I'm just burnt out. I'm struggling at work with my classes. I just need some help.' Anne's voice is muffled through her tears; a sound of anger and defeat. A mixture of calamity.

This is not like her. Anne is never angry.

Rosie lets her cry.

I'm relieved that this is all that it is. I thought of all of these dramatic scenarios. Cancer. Divorce. An affair.

She lets her imagination run wild. At the same time, she feels a deep empathy. A strong connection, as a woman and a mother. A connection they formed from the umbilical cord, when they were one body.

As Anne wipes her nose across her sleeve, Rosie thinks about Phillip's visit.

I wonder if this is the right time to unload this. While we are getting things off our chest. No, no, Anne has enough on her plate. No need to burden her with this shit. This new discovery. It can wait. I know each person's feelings, their dramas, their struggles are real. They are huge to them. Despite comparison.

Trying to reassure Anne as best she can, Rosie places her hand on Anne's. 'Well, I'm here now, so you can begin to relax. Take a break. I can stay for as long as you need. You are so strong, but every warrior needs a rest. Even you, my dear. You are my warrior woman, remember.'

Anne manages a smile through her sunken face as she glances across at Rosie. Rosie smiles back, then looks at Anne's manicured nails as Anne focuses back on the road, taking deep breaths.

Rosie is reminded of the poem she wrote for Anne when she gave birth to Olivia.

'Remember that poem I wrote you, when you became a mother for the first time?'

I was so proud of her. Three generations of women. I read something once about carrying our ovaries when we are just an embryo. So when we are inside our mothers, we are connected to our mothers and our daughters simultaneously. Our womb keep us connected to our line of women, even our grandmothers. I imagine all the women standing on top of each other. Holding each other up. I won't bring it up, bit too heavy for Anne right now. She's not always into my crazy talk.

Anne smiles slightly as she talks through a drowned face. 'Yes, of course. I love that poem, Mum.' A weight seems to lift from her shoulders. Anne takes some deep breaths as they talk about the kids. Tim's work. Her job. Rosie feels a renewed closeness and a deep happiness; the happiness of being a mother and a grandmother.

I'm glad I'm needed. I'm still wanted.

Anne gets out a book from the bookshelf. The kids and Tim have gone to bed. The book is filled with plastic pockets with poems in them.

Anne, of course, being typically so organised, has collected and stored all the poems I have given her over the years. Every time Anne needed support or explanation or understanding, I would be compelled to write her a poem. This was a special thing we shared. I am glad she's kept them. It was not something Tom or Will could understand or appreciate.

Flicking through the poems, Anne picks out her favourites. They reminisce about the times when they were written; they drink cups of tea late into the night. Rosie wishes it were wine but Anne hasn't drunk alcohol since having her children.

I feel partly responsible. The time after Will died, the years of me
drinking in excess. My lack of control. There was a distance between us
then. We were not able to reach each other through the fog of pain and
grief. Now we enjoy our simple tea and talking.

'Do you remember this one?' Anne asks. 'You gave it to me during
my first year of teaching. I've got the painting you did with it. You
know, the pink one, the heart in the centre, with wings.'

'I know the one you're talking about. You are so good, keeping all
this. Treasuring my art, you precious girl.' Rosie gives Anne a warm
smile, squeezes her arm and begins reading the poem.

Fear Not

Beautiful life, in shades of grey
Gracefully flowing within black and white
Sunny days and dark nights
Fine lines between good and bad
Many facets of emotions, drifting amid happy and sad
Confidently ride, the waves of positive and negative
Change is inevitable
Life unpredictable
Blessings and burdens of humanity

Fear not

Strongly sail, the tides of transformation
Transporting you on your treasurable path
Adoration in your grasp
Bursting with each breath-taking opportunity

Master stress, to be your source of strength
Life is short and temporary
No one can escape death
Embrace pressure, to lift you to higher levels
Always giving; not seeking recognition or medals
Selfless and kind
Kindred spirit of mine

Patiently prepare and pray
For brighter days
Wildly dance, in the pouring rain
Fear not, foreseeable pain
Marvel at the rainbows
Create angels, in the snow
We never know
What crazy climate, the cyclic seasons of our existence may bring
Love the bitter winter and the fruitful spring
In all weather
Discover pleasure
Persistently planting seeds of knowledge
Enduring loss with valour
Diligently working for passion, not money
Kind use of sweet honey
Never virulent vinegar or harm
Deep wounds and scars
Wear boldly with pride
Precious soul resides
Vital lessons learnt
Gratitude earned

Not comprehending, the commanding mark you leave
Valiantly chase your wildest dreams

Beautiful soul
Wise and old
Humble and gentle
Beauty beyond the superficial
Loved, cherished and special
Fulfilling a spirited destiny
Leaving an eternal legacy

Fear not

Your own potential and ability
Maintain your peaceful modesty
Warmth wherever you go
A calm and boundless glow
Inspiring
Teaching
Listening with an abounding heart
Generously giving with open arms
Reaching with empathy
Lacking any judgment or insensitive sympathy

Fear not

Your power and beauty
Love yourself in a similar capacity
Relish in your talents and creativity

Don't lose sight
Of your own unique gifts
In the dead of night
Sleep soundly, knowing you make a difference
Achieving a meaningful mission

Within the storms of life
When the weather is unkind
Hold strong to this message
You have a significant purpose
Face it with courage

Fear not

Fulfil all you desire to be
Set your caged bird free

Fear not

You will fly
To new amazing heights
Time will race to catch up with you
Wild winds, beneath your strong wings, will carry you

Fear not

When the dark clouds of doubt are blocking your path
Simply follow your bountiful heart

Rosie remembers how Anne struggled with confidence. Plagued with self-doubt.

Anne was so scared of travelling to the city to study. Facing all her fears. Such a brave, strong girl. Then teaching, placing so much pressure on herself.

Rosie turns to Anne and says, 'I'm so proud of you. You are so strong, darling. So talented and fearless. Look at how much you have achieved.'

'Mum, I wish I could feel that more. I constantly feel like a failure and a fraud,' Anne says, trying to brush off the compliment like a stray hair in her face.

Reaching the end of the book, Anne focuses on the page. 'Here it is, the one I've been looking for. One of my favourites.' Anne reads it out aloud; it feels strange for Rosie to hear her own words read back to her.

Warrior Woman

Warrior woman
Bringing new life into this world
So sacred
So powerful
The most amazing journey of your life
Nothing compares

A new love
A love that will grow
Slowly and powerfully
Each day
Absorbed in a bubble of mothering
Keeping a precious soul alive

Feeding
Waking
Changing
Holding
Physically exhausting
Adrenalin pulsing
Disbelief
As you look at the most beautiful thing
You have ever seen

Moments of sadness and despair wash over you
It feels like a huge mountain you can't climb
Taking deep breaths
Letting the emotions flow
Embracing each high and each low
All part of the journey
One day at a time
You are never alone

A warrior woman
Capable of anything
Endless strength
Fuelled by a love
You have wings to carry you
You are a warrior woman
Who was chosen for this new love

'Oh, I really love it,' Anne says. 'Your words are so beautiful, Mum. How's the novel going?' Anne grins cheekily, sipping her tea. A little sparkle in her eyes.

Rosie takes a deep breath. 'Yeah no bloody good.' A forced laugh is all she manages. 'I just don't know where to start. What to put in. What to leave out. I need a plan or something. I'm just filled with self-doubt. It's not as easy as you'd think starting a project like that.'

'Well stop that crap, and just begin. How about you write to one person. Tell your story. You've lived such an amazing life. You've overcome so much tragedy. You are the warrior woman. With all that wisdom to share with the world. You know, I'd love for my girls, at school, to have a book to read that's about a powerful woman. With an ordinary life. Who overcomes all that life throws at her. That is empathetic, but strong. That teaches them that we all have boundless strength within us, waiting to be tapped into. You know, so many of the girls are obsessed with bloody celebrities and fucking fashion. You know, all that superficial shit. It drives me fucking insane. I'd love you to transport them into your world. To your connection with the land. The wild life. The mountain. Your garden.'

'No pressure, Anne,' Rosie says, chuckling. 'I know you're right. You're fucking right about everything.' Rosie rolls her eyes as she sips her tea.

'I went to this PD the other week—you know, like training to teach English in the middle years—and there were these other teachers from all-girls Catholic schools who felt the same. One lady was saying it's so hard to find texts now that are about a strong female protagonist, written by a woman who's still alive.'

'Really?' Rosie asks with surprise. 'Surely there's plenty.'

'Yeah there are ones, but there's not much to choose from that are contemporary and Australian. Let alone use in the classroom. The curriculum wants us to cover all this shit these days, it's endless.' Anne rubs her face, exasperated. 'My job is not about teaching anymore. It's about ticking boxes and emails. Qualifications and fucking red tape.

I feel like I've lost my purpose. What the fuck am I doing it all for? To pay the mortgage on this fancy house. To send our kids to the best schools. So they can get a good education. They can get good jobs. Buy fancy houses. Pay their large mortgages.'

Rosie feels her irritation. 'Well sometimes we sacrifice what we need to, to ensure our kids have a better life. More opportunities. All I know, darling, is you are amazing. You do such a great job. You were born to teach; we needed a smart one in the family.' Laughing. 'Remember when Will was in preps? You would sit with him. Up on the bed. Making him read. He reluctantly followed your instructions. You helped him sound out the words.' Rosie feels a wave of nostalgia and grief envelope her.

'Mum, I still really love teaching. I love the girls; they inspire me so much. It's just all the other demands that are distracting. Juggling it all. I feel like I fail at everything. If I dedicate too much time to work, I neglect the kids, and if I'm too focused on the kids and getting all the housework done, then I get behind with my school work. Then there's Tim—well, he is just last on my list.' Anne's hands move in a frenzy.

'Well, I think you need to make some changes. If Tim gets this promotion, you should go part time next year. You need a cleaner to come once a week. Be fucked, you doing all that, on top of your work and the kids. It's too much, Anne. You are a warrior woman, but you also need to fill your cup. You can't pour from an empty cup.'

'I know, you are so right.' Anne rubs her face and forehead with her hand, taking a deep breath. 'But you did it, with three kids, and Dad and the farm. You did it all. I feel like a failure that I can't.'

'Well, I had Mumma, she helped me. I was hopeless when you guys were little. I struggled the most when Will was born. He never slept. The first year, I was in darkness and I never worked. I cried all the time, I had postnatal depression and Mumma had to drag me to the doctor's. I guess you remember the times when you were all at school and I had my shit together. Working on the farm. Mumma did a heap of housework for me. You know I've always been hopeless with that. Too focused on the cows and garden. I was not the kind of mother you are. Patient. Reading to them and teaching them.'

Anne rolls her eyes.

'I was always yelling, telling you lot to get out from under my feet.'

'But you were always fun. Dancing. Cracking jokes. Lively. Yes, always losing your shit at us. You weren't boring, like me.' Anne traces the edge of the cup. A look of defeat washes across her face.

Rosie gets up to put her cup in the sink. 'Your crazy, red-headed mother is here now, so, we can have plenty of fun. You need to rest. Let me be your Mumma.' Rosie wraps her arm around Anne and kisses her on the head, like she is a little girl again.

'Yeah, I know. Better get off to bed. What is the time?' Anne asks.

'Just after one.' Rosie looks at Anne for a second longer, as Anne studies her cup.

My girl's not right.

'Night, darling.'

'Night, Mum.'

Rosie lies in bed, slowly drifting off to sleep.

I always see Anne as being so perfect. So independent. She was always the one in charge, even as a little girl, growing up. She was always so wise and sensible. She's married to an accountant, for God sake. A part of me loves to see her so raw. A bit broken and vulnerable. I know that's wrong.

I don't like her hurting. This vulnerability breathes life into her. There are adventures we can go on during the week. I can help you, my dear girl.

Rosie peacefully drifts off to sleep.

GRAIN OF SAND

Rosie packs her bag and puts it over her head, making sure she has her camera. She sprays her perfume.

This fragrance reminds me of Mumma's distinct smell. The perfume she used all her life.

Rosie walks down the footpath. Casting her eyes up, she admires the old trees.

Look at them. Living, surviving amongst the concrete. All these buildings. Reaching up to the sky, so determined. It's frustrating. God, look how severely pruned they are. Just to make way for the powerlines.

Waiting at the tram stop, she checks the times on the list behind the clear plastic covering. She ties her jacket round her waist as the cold wind rushes past her. The tram rattles along the track. Rosie is pleased she wore her boots as she dodges several puddles, stepping towards the tram's entrance with trepidation. After swiping her card, she takes a seat near the window. With intrigue, she watches the shops pass her by.

A foreign landscape. So much to absorb. It reminds me of exploring European cities. The fear and thrill of getting lost. The excitement of discovering new and interesting places. Enjoying it all pass by. An adventure.

Her mind wanders.

I'm excited about the unknown. What I may discover. It reminds me of exploring the streets of Venice, getting lost. Ainsley staying back at the motel. So much freedom.

Rosie opens her notebook, retrieves her pen and begins writing.

A Labyrinth

Streets like intertwined rivers
Weaving their way
In a tangled maze
Lost
Endless discoveries
It all looks different from a different angle
Tangle of languages
Accents
Cultures
Sea of endless possibility
My emotions
Expectations
Mood
Have been like these canals
Streets
Tangled
Twisted
Weaving their way out to sea
To find
Freedom
Space
Breathe again
Relax
Calm waters
No more greed
Or need

Contentment
Satisfaction
God
Love
All the world
Is my home
With God
I am never alone

Reaching the centre of the city, Rosie places her notebook in her bag. Getting off the tram, Rosie recognises the familiar landmarks. She walks towards the art gallery, breathing in.

The air doesn't have the familiar freshness of my mountain air. I can only imagine what I could be breathing in. All these car fumes polluting the air.

Crossing the bridge, she looks down at the river. It is dark and murky. Rosie is reminded of crossing the bridge at home, the clear water revealing the stones at the bottom.

I wouldn't want to go swimming in there, let alone drink it. The city is so interesting and exciting but also so foreign.

The noise fills her head. The colours, the movement. So much to see. After weaving her way through the people, she is relieved to get off the footpath. She retreats to the quiet sanctuary of the gallery, filled with excitement, anticipating seeing an exhibition.

She is one of my favourite artists, Rosalie Gascoigne. I wish Stella was with me.

Rosie walks through the corridors towards the right section, admiring the grandeur of the building.

It is all so clean, ordered, with its pristine white walls.

She looks up, her head and neck arching to see it all. Walking through the gallery space, a surge of life rushes through her, like finding hidden treasure.

This is it.

She reads the sign for the exhibition at the entrance. A friendly smile greets her. A short girl with thick-framed glasses. Rosie returns the smile.

What a boring job, standing there all day. I guess you could people watch, if nothing else.

In awe, she wanders. Looking at pieces she has only ever seen in photos. Corrugated iron placed strategically to form the inland sea.

They seem to float, dance. Look at this beautiful selection of lino. The old crates. Sticks, all placed so carefully.

Rosie is tempted to reach out and touch it. Feel the history. Touch the stories. She notices the alarms and watchful eye of the guard. Perched like a kookaburra on a branch.

Gascoigne has such a powerful relationship with the land. Her amazing observations. Her unique artistic interpretations. Fuck it's amazing.

Filled with inspiration, Rosie considers her own artist journey.

She never started until later in her life. Maybe it's never too late. To begin. To create.

Rosie walks around several times, absorbing it, returning to her favourite pieces.

As Rosie leaves the gallery, the girl with the dark, thick-framed glasses offers her a mechanical smile. Rosie has a spring in her step. She finds a crossing before making her way to the gardens. She waits at the crossing, lining up like a school child waiting for the bell to ring. The little green man to flash green. Rosie walks with the crowd and finds the gardens. She squints from the glare of the sun that has escaped the clouds. Finding a comfortable, dry place on the grass, she retrieves her notebook from her bag and begins writing and drawing.

Hours slip by as she fills the pages with her creative energy. Lost in a world she can't explain. Lost but found, in sync with her soul.

Feeling hungry, Rosie decides to find a place to have lunch. Vaguely remembering a laneway she went with Anne once—filled with restaurants—Rosie goes in the direction she instinctually thinks is right. Rosie lets her memory and intuition lead her. She ventures up a cluttered laneway filled with the smell of food. Walls lined with graffiti. Rosie walks up and back down, nervous to pick a place. Overwhelmed at the choice. Finding a place that isn't too crowded, she sits in a quiet spot.

Eating her burger and chips, she watches the street. A tangle of people move consistently like flowing water. The flavours excite her tastebuds; this is not like the burgers from her small-town fish and chip shop. She studies the pictures plastered on the wall. A cat made of paper looks into the distance, a black-and-white image.

The city overloads Rosie's senses. There is so much to absorb. Such a faster pace than she is accustomed to.

As Rosie finishes her meal and sips on her drink, tiredness flows through her body. Her legs feel heavy. She watches the sparrows scavenging scraps from empty tables, bouncing, fluttering. Picking up her bag, she checks she has everything.

I better make my way back to the train station. On the way, I might look in that art-supply shop.

Rosie steps into the art supply store, escaping the noisy laneway. The smell of sandalwood fills her nostrils. The walls are lined with a plethora of materials.

There is so much I could buy and use.

She touches an art easel, feeling its smooth wood. She flips the price tag over, and raises her eyebrows.

I won't be taking that home. I'm apprehensive to make a choice.

To make a purchase. The city intimidates me. I feel like a stranger in a foreign land.

Stepping back out into the laneway, Rosie continues to walk, avoiding the flow of people walking in the other direction. She goes into a bookshop. Noticing how noise fills the street outside, she scans her eyes over all the different titles and authors.

There's so many stories out there. How could my story possibly compete? So many talented writers. I'm a very little fish in a massive pond. The city makes me feel like a grain of sand on the beach. A beach filled with billions of individual grains.

Feeling small and insignificant, she craves her mountain. Choosing a book by one of her favourite writers, she makes her way to the counter. A young girl scans it, her face a mass of piercings. Rosie looks at the round hole stretched in her ear and the tattoo running up her neck. Conscious she is staring, she quickly diverts her line of vision.

Entering the street into a sea of pedestrians, she notices the darkness the tall buildings create. She feels space shrinking. Rosie feels claustrophobic. Confined.

Standing on the platform, waiting for her train, she watches an old lady, huddled over, dragging her legs slowly up the platform. Pulling an old leather cart. Her grey hair dishevelled.

Is she homeless? No, probably not, too clean. What a place to live and then die. How lucky am I to live where I live? In the expanse of my valley. It's so open and wide. My big, sprawling sky. Infinitely high. I miss that space. I'd love an afternoon nap in my own bed. Sit at my desk, in my wooden chair. I already miss the smell of home.

Rosie moves like a grain of sand on the beach, swept by the wind, onto the train. Surrounded by a flood of people and cascading noise. Staring out the window, she watches the water flow down the putrid drain.

BLACK BOX

As Rosie looks out the window of the train, she is excited to visit Aunty Jassie.

I haven't seen her in such a long time. We have our letters, but it is not the same as eyes meeting. Feeling the warmth of her presence. Her calming presence. A living angel. A saint. Always so calm and wise. Never concerned with worldly distractions. Focused on the ways of heaven; a devout nun.

Rosie remembers the beauty of her salvation.

My baptism. Clothed in a white lace dress. The light shining through the window. The Holy Spirit resting on my shoulders. As I made a promise. A commitment to God. I remember reading Mark's gospel for the first time. Falling in love with the man. The son of God. Jesus. The intense conversations I had with Aunty Jassie. She taught and inspired me to have a deep love and passion for a revolutionary. A rebel. A saviour. A man but also God.

Lost in her thoughts. The train trip seems to go quickly.

I need to talk to Aunty Jassie. I need some answers. A brother. Another family. I know she will know.

As Rosie walks from the train station, leaves dance at her feet, swept up by the winter wind. Rosie admires the gum trees lining the path.

She checks the address before she knocks. A brick building, with a black door. A veranda reaching around the front. A little bit of nervousness runs through her body, anticipating the door opening. As she looks at the crack in the tiles, another gust of wild wind sweeps through the trees. The door opens and an elderly woman greets her. Rosie explains who she is and whom she is visiting. The little nun looks very frail, as though her bones will crack if you touch her. She seems to know who Rosie is and who she is visiting. Shuffling along the floor, she leads Rosie to a communal room with a small kitchenette. Rosie takes a seat. Patiently waiting for Aunty Jassie, Rosie examines the cabinet filled with plates. The place brings her a sense of peace and calm. Looking out the window, she can see the wind blowing through the trees. A line of camellias move in unison as the wind shakes them. Aunty Jassie enters the room discreetly in her typical quiet manner. Rosie gets up and embraces her.

I'm so relieved to finally see her. She looks exactly the same as the last time I saw her. A few more lines around her eyes but she's still so beautiful.

Jassie has a bag she places on an empty chair.

'It's so good to see you,' Aunty Jassie says. 'You look so young. This time of rest has been serving you well. I'll be right back.'

Aunty Jassie has seen me in many different times. Like when I was in hospital. I'll never forget the time Aunty Jassie came to visit me. I was dark and bitter. I asked her why she was taken. How could this happen? I'll never forget Aunty Jassie's response: 'We all have a set number, an allocated time on this earth, and MJ, hers was eighteen years. It is all a plan. There is no explanation for it. This is just the dress rehearsal for our most important life and mission in heaven. God must have needed her sooner than we would have liked.' I mulled over this for a long time. I thought about it a lot when Will died. The same message. The same wisdom. At the time, it gave me an answer, but could not alleviate all my anger. My utter disbelief. My intense grief.

Returning with a jug of milk, Aunty Jassie begins making tea and placing biscuits on a plate. 'How is Tom and Billy?' she probes.

'You know, Tom works too hard, as usual. Billy is the sweetest boy, an old soul; he loves his chickens. Full of energy. Questions about everything. He's doing well at school. He seems happy.' Rosie can't help but smile as she describes her beloved boy.

'Does he ask about his mother?'

'He has. It's hard to know what to tell him, to be honest.'

Aunty Jassie places the cups of tea on the table; she moves to the counter and picks up the plate of biscuits. After carefully positioning them on the table, Jassie cautiously sits down. Out the window, the rain begins to pelt down, moving sideways as the wind continues to roar.

'I want to talk to you about that, actually,' Aunty Jassie says. 'I'm pleased you were able to visit today.'

A large lump begins forming in Rosie's throat, knowing Aunty Jassie has something important to tell her. Aunty Jassie sips her tea. 'I have recently been working in a women's refuge, as you know from my recent letters. By some act of God, Lottie and I crossed paths.' Pausing, Jassie gives Rosie a chance to absorb the information.

What the fuck. What does she mean, they crossed paths? I want to ask a million questions. I better give Aunty Jassie time to explain.

'Unfortunately, she was not in a good way when I first saw her. She had been homeless. Living on the streets, for many years. Lottie recognised me, despite—I suspected at that time—being affected by drugs. Later, she divulged the extent of her drug addiction. For many months we were in contact and we spoke at length about her life. Her choices. I thought we had got to a point where she was making progress but a few weeks ago ...' Aunty Jassie pauses. Time seems to slow. Rosie knows the words before they come. The wind blows through the leaves, as if in slow motion. 'I received news that she was deceased. A drug overdose. I'm assuming unintentional. But the authorities don't put a lot of time and effort into investigating the details of a homeless woman's death. Unless, of course, murder is suspected. I collected all her possessions from the refuge.' Jassie directs her eyes towards the bag on the chair. She pulls out a black box and opens it up.

'This is a box of letters. Written to Billy. I haven't read any of them, but I want you to take this bag home for Billy. When you feel it is the right time for him to have them.' Aunty Jassie speaks with a sadness and regret in her voice.

'Was she with anyone? Any other children?' Rosie asks, taking the big, black box filled with the pile of letters and things for Billy. She places it beside her bag to take with her; it feels heavy, like it's made with lead.

'No partner. No other children. Lottie was a beautiful girl. As I got to know her, she revealed to me that she had many demons. She was abused as a child by one of her stepfathers. I know this is a lot to take in, but I really want to tell you everything while we are in person. Lottie spoke of you, Tom and Billy with such fondness. She missed her boy. She missed Tom and you. The farm. But she never felt like she was good enough for that life. Lottie was broken and damaged, long before she came into our lives. A bird with clipped wings.'

Rosie begins to question why as the news trickles into her ears like water flowing down the window.

'I wanted to tell you in person. She's with God now,' Aunty Jassie explains as she reaches her hand across the table and places it on top of Rosie's.

'How do you know? Do you believe she is in heaven?' Rosie pleads as a tear rolls down her cheek. The reality of the news sinks in. Aunty Jassie hands her a tissue.

'Jesus was there for the sick. The damaged. The broken. Those who struggled; he spent his time with the homeless, prostitutes and beggars.

Lottie is with him now.'

There is silence. The rain falls. The wind blows violently. Time breaks in half. 'I organised a funeral for her,' Aunty Jassie says. 'I tried to look into her family but her mother disowned her. She never knew her father. Lottie spent several years in foster families before running away.' Aunty Jassie takes a breath to continue speaking, then glances at Rosie and pauses, as if thinking better of it. She hands Rosie a Bible story to read. The woman at the well. 'Remember that from when you were baptised?'

'Yes, of course I do,' Rosie whispers, the paper in her hands. 'Have you ever done the wrong thing? How do you always know what is right?' She searches Aunty Jassie's face, desperate for answers.

'Well, I don't always know. You know, over the years, Phoebe and I haven't always seen eye to eye. We had a fight when we discovered Daisy was pregnant with you. Of course, your mother wanted to keep you—her sweet baby—but she was scared that our parents would disapprove. Daisy was struggling to hide her morning sickness. I suspected it a long time before she told Phoebe and me. As you know, we shared the back bedroom. Phoebe was on her own. Phoebe said for Daisy to abort you and keep it a secret. I told her that was wrong. We argued about it. Phoebe didn't speak to me for a long time afterwards. Your mother and I spoke about it. Daisy told me, "I love this child already, growing inside of me." She was adamant you were a girl. She also knew that she was too young and not married. I'll never forget her words. Daisy said, "I feel in the depths of my being, in the pit of my aching soul that I'm supposed to have, to love and to raise this child. It is my destiny to be a mother." We were sitting on the edge of the hill. The stars shining brightly. I wrapped my arm around her and told her, "I'll help you tell them. I'll help you raise this child. We are in this together." I promised her.'

Tears rush down Rosie's face. Aunty Jassie reaches across the table, places her hand on top of Rosie's and says, 'I'll always keep that promise to love. To cherish you like my own daughter. I'm so proud of the woman you have become. Search in the depths of your heart and there the answer will be, waiting for you.'

With her eyes cast down, in a voice that is almost a whisper, Rosie says, 'Speaking of matters of the heart. A boy came to visit me.' Rosie is not sure if she can actually say it.

Now is the time to let it out. We need to talk about this now. Who knows when I'll see Aunty Jassie again?

'He looked identical to Will. Arrived on my doorstep. I thought I'd seen a ghost.'

A frown appears on Jassie's face. She fidgets in her chair. Something flashes through her eyes as she takes a deep breath.

'So this beautiful young man, it turns out, is my nephew. Phillip. He had my brother's birth certificate. With Daisy's name on it. *Unknown* is all it stated for the father.'

'Robert? Dear little Robert,' Jassie says, fiddling with a crumb on the table as her voice trails off, her eyes cast down.

A heat rises. Rosie's heart beats fast. A tingling in her eyes.

'You knew. You bloody knew. You never told me. Of course you knew.' The anger continues rising up her neck, stinging her eyes. A foreign feeling towards Jassie. Reminiscent of a time when she was angry at the world.

'Oh, darling. I knew. Yes, I knew. I wanted to tell you. But it was not my place to tell you. I fought with Mumma and Phoebe many times about it. They wanted to preserve your innocence. They thought that you had suffered enough. In losing your mother. Never knowing your father.'

'How could she give him away? Why wasn't I just given away?

Unwanted. Unloved.' Rosie throws her arms like she is throwing something out the window. There is harshness in her voice, like a knife slicing the air.

'It wasn't that simple. You know in those days women were sent away. They went on a convenient holiday. Daisy actually loved your father. She loved Robert too. Our parents forbade it. He drank too much. They wanted her to marry a local. A respectable farmer, with plenty of money, of course.'

'What, like I did?'

'Well, luckily for you, you fell in love with the right man. That's why you, darling, got the farm. These are simple facts of life. They were different times. Daisy was heartbroken when her son was taken from her. She was forced to say goodbye to the man she loved. That last goodbye was how you were conceived. Then he was run out of town. They were powerless. Daisy planned to find Robert when she could. Find your father. Have you. Run away. Be a family. Your mother, oh she was a victim of difficult circumstances.'

'What was his name? What was my father's name?

'Patrick, Patrick Quinn.'

'Did he love her?'

'From what I knew, he loved her. If he was able to, he would have married Daisy. Look.' Jassie shakes her head. 'Pa was a wonderful, honourable man. We all know that, but he wouldn't let her marry him. They were such different times; women obeyed their husbands and their fathers. I guess I was a coward then. Believe me, I wanted to fight for what was right. But I didn't. I'm sorry. I truly am.' A single tear runs down her cheek. A branch scratches against the window as the wild wind creates fury in the leaves of the trees. A knot forms in the pit of Rosie's stomach.

'Oh Jassie, it's not your fault, I know.' Rosie shakes her head. 'I understand. Oh I know things were hard back then. It's just been such a shock. So much to take in. I haven't thought about my parents in so long. Then this boy, this young man—the spitting image of Will—rocks up at my door, with this birth certificate. There was a note with Mumma's name and address on it. Robert has died; apparently he was going to find his family before he became too ill to travel. The boy grew up in England. His wife and family have moved to Australia. I'm thinking of visiting them.'

'Life is short. Go and see them. Find the answers you need. Don't be scared or foolish, like I was.' Jassie gets up, signalling it is time for Rosie to go. Methodically, Jassie clears the table.

'Before I go. Do you know a Tina? Maybe a pen pal that Daisy had?'

'It doesn't ring a bell, sweetheart. I have told you what I know.' Jassie holds her tenderly on her shoulders, looking into her eyes.

She's telling the truth. She knows nothing of these letters. The box. The photograph. I know Jassie. I'd know if she was lying.

They embrace. Communicating so much left unsaid. As they say their farewell, waves of emotion wash over Rosie. Gratitude for Aunty Jassie. A longing to stay with her a little longer. Grief. Shock. Flood of tears.

'Write, my girl. Please write,' Jassie says. Her soft hands cradle Rosie's face as she looks deeply into Rosie's brown, tear-filled eyes.

'Always,' Rosie replies.

She walks out into the rain-soaked street, her red curly hair sweeping across her face as the wind fights against her.

A part of her wants to stay here, forever in Aunt Jassie's protection and love.

I know it's time to go.

Travelling back to Anne's place on the train, she is in a daze. Trying to comprehend all she has been told.

There is that part of Mark's gospel. I remember reading it for the first time and discovering that Jesus was not concerned with people who were perfect, but the 'morally sick'. Prostitutes. Beggars. Sick people need a doctor. I desperately wanted to know where my best friend was. Again I recalled Aunty Jassie's words as I lay in the hospital bed: 'We all have a certain amount of time on this earth and we don't know how long that is.' Questioning. Searching for the meaning of life. Bible study. All I could understand was that the only thing that lasts is the soul. The soul only knows of love. That is what is important. That is eternal.

Rosie stares out the window; the world passes by in a blur. An aching. A desire burns in the depths of her heart.

I need to write. I know I need to write.

She catches a glimpse of a bird's nest; she envisages the baby birds, the eggs. She remembers a homeless person she saw at the train station.

Imagine the life Lottie had lived. Being faceless. Nameless. Invisible. In desperation and despair.

A deep maternal instinct brings her to tears; a lady opposite her passes her a tissue.

'Sorry, I just received some tragic news today,' Rosie explains to the stranger.

The older lady smiles with warmth and understanding. She has short, curled hair, pressed neatly. Stockings. Skirt. The woman clings to her bag and pulls out her crocheting.

We are probably similar ages.

Rosie looks out the window, trying to avoid eye contact and the obligation of making conversation. Longing to protect and care for Lottie, guilt washes over her.

I wish I had made her stay. I feel so selfish for the happiness I took from her.

Many questions run through her mind.

Do I tell Tom? Do I tell Anne? What about Billy?

Rosie feels very alone, wishing she had someone to share this burden with. Gazing out the window, she looks at the cars in the car parks. Lost in her thoughts. The warm sun comes through the window.

I'm so tired. This day has exhausted me. So many answers. So many more questions. What did my brother look like? What if my mother had survived? What if we could have been a family? All together, like a normal family.

An image of a perfect family posing fills her mind.

She's surrounded by concrete. Powerlines. Fences. Traffic lights. Thick, imposing walls. Rosie feels homesick for her mountain. Her bed. Her garden. The wide expanse of her valley.

Trees interspersed with graffiti. The endless rows of fences.

Doors opening and shutting break her trance. The sky fills with clouds once again. Surrounded by strangers with headphones in and on their phones, detached from the world. Surrounded by all these people, she feels insignificant. Lonely. Rosie wonders what their stories are. The man in the business suit. The man reading a book.

She watches the large buildings. Cranes. Industrial areas. Rooftops. The suburban sprawl flies past her window.

Arriving at her train stop, she picks up her bags and steps onto the platform. The weight of her bags seems impossible to carry. She fights the wind as she begins trudging back to Anne's place. Her shoulders ache, carrying a weight she longs to be free of.

HAPPY WANDERER

Hanging another towel over the clothesline, Rosie straightens it before she pegs it on. Admiring the gum tree in the neighbour's yard, towering high into the sky, she hears the foreign noise of traffic in the background.

I feel so far from home. I'm such a silly old lady. Longing for home, my beloved gums. It won't be long now. I'll be surrounded by them again. I just want some normality. The world feels crazy. First Phillip arrives, now the news of Lottie. Aunty Jassie had plenty of answers. I'm just not sure if they were the ones I wanted. Her face is in my head. Her glasses. Her short, curly hair going grey. Aunty Jassie's voice. I can't stop the conversation playing on loop in my head.

As she spins the Hills hoist around, she notices the cherry blossom in Anne's backyard is bare and stark.

It reminds me of the one in my garden. I remember giving it to Anne when they first bought the house. I was so proud of Anne and Tim. They had bought their very own place. They seemed so determined. So successful. For a long time, I had doubted they would ever have kids. I accepted that, as I wanted Anne to feel no pressure.

Rosie decides to go for a walk in the park. She puts the laundry basket back in the laundry, then packs her camera in her bag. As she walks out the gate, she checks the letterbox, then turns and admires the old house. The dark-red bricks. The hydrangea under the front window.

The large oak trees lining the street expose their light-dappled skin. Clouds drift peacefully in the winter sky. Inspecting the gardens as she walks, Rosie imagines things she'd do to the gardens. Waiting at the lights, she watches the cars stream past and imagines Anne in this chaotic world.

Anne was riddled with homesickness in the early years, when she first moved to the city to go to uni. I can really understand why. The long phone calls to her father. Searching for home. They always had a special bond. I guess Blake was always such a good listener. The stable, consistent one. Anne needed Blake when Olivia was born. I guess I was there after the caesarean, in those early weeks. We bonded, a mother and daughter, through the shared agony of being a new mother. How she agonised over breastfeeding. Feeling inadequate because it wasn't working. Then she started bottle-feeding Olivia. Anne has become the most amazing mother. How Blake would love them. He'd be so proud of her. God, he's missing out on a lot. Why me? Why would you let me stay and take Blake away?

Rosie crosses the road and enters the park. The green grass is lush. Contained. Manicured. She follows the curve of the garden beds as she tries to name all the different species. Rosie remembers Mumma teaching her different names of plants as a child. Rosie always had a thirst for knowledge. Taking several photos, Rosie works on the different frames and positioning of objects in the photo. She trials different compositions: placing the gazebo in the background, the long, slender reeds in front. The bright-purple happy wanderer in the centre. Pink and orange grevilleas to one side.

As she moves, she tries to capture all the beauty she can see in just one shot. Noticing a gorgeous flowering gum, she zooms in to see the delicate and intricate beauty of a single flower. The pink fingers spreading. A golden centre. Rosie marvels at its perfection. God's creation.

After she exhausts her ideas for taking photos, she sits for a while on the soft grass and begins drawing—her pencil moving with ease across the paper as she copies the straight, rectangular shapes of the gazebo. The rambling vines. The chaotic spread of leaves of the happy wanderer. As the pencil glides, Rosie builds the images. She thinks about Lottie, remembering her when she first arrived.

It was such a surprise when Tom brought this wild filly home. Lottie was always laughing. Having a joke. So bubbly and charismatic. She was so loud and friendly. Always making everyone feel at ease.

The memory brings a smile to her face as tears well in her eyes.

The first time I met her, I thought, She's so much fun, so wild and beautifully rough as guts. I really liked her, instantly. Lottie was the antithesis of Tom. I thought at the time she was perfect, exactly what he needed. She rubbed Mumma up the wrong way, of course. Her vibrant personality and confidence. I remember Mumma saying, 'She's got too much of what the cat licks its arse with.' I could always empathise with our dear Lottie; she had a fire burning inside of her, an unfulfilled potential. A roller-coaster ride of emotions, wearing her heart on her sleeve. I remember that late-night conversation with her. Everyone in bed. Those scars on her legs. The pain she had endured. Her tales of running away from home. Where would she have been? I should have known then. To keep her closer. Keep her safer.

A leaf drops from the tree; it floats, drifts on the breeze, twirls and gently lands on the grass. From the corner of her eye, she notices a blue wren dancing on a branch. Then it disappears.

I can only imagine the places she'd been. Maybe being adopted is a good option. Robert's life sounds like it was normal, or at least comfortable. Growing up overseas. They must have had plenty of money, especially back then.

As Rosie begins to venture back to Anne's place, she decides to go into the library.

She walks amongst the books, not looking for anything in particular. A little girl with long, red hair walks past, holding her mother's hand and chatting. Her thick hair tied with a white bow. The little girl looks around three years old, reminding Rosie of the granddaughter she wishes she had. Reminded of broken dreams.

She makes her way to the children's books. Picking one up, she skims through it, admiring the illustrations.

I'd love to do this. I should try this.

She checks the time. The ticking clock on the wall.

It won't be long until the kids are home. I better get back and get some housework done for Anne.

She walks briskly. The breeze moves her hair in front of her face; she pushes her curls behind her ears.

Imagine all the different picture storybooks I could write and illustrate.

The footpath leads her back to Anne's house. The large oak trees stand guard.

Sitting down, she starts writing a list of ideas. Feeling free and inspired. She looks over to the painting leaning against the wall. The bright pinks. The caged bird released.

I should take my own advice sometimes. I still have two hours before the kids are home. Plenty of time.

Uncovering the name and address on the paper in her notebook, she feels compelled to go. They are in a neighbouring suburb. A short tram ride. Rosie quickly works out the route, still doubtful if she wants to see them. Meet Robert's wife. Meet Phillip's wife and children. Looking at the painting, she packs her bag. She locks the door behind her.

A cold wind brushes past her as she enters the street. Hearing the tram coming, she quickens her step to get to the stop in time. The tram approaches in perfect time for her to climb on. Filled with nervousness and excitement, she takes in all the city has to look at. People and shops sweep past the window.

As she gets off at the stop, she checks her mud map to work out where to go. It is clear this is an affluent suburb. The leafy street is filled with large properties bordered by tall brick fences and iron gates.

This is a foreign world. I wonder if I've got the wrong address. How could I be related to people who live in a house like this?

Rosie presses the intercom. A muffled voice comes through the speaker. 'Hello?' It is clearly a British accent.

'Um, yes. Um, hello. Um, this is Rosie. Rosie Lane. I am here to see Phillip, if he's about, please.'

'Hello, Rosie. How are you? I will just unlock the gate.' Rosie recognises Phillip's voice as a loud buzzer sounds. The gate unlocks and she hesitantly opens it and walks down the path. A small, neat hedge lines the path. A tall tree fills the front yard. A two-storey house stands before her, lacework trimmings along the verandas. The place looks pristine. As she approaches, the door opens. Phillip's warm smile is there to greet her. Rosie's breath is taken away at the sight of him, as her son is momentarily returned to her.

'It's so lovely to see you,' Phillip says. 'Please come in.'

Entering the house, she wipes her feet at the front step, unsure how to behave in a house like this. Her neck twists around as she takes in all the architecture, decor and antique furniture filling the house.

'Come through. We are in the kitchen. My wife, Kylie will be so excited to meet you.'

'I hope I haven't come at an inconvenient time. I'm staying with my daughter, Anne—she's only a suburb away, so I thought I would come and see you.'

'Kylie, this is Rosie—um, my aunty, I guess you could say.' Phillip holds his hand out, gesturing towards Rosie.

'Rosie. How are you? It's such a pleasure. Can I get you a cup of tea?' Kylie reaches out and gives Rosie a hug. 'Sit down, please. Make yourself at home. The kids are outside. They are loving this Australian weather. All this time to be outside.' Kylie's accent is Australian with a dash of British thrown in.

'I'd love a cup of tea. Thank you so much.' Rosie feels a warmth from Kylie, as though she already knows her.

'How do you have it?'

'White. No sugar, thanks.'

Rosie takes her bag off from around her shoulder and looks at the beauty of the house. There are artworks and family photos on the wall. It looks like a professionally styled house by one of those designers from TV. Filled with anxiety, part of her wishes she didn't come.

'Shall we move into the living room?' Phillip asks.

'Yes.' Rosie smiles and follows Phillip and Kylie into a large room. The ceilings are high, a large brick fireplace dominates the space. Rosie looks around while trying not to look too nosey. Her heart races; her breath is shallow.

This pain will go. It always does. I will be glad I came.

The call of children can be heard from outside.

'Here you go,' Phillip says as he places her cup of tea on the coffee table.

'Thank you, sweetheart. Nothing better than a cuppa.' Rosie wraps her hands around the mug.

'So, you are staying with Anne; that must be nice?'

'Yes, I don't leave the valley very often. So it's nice to get away. I spent some time overseas when I was younger, but the rest of the time I've been on the farm. I was able to visit my aunt yesterday, actually. She has filled in some gaps for me.' Rosie sips her tea and hesitates. 'Phillip, I've been wondering what your grandparents were like? Your father's adoptive parents.' Rosie runs her hand around the rim of the cup.

'Well, my grandfather was Charles Butler and my grandmother was Tina.'

'She was a beautiful seamstress,' Kylie interjects. 'I'll show you some photos if you like.'

'That would be lovely, if it's not too much trouble,' Rosie responds with a warm smile, relieved Phillip's wife is so friendly.

Kylie returns to the table with a box of photos. She sits a pile of photos on the table.

'This is just a random bunch we collected while cleaning out Robert's study.' Kylie places more photos on the table and spreads them out.

Rosie glances across the table; an identical image to the one she saw in the box at home is there staring back at her.

NO PLACE LIKE HOME

Awaiting the train that will take her back to the country, Rosie has mixed feelings. She's excited to be going home but sad to be leaving Anne and the kids. She gives them all a warm embrace.

Maybe I should tell Anne about Phillip before I leave? I know I should have last night but I need to process this before I tell her. I can't tell her right before I go. It can wait. There will be a right time, just not right now.

Anne hands her a book. *The Alchemist.* 'You must read this,' she says adamantly. Conviction in her eyes. Rosie looks down as she wraps her arms around them. Olivia and Lachlan's faces are pure and innocent.

They look like little angels. Oh, I miss them already.

Picking up her bags and walking to her seat, she holds back tears.

Tom and Billy pick Rosie up. Their faces glow at the sight of her. As they drive over the big hill, the valley is exposed. Her heart leaps; she feels a sense of relief knowing she is home.

Billy is excited. 'There's a surprise when we get home. I got an early birthday present.'

'What are we going to do for your birthday?' Rosie asks. 'It's the one day you get to do what you want.'

'Can Jimmy come over for a sleep over?'

'Yeah, that's easy,' Tom responds.

'What about a cake?' Rosie asks. 'You'll need to check the book and pick a design for this year.'

'Can we go for a drive up the top of the mountain?' Billy pleads.

'Yeah, but you've been there heaps of times,' Tom says. 'Don't you want to do something different?'

'I know, but that's my favourite place.'

'What about if we take you to another mountain? To a bigger, taller one?' Tom inquires.

'Aw yeah, really? That'd be awesome.' Billy bounces in his seat. Tom's face lets in a slight smile.

'That friesian bull showed up,' Tom mentions.

'Oh yeah, where did he get to?'

'Got through right up in that top corner of the Selection. Anyway, I managed to get him back on the bike. The neighbours might have some black-and-white calves next year.'

'Sounds like I missed out on all the fun while I was gone?' Rosie glances to the back seat. Billy is sitting forward, eager to be part of the conversation.

They drop Rosie home. She feels a sense of relief while opening the gate. She misses her old dog's greeting as she carries her bags inside. The bitter cold has nested in the house in her absence. After placing her bags on the table, she prioritises getting the fire started. When she goes out to the woodshed, she notices that Tom has placed a fresh load of red gum there for her.

Always so busy, but can always look after his mother. I wish he'd waited until I got back, so I could've helped.

She cuts some kindling from the fence palings using the little tomahawk axe. Filling her arms with bigger wood, she goes to stand up as a small snake wriggles from between two logs. Rosie instinctively drops the wood and grabs the axe; with two swift cuts, the snake is in pieces.

I'll leave it there. A nice feast for a bird or cat. What's it doing out at this time of the year? Maybe it got carted back. I'm relieved it didn't get a chance to make a permanent home in the woodshed.

Rosie picks up the kindling and wood again, eager to feel the warmth of the fire. Moving inside, she turns on all the lights. Trying to create warmth. A familiar feeling of home.

Dumping the wood at the base of the Coonara, she opens the door. Searches for the firelighters and matches. Rosie places the firelighter in the centre, surrounds it with kindling in a tepee shape and lights the pile. The flames engulf the stack of neatly placed kindling. Rosie goes into the kitchen to make a cup of tea while it takes light.

It's good to return to this familiar smell. My kitchen. Home. I wonder what's in the rest of those envelopes. I'll have to wait for Billy and me to look through them. Now I have another bloody box full of letters. I don't even want to think about it right now. How did life become so complicated?

Rosie crochets beside the warm fire and sips her tea, the cold slowly being chased out. She rocks gently in her chair. Melodic music plays. Rosie closes her eyes; an image of Lottie when she was pregnant fills her mind.

Lottie was bursting with warmth and life. Possibility. Vibrant. I don't remember ever being like that when I was pregnant. Just tired and sore. But Lottie was your stereotypical, glowing pregnant woman. A ball of inspiration.

Rosie places her hands over her chest, feeling a deep pain; regret and sadness.

This image is how I will remember her. That is how I imagine she will be in heaven. That was Lottie, in her purest state. If only her demons weren't so strong.

With a long sigh, Rosie crochets, rocking slowly in her chair. The wind howls; a purple petunia rocks in a hanging basket outside the window.

I send you love and prayers, my girl. A beautiful soul. My daughter. Billy's mother.

A single tear runs down her cheek and onto her neck. Glancing out the window she sees the flash of a little blue wren. It dances on the clothesline under the veranda. Before flying away. Closing her eyes, Rosie keeps rocking. A mad woman rocking.

Winter's Day

The rain is falling
Rain drops on the windowpane
Cleansing corrugated iron
Painting it like glaze
Tall gum trees sway gently
Looking out the window
Warmed by the wood fire
In the distance, clouds dance
Like a rhythmic waltz

Blue skies
Bright clouds
Setting sun shining a spot of light

Edges in gold
Contrasted with dark storm clouds
Mountain range, blanketed in white
Draped in grey soft clouds

Boy dances to the music
Craving liberation, inspiration
Seeing God on a miserable winter's day
Rain clears
Setting sun brings calm and peace
Looking at the mountain
I know as home
Pray for winds of change
Sip the moment of contentment

Last remnants of light are like fire
A final blaze before darkness descends
Sun's goodbye before sleeping
Moon rising
Grass, soaking in fresh rain like a thirsty sponge
Droplets of water cling to the cage
Cockies nest, seeking shelter and warmth
From the cold
The night's approach
On a winter's day

BLESSING OF SURRENDER

The sun rises; a new day dawning. Pink streaks through dark clouds. Birds wake. Singing softly. Wispy clouds drift gradually. Rosie is enamoured by the colours. The changes and variations.

Look at the colours; greys, whites, pale blues, violets and pastel pinks. Each day an artwork. A masterpiece. Each day a surprise. A revelation.

Rosie peers out the window, holding the lace curtains back. As the sun continues rising, the colour becomes more vivid. More vibrant.

Slowly pacing through the garden, Rosie watches. Bare feet; one with her garden and her God. Dew on the ground. Wet on her feet. As she walks through the front gate, she sees the yellow of blooming daffodils. Rosie pauses to admire them.

Such a blessing.

As she walks around her garden, she thinks of the daffodils. When the bulb was lying dormant, hidden beneath the ground. Rosie walks inside and sits down at her desk. Finding her pen and notepad, she writes. She visualises the daffodil; her words flow onto the paper with ease.

Golden Armour

> *Beneath*
> *Cold*
> *Hard ground*

Planted
Wrapped in darkness
Silenced
Stultifying protective dirt

Complete
Whole
Waiting patiently
Dormant
Still
For warmth
Illuminating sunshine

Bulb comes forth
Breaking open
Emerging victorious
Against the winter's imprisonment
Growing towards the sky
Breaking through crust of earth
Fighting for freedom
Fulfilment
Time to bloom
As days get longer
Skies get brighter

The daffodil
Spring's signal
Celebration
Reaching for the sun
Unapologetic

Unveiling its glory
Flowering gracefully
Powerfully beautiful
Shining brightly
Lighting up the world
Cloaked in golden armour

While finishing the poem, an idea for her blank canvas comes to her. Images fill her mind; an empty bird nest in the foreground. The sunset in the background. Sitting on mountains. Circling the wide expanse of a valley.

Beginning to mix the paints, she doesn't know what to do with this new information she is burdened with.

I don't know what decision to make. There's a part of me that wants to bury the truth and keep life the same. Billy believing his mother is on an adventure. Don't be stupid—that little boy knows. He has insight. You can't fool him. How will Tom feel if he finds out I hid this? Isn't he entitled to closure too? Isn't it time for him to stop punishing himself? Won't he punish himself more? What about Phillip and Robert? My parents? I haven't told Tom or Anne about all this either. How did I all of a sudden get wrapped in all these secrets? Why now?

Back and forth, her thoughts explore different options and approaches.

At the end of the day, I know there will be pain.

The paint flows across the surface of the canvas. Rosie lets out a deep sigh. Massages her forehead. Soothing her momentarily. The thoughts keep running like wet paint. Anxiety infiltrates her body. Nervousness, like the phone will ring at any moment with bad news.

This fear. Of nothing. Of the unseen. The unknown.

Rosie takes some deep breaths, watching the colours and shapes take form and begin to emulate something. The creative process gives her some relief.

I could talk to Stella. What about Polly? Even Tilly, which might make it even harder.

The painting begins to look complete; she adds finishing touches. Standing back from the painting, she moves around the room to look from different angles. Checking the perspective. Looking at the shapes and recognising imperfections. Moving back and forward, she makes touch-ups. Knowing after all these years that there is a point when you should stop; know when it is complete. Finished.

Rosie inspects the mountains. Looks to the swirling twigs forming the bird's nest. Feeling the loneliness. Hearing Lottie's laugh. Remembering her, days before giving birth. Bursting with baby. Pride and love. She holds on to the image for as long as she can. Then it comes crashing down, like a bird cast from the nest. The images of Lottie living on the streets. The last time Rosie saw her, Lottie's face was drenched in tears and rain. Breathing deeply, Rosie prays.

Dear God, I give you this painting. I give you Lottie. I give you these decisions. This anguish. Take away this anxiety. Soothe my restless soul. God, I'm placing this in your hands. Guide me. Protect me. I surrender, God. I surrender.

A sound out the back interrupts her thoughts.

It sounds like someone is here.

She wipes her hands on her white jacket. It is speckled with paint. It has served her well, for many years. Protecting her clothing. Becoming a canvas of its own. Hearing the back door, she walks along the hallway and through the lounge room, eager to see who it is.

'Oh, what a pleasant surprise,' she says as she is greeted by Tilly's smiling face as she closes the back door. Sparkling green eyes. 'What's goin' on?'

'I'm on my way to town,' Tilly replies. 'Thought I'd stop in and have a cuppa and a quick hello.'

'Take a seat. I'll put the billy on,' Rosie says warmly. She fills the kettle and turns it on.

'I see Billy's got a nice mob of chickens kickin' round down there. How many eggs he gettin' these days?'

'Oh, I don't know. More than I can eat. They're the best-cared-for chickens in the district. That's for sure. He mothers the darling things, just like Tom used to. Remember him back in the day?'

Tilly chuckles. 'Yes, I do. He bloody threatened Will and I with the four-ten one day, for goin' near the bloody things. We decided to leave 'em be.'

'What's news around the place?' Rosie asks.

'Don't know. Haven't really seen anyone of late. Been keeping to ourselves, pretty much. Keepin' out of trouble.' Tilly scruffs her short, blonde hair as she scratches her head.

'How's things with Ash?' Rosie asks. Trepidation in her voice.

'Ash and I had a pretty big blue the other day. I found out she had sent money to her brother.' Tilly shakes her head, focusing on the table as she explains. 'He's nothing but a good-for-nothing, useless, fucking drug addict. I don't know how she continues to get sucked into his bullshit.' Tilly takes a sip of her tea. 'He said this shit to her, about needin' it for the kid, and she believes 'im. He ain't spending a cent on that boy. He's just putting it straight in his arm. You can't tell her though; she's fucking bull headed. Anyway. We had words. She eventually agreed that it's unfair to use our money for her brother.' Tilly sighs.

Rosie passes her the biscuit tin. Tilly takes out an Anzac biscuit and dunks it in her tea, soaking it in the liquid. Softening it. Tilly eats it, looking like the teenager Rosie knew all those years ago. A bond is woven between them. An unspoken connection. Formed through loss.

Tilly has been a blessing; we share so much love and mutual respect.

'Tread carefully, Tilly,' Rosie warns her sternly, looking deep into her eyes. 'You will only ever find one Ash. You know she's one in a million, my girl.'

'What are you saying? "Don't fuck it up, Tilly"?'

'Yes, darling,' Rosie says as she reaches a hand across the table and places it on top of Tilly's. Tilly's eyes are cast down, fixated on her tea. 'Try be a bit more empathetic; it's her brother and nephew. You know she'd give any poor bastard the shirt off her back.'

'Yeah, I know.' Tilly takes a breath. 'You're right; you're always fucking right. That's why I haven't fucked things up too much, 'ave I? You've kept me on the straight an' narrow. I better make a move and get these jobs done in town.'

They get up from the table in unison and make their way to the back door.

'Someone's got to keep ya in line. My wild child,' Rosie says as she ruffles Tilly's short blonde hair. Adding to its messiness. Like she used to when Tilly was a young girl. Their eyes meet. They knowingly smile.

'I'll walk you out,' Rosie says.

Tilly puts on her boots. Zips up her jacket over her flannelette shirt. Her jeans are tight over her skinny legs. She rolls a smoke as they admire the begonias under the protection of the veranda. They are dark green with wide round leaves. Lighting her cigarette, Tilly takes a deep drag.

'I'll grow some cuttings for you, if ya like,' Rosie says. 'You just need to keep them out of the frost.'

'That'd be good. I like this one here,' Tilly says as she strokes the leaf of the begonia. Admiring its texture and shape.

They walk out the front; Tilly finishes her cigarette as they watch the chickens scratching in the garden.

'Wait here a minute. I'll go in and grab ya some eggs to take home. I nearly forgot.' Rosie races inside. Tilly stands by the gate, transfixed on the mountain. Rosie returns with some eggs, stands beside Tilly and takes a moment to be absorbed in the grandeur of the mountain. Rosie farewells Tilly with a caring embrace. She watches her wave. A cheeky grin spread across her face. The same twinkle in her eye she has always had.

She's like a daughter to me. My beloved friend. What a blessing.

Rosie prays for her as she watches her drive down past the dairy. Feeling a cord, not unlike the umbilical cord, holding them together.

HOPE

Rosie wakes dozily. The clouds drift from the mountain to expose the snow. A light dusting at the top. Rosie thinks her eyes deceive her at first.

This is a unique event to have the snow so close, for it to fall and settle. It feels like a strange gift. A sign. A message. Interpreting all these signs of the weather. The valley. A way to communicate with the magical. The spiritual. Another dimension. Another level. A higher realm. People would think I'm crazy if they knew what I thought. How I saw life. I'm getting too old to really give a fuck what people think.

She looks at the orchid on her windowsill. A flower has just slowly opened.

I've watched it swell and show promise and possibility. Now it has burst into life.

It is speckled with purple on a light-green backdrop. A shape like a four-leaf clover.

I'm impressed I've kept it alive; nearly two years now, since Polly gave it to me. Must have been for my sixty-eighth birthday. I love its embodiment of hope. Showing promise. Resilience. Growth. Limitless possibility.

As she stands at the sink doing the dishes, Rosie remembers her Uncle Rex telling her, 'You shouldn't be doing all that farm work. You should be in the bloody kitchen. Where ya bloody well belong. It's a disgrace. Trying to work like a man.'

Well, he's bloody where he belongs now. Dead. In the bloody ground. That chauvinistic, drunken pig of a man. I certainly didn't shed any tears when that fucking bastard died. Drank himself to death. The ignorant prick.

Rosie thinks about her plight as a woman. Anne juggling her competing roles. Olivia, at ten years old.

What will the future hold for her? Will this world give her the ultimate equality she deserves? Will she need to fight and struggle, like the women before her?

Glancing out the window, Rosie admires the happy wanderer climbing the fence. Flowering a beautiful white.

I'll prune that grapevine out the back today. Prune the fruit trees tomorrow. Maybe pick some daphne from the bed at the corner. It will be nice in a vase on the windowsill.

The sun slowly casts light across the landscape; fog has lifted, showing promise of a clear day ahead.

Rosie thinks about an artwork she painted.

The black-and-white silhouettes of a male and female head, with a butterfly in the centre. I called it Coconut Island. *About the fallacy of equality. I thought it would be foolish to think there would ever be a thing. The song that inspired me. What was it? Those lyrics, something about a coconut island.*

After wiping her wet hands on the tea towel, she goes into her study to search for the song. Finding the CD cover, she searches. Thinking she knows the right one, she skips the songs and presses play.

This is it. It's the right one. 'Anna Begins'. Counting Crows.

Rosie listens to the lyrics. Wondering what they mean. What it's all about; she is lost in the words. His melodic voice.

As Rosie listens, it means many things to her.

My love of art is that there is no fixed answer. My interpretation and interaction is what the art strives to achieve. That is why I never attempt to explain my artwork. Or talk about the purpose or my intentions. I love to discover what the viewer sees. What they feel and interpret. If only I could write to make people feel the intensity of emotion that this song evokes in me.

Standing up after the song has finished, she puts on her coat. She ventures out the front door, placing her striped beanie on her head. Picking up her secateurs from the windowsill, she places them in the wheelbarrow. She lifts it up and wheels it out. There is brightness. A freshness in the air. Placing the wheelbarrow beside the front rose beds, she starts from one end and begins pruning her roses. Selecting each branch to be cut, Rosie considers how much she loves them.

They are strong, ugly, with thorns, like blackberries. Love to be savagely pruned. The flowers possess such power, colour, form and beauty; their provocative scent. It's like the drawing on the wall. My mother's favourite flower. A gift my mother gave to Mumma.

In the silence, she sits. Taking the moment to pause. To be. To stop. Her mind races over things to do. Sitting wrapped in silence, she reflects. Rosie faces this moment in her life. The wrinkles on her hands remind her of the passing of time as she looks at her wedding ring.

My diamond. A symbol of our commitment. 'Til death do us part.

My old body and mind are tired. I have earned this rest. Enjoy it, old girl. Just enjoy it.

The wind whistles. Whispering through the trees. Rosie wonders what words will be enough.

How do I explain this to Tom? What will his reaction be? Will it alleviate guilt? Fear of her returning? Will it pile on further pain? Should I lie by omission, make it sound better than it was?

A lone magpie flies, floating on the wind, being lifted. Cows feed. Roaming in the paddock. Her heart is heavy. Beating strongly. Rosie takes deep breaths as she looks at a pile of wood on the side of the hill Tom has cut and left to dry. The wind is like her anxiety; she fears she'll be swept away.

As she prunes the roses and considers the path ahead, she feels a pang of nausea. Rosie knows a methodical job like pruning roses is good for her anxiety. She thinks of times when the children were young and she spent endless days in the haze of motherhood, stuck within the confines of her house.

My manic compulsion to line things up. To clean. Wanting control, its draining effect. I've come to know myself now. I want to take a handful of pills but I know that road. I've been down that road before. The gifts of age and experience. I know where most paths lead. I crave a cigarette and a straight whisky, on the rocks. I know that road. I know that road well.

Rosie lies down. In the warm sun. On the soft grass. Taking deep, slow breaths. She closes her eyes, and her racing mind goes on a journey.

I'm happy to let those days fade away. Embrace this time of a slow pace. May it be filled with energy. Life and vitality. Move to the rhythm of my body. My garden. The weather. The seasons. Devoid of pressure or commitment. Free like a butterfly fluttering through my garden. My fear and doubt, a beautiful beast. I must love and accept this part of myself. Both a blessing and a curse.

There is a palpable excitement as they venture off together in Tom's ute. Billy is beyond excited to be with Jimmy and on their way to the tallest mountain in Australia. Though it is close to them as the crow flies, it is a long drive. Around two hours. Rosie has packed snacks and books and the boys have iPads to endure the trip. Tom was up extra early to milk the cows so they could leave early enough to get to the mountain and back before the evening milking.

The road weaves over and around the mountain ranges. The trees grow thickly beside the road. They feel the temperature drop as they drive into the mountain range. Billy asks lots of questions. He wants to see a brumby. Jimmy chews on the lollies; he is always the Yin to Billy's Yang. So nonchalant, when Billy is so hyperactive and energetic.

As they drive towards the peak, the trees change. Rosie explains the type of trees and how they grow in this climate. They observe the shapes and their adaption to snow weighing them down.

They arrive at the ski resort and catch the ski lift to the start of the walkway. Rosie is scared of heights so she rides beside Billy, who has no fear and a love of heights. Tom rides behind them with Jimmy. Rosie closes her eyes and clings to the bar, breathing deeply, unable to look down. A sudden gust of wind rocks the chair lift. Her heart leaps.

'Don't worry, Nanny, we're nearly there.' Billy brushes against her.

'I might need new undies when we get there, my love.'

Rosie is relieved when they reach the top. They walk along the walkway; it is a steel frame that allows the vegetation to grow underneath. Billy wants to run. Jimmy goes at the same pace as Tom, slow and steady. Following along, feeling the cool wind and soaking in the sunshine, Rosie feels contentment. Taking in the scene as they walk.

A loud noise breaks through the crisp air.

'What the bloody hell's that?' Tom yells, putting his hands over his ears.

'Sounds like bagpipes.' Rosie frowns.

They turn around; Rosie spots a man in the distance playing the bagpipes.

'Well, ya never know what you might see up here!' Rosie yells as they continue walking, the bagpipes playing as they stride ahead.

Reaching the top, Billy runs around like he is on the top of Mount Everest. He and Jimmy pose like winners on a podium. Rosie takes photos of them. Tom quietly stands back. His hands in his pockets. A slight grin on his face.

This reminds me of the photo of Blake and me taken in this spot. Probably over twenty years ago.

As they walk back, the boys run ahead. Joking. Laughing. Tom and Rosie walk in silence. No need to speak or explain. Enjoying Billy's adventure. Grateful to share the journey.

Maybe this is a good time to speak to Tom? No, not now. I can't ruin such a good day. I'll find a good time.

The drive home is quiet. Billy reads his book. Jimmy rests his head and eventually falls asleep.

'So you never told me what your surprise was, lovey?' Rosie glances over at Tom to catch his smile. Tom looks in the rear-view mirror.

'It was a slug gun.'

'What! Aren't you excited, honey?'

'Yeah, at first I thought it was a toy one and then Dad cocked it and nah it's a real one. I just have to wait for Jimmy to go home. It's in the gun case.'

'Well, just be careful not to shoot any native birds with it. Maybe tin cans for now.'

They arrive home in time to milk the cows. Rosie retreats to her kitchen to prepare Billy's special birthday dinner and ice his cake.

'Get outside, you two! Tonight's feast is a surprise!' Rosie shouts to the boys as she flings her arms, stopping them from following her inside.

'Oh, Nanny, can't we have a sneak peek? Please, Nanny,' Billy pleads.

'No, go find something to occupy yourselves.'

'Alright,' Billy says with defeat. 'Let's go to the meat house. I'll show you my cubby.'

Rosie watches Jimmy follow Billy as they run down to the stone building.

How boring life would be without that boy. My precious boy.

LITTLE BLUE WREN

Mad Song

The wild winds weep,
    And the night is a-cold;
Come hither, Sleep,
    And my griefs infold:
But lo! The morning peeps
    Over the eastern steeps,
And the rustling birds of dawn
The earth do scorn.

Lo! to the vault
    Of paved heaven,
With sorrow fraught
    My notes are driven:
They strike the ear of night,
    Make weep the eyes of day;
They make mad the roaring winds,
    And with tempests play.

Like a fiend in a cloud
    With howling woe,
After night I do croud,

And with night will go;
I turn my back to the east,
From whence comforts have increas'd;
For light doth seize my brain
With frantic pain.

— William Blake

A wild wind blows, whistling through the trees. Making wind chimes sing. Branches scrape on tin. Rosie feels sick and forlorn; her throat is sore. Her body aches. Fighting the pain, she walks around the garden. She admires the plump, lush, voluptuous camellias in shades of pink and red. They line the veranda and scatter their dead flowers on the path, creating a thick rug. Weighed down by her heavy head, she succumbs and goes back to bed. She knows her body is telling her to rest; she has learnt to respect its wisdom. To listen to it. The exhaustion is deep in her bones. Stress hangs over her like a dark, thick cloud. Lying down, pulling the covers over her shoulders, she lets her tired eyes slowly shut.

Drifting in and out of sleep, she tosses and turns, trying to get comfortable. She opens her book and tries to read for a while. Anxiety crawls over her body like a spreading rash. Restlessness races over her body like an incessant itch she cannot reach to scratch. Pulsating legs. Twitching. An aching body; tired and sore. Unable to rest and relax as she continues to toss and turn. Head swirling. Cramping limbs. Rosie feels no relief. Reminded of her time in hospital.

Being dragged to the psych ward; a broken teenager who had lost everything. At that time, she was my everything. My best friend. My support. My comfort. It was like losing that part of myself.

A moment of regret makes her chest tight. Thinking of MJ.

Crumbling under the weight of tragedy.

Not being able to leave the house. Needing to hide. Avoid people from school. Polly and Ainsley, both trying to deal with their own grief. In vain, trying to rescue me as I slowly drowned. That was my first meltdown. A teenager, spending a month in a psych ward. Well, I guess now I can see it was a turning point. The catalyst for change. A moment to acknowledge and embrace my 'madness'. I remember a conversation with Anne, in the kitchen, when she was only young; her asking, 'What was it like? How did you manage to recover?' It was hard to answer at the time but what I said still makes perfect sense. 'It was like being trapped in a dream or a nightmare. I wasn't able to decipher what was real and what was an illusion. Medication. Family and friends. That's what saved me … and of course, myself. I had to drag myself from the depths of despair and I did. You, darling, you have the same inner strength that will allow you to always drag yourself out of the shit. Don't ever forget that.' She is so strong, Anne. So bloody strong. Stronger than me; she's like her father. Stoic and courageous. How I've wished I wasn't such a fuck-up sometimes. But this is my story. This is my beautiful contradiction. My blessing and curse. Teenage years, they are so passionate and intense. A storm of hypersensitivity; trying to lay the foundation. Write the script of your adult life. I wouldn't want to go back. I'm happy with this time. This precious time, now.

Struggling, she crawls out of bed and takes a swig of olive leaf extract, grimacing with the harsh taste.

This shit must be good for ya. It tastes so bloody awful.

She retreats back into her bed. She knows there's plenty to do, but all she wants is to stay in bed all day. Head aching, she can't help but think of Lottie.

I should have helped her. I should have helped her stay. I shouldn't have let her go. I let her down. I should have supported her. What was I thinking, letting her walk out that door?

Rosie hears the clang of thunder. The rain begins to forcibly drum on the tin roof as she feels the dark clouds surrounding her, filling her with both comfort and fear. The earth speaks of her dismay. Failure. Voicing her regret. Releasing tears, in pelting rain.

I just want to crawl into a ball and let the tears wash me away. I feel so trapped and helpless, like I will never escape.

Imagining Lottie living on the streets, she can't help but place herself there. She imagines being Lottie, trapped in filth and addiction.

The excessive public exposure. Vulnerability. Disconnection and loneliness. I can just imagine how she felt; lost, sad, traumatised. Imagine people ignoring her as they walked past. Cold and hungry. Trying to survive. Devoid of shelter or safety. The rain, wind and cold.

Her mind writes a million stories of survival and deprivation and she drowns in shame and sorrow.

Letting the tears dampen her pillow, she battles drifting off to sleep. Eventually she falls into a deep, restful sleep. She dreams, transported to another time and place. Her dreams carry her; she is flying high above the valley, high above the mountains ... weightless, free. A mother bird pushes the baby bird out of the nest, exposes it to the harsh world. A little blue wren. Abandoned. Rejected. Reaching out, she desperately tries to catch it, but it is too late.

She wakes dripping in sweat. Her dream still fresh in her mind.

She turns on the shower and waits for the water to heat up as she gets undressed, placing her sweat-drenched clothes in the dirty clothes basket. Feeling the temperature of the water, she adjusts the cold-water tap to the right temperature before stepping under the water. Hearing the storm outside, she enjoys the warmth of the cascading water. Soaking her hair, creeping over her skin. Rosie runs her hands through her hair, closing her eyes as she lets the water cleanse her face.

If only I could crawl up into a ball. Hide from the shame. This harsh reality.

She washes her skin, trying to remove the dirt, the dirty filth from her body, from her mind. In this moment, she again remembers herself as a teenager.

In the hospital. Psychotic. Depressed. The nurse talking to me in mumbled words. Her calling out as I sat on the floor of the shower. Rocking. Calling out, 'I just want to die! Please. I just want to die.' The lowest point in my life.

Letting herself go there and sit in that memory, Rosie imagines holding that young girl. Comforting that part of her, that precious moment; holding the mad woman rocking.

PART THREE

Home is a place we all must find, child. It's not just a place where you eat or sleep. Home is knowing. Knowing your mind, knowing your heart, knowing your courage. If we know ourselves, we're always home, anywhere.

— Glinda the Good Witch, *The Wizard of Oz*

Sweet Song Flying

The rested earth spoke quietly of her tenderness and tenacity. A warm feeling of contentment sweeps over her like a leaf floating on the breeze, gliding through the valley. An honourable purpose, to create and sustain life. Embracing the wind, rain, sunshine, snow, stars, moon and the plethora of change the seasons offer. Transforming whilst simultaneously remaining whole.

BUTTERFLY

Rosie tosses and turns with pangs of doubt.

It all seems like such a mess. How do I put it all together? Now I have all this new understanding. A brother. A father. Boxes of secrets.

Rosie climbs out of bed and wraps her brightly striped dressing-gown around her. Her legs feel heavy and sore. Putting on her striped beanie, she slides her stiff feet into her pink slippers. Hunched over, she makes her way to the kitchen. Crouching down, she grabs the metal stoker and stirs up the remaining coals in the stove, then strategically places some kindling over the coals to get it going again. She blows it gently, giving it oxygen. The flames ignite.

Having made her tea, black and strong, she ventures to her desk. Sitting there, she wipes the sleep from her eyes and stretches her back. The smell of the fire wafts through the house. Rosie tries to write. The events, ideas, memories and emotions swirl around in her head. Rosie has wanted to do this all her life, but has always waited; waited for children to grow up and the work to end and for there to be time. Rosie knows time can quickly run out. She tries to start.

Who cares about my silly life? How stupid and boring.

The eloquent voice of Anne rings in her mind.

'I'd love to know about your childhood. You should write about it. Your poetry is beautiful, Mum. I can see it, feel it. Why don't you write a book? Oh, Mum, don't be so ridiculous, you are so talented.'

Rosie begins flicking through her journals, discovering snippets of time and place.

It seems like a big mess; how do I make it interesting? Where do I start?

She thinks about the highlights, the good times, her happiest memories.

Getting married, having children. We never had a honeymoon; being pregnant, we decided to go back to work the following day. Oh, the rush of excitement, moving into our quaint two-bedroom house. Down on the flat, near the creek. We had our new home; we could finally be together as husband and wife. God I loved decorating it and making it our own.

Rosie flicks through a journal, an old one, and begins to read.

It wasn't until Anne was 2 years old that we took a holiday, the three of us and my grandmother, 'Mumma', as we called her. I could never say grandma as a child and started saying 'Mumma' and it stuck. She was always more like a mother to me than a grandmother. It was some of the happiest times of my life. The excitement of travelling. Away from the work and the responsibilities of the farm. Blake had to relax. It reminded me of the fun times of our youth. We had always been friends growing up. Neighbours. Only children. In the same year at school. Catching the school bus. It had never occurred to me that he was ever more than just a friend, until he got his first girlfriend, Zoe. She was so pretty. Smart. Blonde and petite. I felt so much anger and jealousy; these foreign feelings I hadn't felt before. I accepted that he had found his right match. I buried the feelings for many years. Always thinking I'd never get married or have children. I thought I might even become a nun like Aunty Jassie. Here we were, married.

With our little girl on a big exciting adventure. It was a long flight with a toddler but darling little Anne slept most of the way in my arms.

Rosie remembers one of the best days they had on the trip. She continues reading. Sipping her tea. Light streams through the window.

Anne was with Mumma and we hired some bikes to explore the mountains. The tropical paradise. Our guide took us to the most beautiful, pristine waterfall. We trekked through mud. Hidden at the end of the track was the cascading water, a vast pool at the bottom. We spent the day swimming, eating and sunbaking. I felt so much love and contentment. How I treasured the moment. Knowing the many dark days I had seen. Knowing you must make hay while the sun shines. We rode back on the motorbikes, happy and playful. The sun was warm and inviting. We rode on the dirt track. A lone horse feeding beside the road. Dogs barking as we passed. Small houses scattered amongst the hills. The green paddocks spread across the valley. They were lush; a tropical paradise.

The following day the four of us went on a short boat trip to a small island where we went snorkelling, seeing fish of all colours. Anne played in the sand and splashed in the water, Mumma watching her dutifully. She didn't articulate it but it was obvious Mumma was having the time of her life. I was so grateful for her presence and her company.

Rosie looks at a leather-bound journal Anne gave her and the nice pen.

I want to begin. I want to start to write the first words in it but I don't want to make a mistake. I try to have faith the right words will come at the right time. I really miss Anne and the kids.

Deciding to go for a walk to clear her head, she picks up her camera and hangs it around her neck. Changing into her overalls and putting on her boots, she sees sunshine streaming through the window.

Striding through the front gate, she admires the blooming paulownia tree. The promise of fresh leaves on the elm trees. Pacing down the hill, she happily soaks in the soul-quenching heat of the sun. The dairy is quiet. Chained dogs bark. The rooster crows. Calves bellow in the distance. Over the ramp and into the Hill Paddock she strolls. Relishing in the warmth; the sun is shining with intensity and strength, covering her like a vast, thick blanket. Pacing up the incline to the stony gully, Rosie thinks of her grandchildren playing here. Lachie throwing rocks. Clapping with excitement. Liv stacking the rocks neatly in a pile and making patterns. Rosie ponders over the precious memory.

Anne is so patient with them. Little Lachlan is such a handful. She is such a good mother. So attentive. Much better than I ever was.

Hearing the thunder of a plane flying overhead, she longs for their company, laughter and joy. But she holds the memory instead. That is enough to fill her with happiness and gratitude.

As she glances across the paddock, a swarm of small blackbirds fly in formation, like an orchestra, well timed and rhythmic. A sweet song flying.

Passing the stack of old cars—'the graveyard'—she marches on through the open gate. The hay shed is empty.

It won't be long now. Time to make more hay to fill it. Harvest. What a time of fervent activity. So much stress and poor Tom doing all those ridiculous long hours. I know all too well this is the way of the farmer;

make hay while the sun shines. I remember my exhausted grandfather arriving home late, eating his cold tea and heading straight to bed. Raised seeing the sacrifices. I'm so deeply grateful.

Rosie walks energetically over the track, getting lost in her thoughts and memories. Eagerly striding through another open gate, she watches the sheep feed in a mob over the ridge. She looks for any signs of newborn lambs. The sun warms her back as she breathes in deeply; the air is fresh and invigorating. Rosie passes the beautiful old gum trees, over the ridge and through another gully. Appreciating the easier walk with fewer gates to open. No fences to climb through. Rosie gets to where the old road had once been; it still shows signs of being a road. Looking both ways, she walks over the new bitumen road, hearing the hum of a car in the distance. As she opens the gate—it easily swings open—and shuts it behind her, she hears magpies singing. A feeling of delight.

I love spring. My favourite time of the year. The sounds. The sunshine. The smells. It's magical.

She stops. Her eyes are drawn to the sight of a bright orange fox with a thick tail and healthy coat. It runs along the edge of the dam. Pauses. Their eyes lock for only a second and then it runs up the hill, out of sight. The look is quick and penetrating. Taking a deep breath, Rosie puts her hands on her hips.

I wonder if it's the same fox I've seen down on the flat, near the house.

Rosie walks past the dam. The water is calm and flat, reflecting the trees and the clear, blue sky above. Evoking an image of her cold early-morning walks through the London park to mass.

The small lake with a mother duck swimming, her ducklings following along in a perfectly formed line. It is funny the things that have stayed with me all these years.

Rosie reflects with a grin.

It seems like a lifetime ago now.

With her head down, watching the placement of her feet, she strides over to the big rock. It is grand and permanent. Sitting proudly in the clearing below the line of thick bush. Cautiously climbing up to the top, she crawls, placing her hands and feet in the right spots to keep her stable. At the top, she catches her breath and makes herself comfortable. There is an open view of the farm. The paddocks and valley below. The town framed by the snow-covered mountain range. The clouds have lifted and reveal the splendour of the remaining snow; it shines and glows in the splendid spring sunshine. Taking some photos, Rosie is disappointed that the camera can't capture the beauty she sees.

It never conveys the grandeur of the scene in the same way I perceive it.

The big rock evokes childhood memories.

Climbing on it. Playing games. Creating fictional scenarios with my cousins and MJ. How much pleasure it brought me to watch my own grandchildren climbing it. How they loved it as much as I had as a child. Cautious Olivia climbing carefully. Wild Lachie running up, racing to recklessly climb it without care or fear of danger. Anne calmly guiding, helping and encouraging them. Their beautiful blonde hair glistening in the sun. If only they could stay longer. If only they could move closer. I know Anne has work and a life she has built. A teaching job. A husband. I will patiently count down until the next holidays. Summer holidays and Christmas. Always my favourite time of year.

Admiring the moss on the big rock, she runs her hand over it. Feeling its texture. Illuminated by the sun, the different shades of teal with patches of green and grey gleam. Rosie hears a crow calling and sees Tom feeding the cows in the paddock below. The cows gather around the hay. A willie wagtail moves amongst the trees and rocks, darting and energetically swishing its tail.

Rosie stares across the bush line. Admiring the gum trees. An echidna walks down the hill near the dam. Rosie holds her breath.

What a precious sight. They are rare to see. A sign of rain.

It waddles; unaware she is even there. Large prickles move with the motion of its back, its long nose surveying the ground beneath. Rosie tries to capture it.

I'm tempted to follow it, but I don't want to scare it. No need to disturb the poor thing. I want it to not even realise I'm here.

Zooming in, she gets a shot.

It is something, at least. My camera never seems adequate to capture the world exactly as I see it. A never-ending frustration of mine. I've painted many images in the past to try and express my love. How it looks through my eyes. It never feels enough. I've searched for the right words all my life to express my emotions. The right words to paint a vivid picture. They often seem insufficient. I will search still.

The echidna waddles out of view. Rosie soaks in the moment. Breathing in deeply.

I'm tempted to lay back, close my eyes and drift off to sleep.

The sunshine excites her, though. Thinking of the list of jobs she has to do, she is eager to get into her garden.

Climbing down from the rock, her heart is filled with gratitude.

This big rock has served many generations as they have climbed, explored, and admired their surroundings.

Rosie feels alive, light and free. Rejuvenated by the glorious sunshine and vibrant surroundings. There is weightlessness to her body. Excitement surges through her as she walks eagerly through the gate and over the road. She thinks about Olivia elegantly skipping and twirling in the green grass of the paddock.

What a precious gift it is to be alive.

Walking down through the paddock, she sees Tom checking on the cows. He drives in her direction.

The poor man. He works so bloody hard.

Rosie empathises with the demands of dairy farming. Its challenges and relentlessness. Rosie remembers Tom as a little boy, destined for farming.

He wanted to leave school as soon as he could. All his spare time he spent farming. He loved it. He was born to do it.

Tom drives up beside her. 'What's going on?' he asks.

'Just out for a walk,' Rosie replies. 'Thought I'd get a few photos before all the snow melts.'

Thrusting his head to one side, he says, 'There's a heifer down there in the flat—she's havin' trouble calvin'. I think I'll take her down, ya wanna give us a hand?'

Always eager to get involved, Rosie doesn't need to be asked twice. She jumps in the ute and places her camera in the glove box. They head off to find the cow.

Tom pulls up and Rosie gets out to inspect the young heifer: a small black cow with a thin line of white along her side, reaching up to her udder. Observing her obvious distress, Rosie can see she is struggling to have the calf. Beginning to encourage the heifer to head for the dairy, she walks beside her while Tom drives slowly behind.

'I think she definitely needs a hand. Do you have any string in the back?' Rosie asks.

'Yeah but I reckon we might need to get her in the yards,' Tom answers. 'She's pretty mad. It's good to have a hand to chase her down.' They let the heifer set the pace. Rosie gives her empathetic words of reassurance.

'I know, little girl, you'll be alright. We'll get you down there and help get this big lump of a calf out of ya.' As they walk slowly, Rosie remembers giving birth to Tom.

He was born in spring. The snow was still on the mountains. Tom didn't want to come out. I was induced. A long, painful labour. Followed by forceps to finally get him out. He was a big, healthy ten-pound baby. I thought after the birth of Anne I could never again feel such intense love, but then Tom arrived. He had the most beautiful spirit; he was so calm and content. An old soul. The most perfect baby. He slept contently and fed easily.

A kookaburra flying by interrupts her thoughts.

It is unusual to see them in flight; I only ever seem to notice them when they're sitting. Observing or laughing at the world around them.

The heifer is herded into the yards; Tom directs her up the race to keep her confined and easier to manage. He grabs the string from the ute. Rosie pats the heifer and tries to keep her calm with her soothing voice. Tom ties the string around the calf's legs sticking out. When the heifer strains, he pulls on the string to help bring the calf out. The legs come out further. Tom sticks his arm in around the legs to try to check the calf and make sure it's all coming out straight. He pulls again as the heifer bellows and strains. The calf's head comes out. The heifer goes quiet with some sign of relief.

'Good girl. We're nearly there, keep pushin',' he murmurs with encouragement. 'I think it's a whopper by the looks of things! No wonder she's havin' trouble!' Tom yells out. With another strain and tug on the string, Tom using the heavy weight of his body, the big, healthy calf comes out, falling to the ground with a thud. They both reach down to check it. It's not breathing.

'Quick, get it up and clear its lungs,' Rosie directs Tom with urgency, panic woven through her voice. They drag the black calf out of the race and over to the ute. The heifer is bellowing. A desperate cry for her newly born calf. Tom climbs up on the back of the ute. Rosie hands him the calf's back legs and he lifts it up. Tom shakes it up and down as fluid drains out of its mouth, onto the ground. They rest the calf down on the tray of the ute and massage its chest. It coughs and splutters. Its eyes flutter as it begins to breathe. They both sigh with relief.

As they cart it over to its mother, Tom checks under its leg and exclaims, 'It's a bull calf!' They stand there for a moment and watch the calf struggle up onto its wonky legs. The mother smells and licks her calf as it goes in search of her udder. Watching the calf and mother, Rosie and Tom share a short moment of contentment and relief.

'Better go,' Tom says, cutting through the silence. 'Got a few jobs to do before it's time to get Billy from the bus stop.' Rosie follows Tom out of the gateway.

'Can you get him to bring us up some milk when he's done with the calves?' she asks. Rosie watches him climb into the ute.

'Yeah, no worries,' he answers as he starts up the ute. Tom has a slight grin as he motions with his head. Rosie glances over and they watch the calf have its first drink from its mother. He puts the ute in gear and heads off down the laneway.

Always bloody working, that boy. Always doin' a few jobs.

Rosie shakes her head. After making sure the gate is shut properly, she walks up into her garden, remembering Tom as a little boy.

He could never keep still. He was always on the move at his slow and steady pace. Nothing's changed. He's always moving. He's certainly slow and steady wins the race. Will was fast. Bull at a gate with everything. Two speeds, flat out and stopped. I love them equally but sometimes I wonder if I've loved Will more because I have mourned him. Idolised him in the process. I guess I've only done what any mother could.

The daffodils catch her eye. They are a sight to behold. They shine brightly. Each one a golden sun. She recalls planting them with her grandmother. Digging them up and spreading them out. They are beautiful shades of yellow. Rosie begins weeding around them whilst admiring them. Moving amongst the piles of weeds on the lawn, she checks to see signs of the tulips flowering.

They are poking their heads up but no signs of blooms yet.

Rosie pulls some weeds creeping through the sugarcane mulch. Looking at the arbour on the side of the hill, she is reminded of her wedding day.

The sky was the most vibrant blue. Not a cloud in the sky. The snow was still on the mountains. The magnolia had just flowered. It was just a simple affair. My grandparents and his parents. Blake standing tall, blonde hair glistening in the sun. I can still remember looking into his sparkling blue eyes. The son of the neighbours. I was tiny then, even at three months pregnant. No fat rolls round the middle like I have now. Just a modest dress. A simple ceremony. We remained married though, until death did we part. Taken suddenly. Taken too soon. Will's words will forever ring in my ears. 'Only the good die young.'

As she glances out over the valley, the vivid yellow of the wattle along the creek catches her eye.

It is my favourite. Oh, I love the smell. I must get down and pick some. Noticing the acacia trees are getting their leaves, she eagerly awaits them flowering.

I love the long white flowers. Hanging like magnificent chandeliers.

Time slips away from her as she is lost in the world of her garden. She hears the reliable sound of Tom's ute coming down the lane to milk the cows. Looking down the hill, she watches the dairy cows beginning to make their way home. She watches Tom and Billy get out of the ute.

Look at Tom, he's the bloody spitting image of his father. Tall and lanky. The same slow, consistent walk. Blonde hair and beautiful blue eyes.

Rosie watches Billy make his way to the chook pen.

His favourite job, collecting the eggs.

Rosie hears him talking to himself.

'This one's still warm.' Billy studies each one and then places them considerately in the carton.

Rosie smiles, marvelling at his innocence and the miracles of nature. Bending down, she continues to pull some weeds out and add them to her piles. She collects the wheelbarrow and loads them in.

It feels satisfying to achieve something today.

As the sun is slowly setting, a chill comes into the air. The days are stretching out. As Rosie takes her boots off at the back door, a feeling of satisfaction makes her feel as though she has earned her rest today. Sitting down by the fireplace in the lounge room to warm her hands, she thinks about delivering the calf today. Remembers the premature calf her grandmother brought home and placed beside the fire.

Right where I'm now sitting. I was so young, one of my earliest memories. It was before I went to school. I still remember jumping up and down with joy and excitement; it was my new friend to love. The little jersey calf was so tiny and petite. She looked like Bambi with her soft coat and long eyelashes. We called her Betty and I loved to pat her, help feed her. I wanted to cradle her like a baby and rock her. Betty eventually got too big for the lounge room. I would feed and talk to her in the paddock. It reminds me of rocking my own children in the old wooden rocking chair. The exhaustion of newborns. The magic of holding my own grandchildren in my arms for the first time.

The memories coalesce, creating a swirl of emotion and bringing tears to her eyes. She looks up at the painting hanging on the wall that she painted all those years ago—as a new wife, a young mother. It still feels so relevant. The butterfly, painted in shades of deep blue, rich purple and dusty pink, soaring above a mountain.

The symbol of transformation, of strength. Flying and fulfilling dreams.

A deep restlessness stirs in her.

TWO BLACK CROWS

Driving up and over the hill, she takes her time. She admires the paddocks. Birds flying past. When Rosie arrives at Polly's, she feels excited to see her friend. Knocking on the door, she can hear Polly banging and crashing before she comes to the door and lets her in.

Short and round. So warm and inviting. Polly has never changed in all the years I've known her.

Her familiar face makes Rosie smile as she hugs her.

'This is a nice surprise. I'll put the billy on!' Polly exclaims. Her eyes twinkle. Rosie notices the light reflecting off the dam in the neighbouring paddock.

As they drink tea together on the back veranda, there is warmth in the air. Rosie sips the tea while admiring the large silver birches, their white, striped bark.

This tea is good; Polly knows exactly how I like it.

'What's news around the place?' Polly interrupts her thoughts.

'Oh, not much, you know me. I keep pretty quiet,' Rosie responds, avoiding eye contact.

'Yeah, it gets like that. There used to be a time I was out every night at a different committee meeting. You know, I don't have the energy for it all now. I've been getting some gardening done, which has been good. Come down the back and have a look.' Polly scoops the air with her hand as she places her cup down, pushing against the chair to get up.

Walking through Polly's garden, Rosie admires every part—the colours and variety of plants.

I love this cottage garden. It is cluttered and beautiful. Nasturtiums scattered with wide leaves, bright orange. Tulips standing tall. Look at the wall of bike wheels against her side fence, creating a trellis for vines to weave their arms. Daisies are hugged with lamb's ears as they flower brightly in luminescent shades of pink. There is no space; it all fills a place, abundant like Polly's love and generosity.

Rosie asks Polly, 'What kind of reception do you think we will get out of Ainsley when she visits?'

Polly chuckles. 'Who bloody knows? Does she ever change? She'll be bloody painful, as usual. Complaining about everything. Wanting more excitement. I don't know why she bothers, to be honest.'

'I told you about her latest letter, didn't I?' Rosie asks Polly, her hand on her hip.

'I imagine it's like all the ones she sends, about herself. It's never been any different. She has always craved attention. Does she ever think about other people, what they are dealing with?' Polly pauses for a while, her hands on her hips. Her dress creates round mounds, like mountains covering her breasts and stomach.

Polly has always been beautiful; she looks like a grandma now, wholesome and cuddly.

'I'm getting too old for this shit, worrying about pleasing people. Did I tell you about Kate? You know, Trevor's wife? She is upset because she wants to do Christmas at their house this year, because of the kids and the travel. Now Coby is upset because he wanted to come to my place because that's where we always have it.'

'What does Alice think?' Rosie asks.

'She stays right out of it, but she gets frustrated because she feels like 'cause she has no children, she has no say. But you know what she's like. Alice is so easygoing, she just wants everyone to be happy.'

'So, what do you think you will do?'

'I'll just let them thrash it out. It doesn't bother me. As long as we are together. Too many people getting wrapped up in stuff that isn't important. Like bloody Ainsley, always obsessed with money. She's always got the most. She's barely worked all her life. Married into money, she's the one always going on about the cost of things.'

They sit on her back veranda and admire the garden.

'We should be old enough now to focus on the important things we have,' Polly says.

They sit in silence. Rosie considers what they have lost.

MJ. Our husbands. The baby Polly lost, her fourth child, stillborn. I will never forget Polly's trauma and grief. Sitting there, rocking with her, trying to comfort her.

Rosie goes over and puts her arm around Polly; she smiles as their heads touch. 'Well, all I know, deary, is, thank God we are perfect,' Rosie says. They laugh in unison.

'Want another cuppa?' Polly asks.

'Yeah, I'm in no hurry,' Rosie responds.

Polly gets up in an awkward, crotchety way. 'It's hard work getting old,' she says as she moves inside to make the cups of tea. Rocking side to side as she walks.

Looking out into Polly's backyard, Rosie watches two crimson rosellas feeding in the trees. Rosie is grateful for this moment.

My dear old friend who knows me so well. Who knows my story. Who I can speak freely with. We can say so much even in the silence we share. I should ask her about that day. The day MJ died. Fill in the gaps.

Polly brings out two cups of tea. Hands Rosie's to her carefully. They sit and drink their tea. Chatting and letting time slip away without a worry in the world.

'Polly, I'm trying to write a book.' Rosie tries to stop the words as they fall from her mouth.

'Geez, that's good. How's it going?'

'It's been a bit of a struggle. There's things I can't remember. They've been lost.'

'Well, we're getting old. Of course we forget things these days.'

'Yeah, that's true.'

'You have always been a talented writer, ever since we were kids. MJ cherished all those poems you wrote. Remember that box her mum gave you? She had them all in there.'

Tears and smiles simultaneously fill their faces.

On the drive home, dark clouds roll in. Feeling sadness descend, Rosie wishes she could stay with Polly. Wrapped in the protective moment of friendship and support. She feels loneliness creeping through the cracks of the ute. She knows the turns of the road so well. She looks out the window at the sky, overcast and gloomy.

I hate the thought of going home to an empty house; this is strange for me to feel so lonely. I feel lost.

As she turns up her driveway, dodging the familiar potholes, hope and despair compete for her affections, shifting back and forth. She drives into the garage. Two black crows sit on the front fence, watching her, and she feels drawn to the back garden.

Rosie wanders through the back garden. She passes the pump shed and moves to the caravan sitting on the side of the hill in the shade of the kurrajong tree.

Sitting in the caravan, she inspects the walls as memories come flooding in, bleeding onto the carpet.

A place I used to always sit when I missed Will. Before this was Will's space, this was our hangout. The four of us. Polly would sit over there. MJ and I always along the bench seat. Ainsley that side. The hours we spent playing cards or drawing, singing. We were inseparable. MJ's laugh, throwing her head back. Raucous laughter. Telling secrets. Talking about boys. If only I could go back, just for a little while. My old memories are all I have now.

Rosie collects *Travels with Charley* from her study desk and returns to the back garden. Finding a spot at her table, she begins to read.

Moving inside to make a cup of tea, Rosie reflects.

Steinbeck simultaneously inspires me and incites fear and loathing for tackling the task of writing a novel. He makes me want to go to America. His beautiful descriptions make it come alive. I see it. I feel it. I want to write a novel that celebrates the Australian flora and fauna so people would want to see a kookaburra and admire a gum tree. I want it to be quintessentially Australian.

Returning with her cup of tea, Rosie sits outside the caravan; memories come flooding back to her.

Picking up Will and Stella at three in the morning. They had been at a party. Drunk. Laughing. Tired. His arms wrapped around her as I looked in the rear-view mirror. The night they had a fight. Stella coming to me for comfort. I took her side; spoke to him about respect, about how to treat women. I can see Stella's tear-drenched face. Will and Stella living in the caravan out the back. Helping Stella buy her property. So long ago but also feels like yesterday.

The crickets sing, reminding Rosie of going to Salvador Dalí's house in Spain.

The small cage he had in his bedroom to keep a cricket; for him to hear the soothing sounds to assist his sleep. Dragging Ainsley there. She thought everything about him was so weird. I felt so inspired. His house an artwork. Seeing the place he worked, sat for hours creating famous masterpieces. I fantasised about becoming a famous artist and my humble home becoming a museum. I know they're frivolous dreams. I love my art. I pursue it without a need for fame or recognition.

The sprinkler sprays the garden bed. Drenching it. Leaves glisten in the sunshine; a brown butterfly flutters by, drifting on the gentle breeze. Sitting, sipping her tea, she takes a deep breath and sinks into the chair. The butterfly flirts with the yellow daisies in the lawn. The leaves of the peppercorn tree sway. Rosie often sits in this spot in front of the old caravan.

It's still the same, not a thing moved since Stella left. Sometimes I go inside to dust but can't stay too long. The memories. The sadness becomes too thick in the air for me to breathe.

Looking up into the branches of the elm trees, Rosie sees signs of their leaves slowly beginning to return.

PROMISE

The sky is clear, apart from a thick cloud stretching across the horizon, the sun concealed behind it, lighting up the edges. Showing promise. The cloud disperses, revealing the golden sun. Vibrantly shining with strength and purpose. Opposite, the large moon hangs in the sky. Patiently waiting for night, to shine brightly in the evening sky.

The sun shocks Rosie as it comes bursting through the window. She looks out; it looks clear, showing promise of a bright, sunny day. Sign of warmth and hope. After the depths of winter, when darkness and dreary fog blanket the valley, the sunshine is a welcomed visitor. The precious promise of spring. The promise of change brings joy.

There have been many times I thought the sun would never shine again.

Remembering she had promised to visit Wally, she decides the sun is a perfect invitation. Searching the cupboards, she fills a box with supplies to take him. She packs her basket and secateurs.

I might pick some wattle from beside the creek, at Wally's place.

The ute seems to appreciate the increase in temperature and starts with greater ease. Driving along the road, looking into the bush, she sees the splendid wattle glowing brightly.

I remember picking it as a child; I have always loved the glorious colour. Every year I find some to brighten my old farmhouse.

Rosie parks her ute at the front of Wally's house. She can hear the creek flowing as she climbs out. Appreciating the warmth of the sun on her back, Rosie goes to the passenger door, picks up the box and carries it towards the door. Opening the gate, she listens for signs of life or movement. Banging on the door, Rosie hears the television.

I assume it's the races; his one vice in life is betting on the horses.

Wally opens the door. 'Aw, by Christ, look what the cat's dragged in. Come in, girl. What's this you got? More junk I suppose.'

He makes her laugh.

I always feel like a young girl when I'm around him. He talks to me the same way he spoke to me when I was running around the farm as a young teenager.

'A few things,' Rosie says as she puts the box on his kitchen table. The house has a layer of dust. It is dark. 'How are you, Wally?' she asks.

'No bloody good.' Wally shuffles his feet along the floor—his back hunched over—letting his arms swing relentlessly. 'I suppose you'll want a cup of tea, then. Let me wash a mug here for ya.'

'That'd be lovely,' Rosie replies as she sits down at the table. 'What's wrong with ya now, Wally?'

'I'm buggered. It's no good this gettin' old, ya know. Me bloody, poor old body's giving out on me.'

'That's no good. Maybe it's time you move into town. Make yourself more comfortable, you know,' Rosie says. Casting the rod. Waiting for a bite any minute now.

I wonder how this suggestion will go down.

Wally places tea bags in the cups and struggles with a drawer that is stuck as he searches for a spoon. 'Don't be bloody ridiculous. I'm not dying. I've got everything I need here. What would I do in town? I need my peace and quiet.'

Exactly the response I was expecting. Rosie grins with satisfaction.

His beloved cat, Molly, weaves around the table legs, brushing up against her with her matted hair.

I wonder if the poor thing is nearly as old as Wally.

'Have you heard from the boys?' she inquires.

'Those useless mongrels. Sometimes I wonder if old Marge jumped the fence with those two. Don't see 'em or hear from 'em. But little Bessie, she comes to visit,' Wally says as he carries the tea to the table, shaking as he walks. He moans as he sits down, then arches his back.

'Thank God for your granddaughter. How old is she now?' Rosie asks as she watches Wally lift the cup shakily to his mouth.

He still wears a worn-out cap, dresses like he is about to do a day's work ... apart from his slippers on his feet.

'She'll be seventeen in November. She's a good girl, like her mother. I don't know how Laura has stayed with that useless prick all these years. Buggered if I know.' Wally opens up an old biscuit tin. He passes it to her.

'Take one. Bessie brought them over.'

Rosie politely takes a biscuit, biting into a round shortbread. 'Have you been up to Ash and Tilly's and checked the stallion?'

'I went up last week. She's good with that beast. Many would not have persevered. He's quietened right down. She will be riding him by Christmas.' Wally dips a biscuit into his tea. 'How are the cows milking?'

'They're giving plenty of milk this time of year. The last of the cows are calving and fresh ones are coming in. Tom's got his hands full. Ash is coming over to give him a hand during harvest. I might even get a guernsey myself, if I play my cards right.' Rosie laughs and winks, stirring him up.

'Desperate times call for desperate measures, I guess,' he responds with a cheeky grin. 'How's Tom going with that mob of sheep over there? Is he still killin' a few?'

'Well, I'll tell you a funny story about the sheep you'd be interested in hearing. You know old Billy Baxter, from over the hill; he bought a few off Tom, back last year. You know Tom, as honest as the day's long; he charged him a fair price, well below market price. Old Bill said he'd pay whatever he wanted and Tom told him a hundred a head, so for four sheep, that's four hundred, right? He drove them out to his place and dropped them off. He says to Tom, "I've got no cash on me; I'll get the missus to drop the cash off next week, on her way to town." Tom was fine with that. So old Mrs Baxter, she rocks up the next week with the cash, and it's sixty dollars short. Tom didn't say anything.'

'That fleecing mongrel, just like his bloody father. Rob ya blind, those bloody Baxters.' Wally shakes his head and sips on his tea.

'Well, a bit of time passes, ya know—probably about six months— and last week, old Bill Baxter pulls up to see our boy Tom. So, Tom was moving and cutting up this branch that had fallen on the road. Before Bill could open his big trap, Tom says to him, "No. The answer is no." This puts him right on the back foot. Right from the word go. Silly old Bill laughs, then has the audacity to hit him up for some more sheep. Tom just says, "I'm only killing for myself, there's none for sale." Put old Bill Baxter in his place. Tom said he'd never seen the old bastard lost for words before. No sheep for you, Baxter. No sheep for you.'

'Fair dinkum. Ya wouldn't read about it. The bloody hide of 'im, good on the boy. He mustn't let anyone walk all over him. Ya grandfather never did, you know. He was a quiet fella but he didn't forget a single thing. Memory like an elephant. He remembered every bastard who'd ever done him a wrong turn in his life.'

'Well, he's a lot like my grandfather, my boy Tom.' Rosie places her empty cup on the sink. 'I was wanting to go down and pick some wattle from the creek.' She washes her hands and she dries them on a worn-out tea towel.

'Go for it, take the bloody lot with ya, if ya like. It's no use to me.

Mum loved it though. She planted them along there. The old man never let her plant it close to the house—he had hay fever—but he let her plant it all along the creek. She loved the colour.'

'Well, I love it. So I'll grab some before I head home. Thanks for the tea and biscuits. Always good to see ya, Wal.'

Wally smiles. In a rare moment of tenderness, he says, 'You're a good girl, Rosie. A good girl. Look after yourself, alright?' She notices the sparkle in his eye.

'Always, Wal, don't worry about that,' Rosie says, smiling.

As she says her farewell, in the back of her mind she wonders if this will be their final goodbye.

Rosie paces over to the wattle trees along the creek. Magpies sing a sweet song. Rosie begins to pick the freshest flowers. They are bright and vibrant. The sweet, strong smell fills her nostrils. She soaks in the warmth of the sun. The sound of the creek. The birds chirping. It fills her with contentment.

Walking through the paddock, back to the ute, she looks at the mountains. They are grand and captivating. She places the large bunch of vibrant yellow wattle on the passenger seat.

Wally's mother, how wonderful that she planted those wattle trees. She was a keen gardener. A woman who must have lived a tough life.

The wattle fills the cabin of the ute as she drives home. Winding down the window to let in some air, she admires the snow on the distant mountains. As she goes over the hill, the sight fills her with awe and wonder.

It is home. My valley.

Rosie slows down; the neighbour is moving cattle along the road. Moving steadily through the cows, she gives the neighbour a wave. Rosie can hear the kelpie barking and the roar of the bike. The black angus scatter across the road.

It reminds me of many hours on a horseback, moving cattle, from a young age. The stress, all the excitement. My grandfather was a great horseman and taught me how to read cattle and anticipate their movements. To plan and respond accordingly. To train our horse to move them the way we needed. A part of me misses those days. Another part of me is grateful. Life is simpler now. Less stress. Moving at my own pace. I have very little responsibility. All this freedom. There is a price. This time has moments of loneliness. Moments of contemplating that life is coming to an end. The inevitability of mortality. This also inspires me to make the most of my life. The years inevitably tick away. Nothing lasts forever.

As she drives along the laneway, she slows down and takes in the scene. Admiring the calves in the paddock, the bark of the gum trees, Rosie breathes in the fresh air. Rejoicing.

This is a magical life. A magical place.

Rosie pulls into the garage and gets out, looking towards the gate.

I miss my old dog. I miss his tender greetings.

Taking the freshly cut wattle inside, she puts it on the table and searches through the cupboard for a vase. She finds the one she always uses; it is wide and round, decorated in blue and white. Placing the wattle carefully in the vase and positioning it up high on the cupboards, she admires the vibrancy of colour. As she turns on the kettle, a slight smile creeps across her face as her heart is filled with golden hues.

The clang of the front gate, fast footsteps interrupt her thoughts as a flash of somebody goes past the window. The banging of boots on the step. Turning around, Rosie sees Billy as he comes in the back door, his face plastered with a grin.

'Hi, lovey, I've just made a cuppa. Ya want a milo?'

'No thanks, Nanny. Ya reckon we could open the rest of the letters now?'

'Yeah, go grab them from out the back. We'll have a look at them in here. I need to rest my weary body.' Rosie sits down slowly, sips her tea.

I wonder what little surprises the last letters have for us, hey.

Billy places the last four envelopes gently on the table.

'You can look in these two and I'll look in these two.' Billy hands two envelopes to Rosie. Sitting opposite her, he begins looking at his. There is silence as they look at their envelopes.

'What's in yours, Billy?'

'Look—a card. There is a little red-breasted robin on the front. This doesn't have Tina's name on it.'

'What does it say?'

'*To my darling,*

> As the sun rises and falls,
> The moon chases the earth,
> The stars shine brightly at night,
> My love is eternal.
> Until we meet again.

That's it. A bit weird, isn't it?' Billy says.

'Show me.' Rosie motions with her hand for Billy to pass it over. Billy passes it across. Rosie puts her glasses on and looks intently at it.

I wonder if it's from my father? The brooch, maybe that was from him too.

'Is there anything written on the envelope?' Rosie looks across the table, curious.

'No, nothing. It's just blank. What's in yours, Nanny?'

'This one has a different address. It is different to the others. This other address is in the city, I assume. This other one is a journal entry. It has to be written by my mother.'

'What does it say?'

A tear rolls down Rosie's face. Breathing in deeply. 'Um, it just says how she loves me. It is about me before I was born.'

Handing it across to Billy, she takes out a handkerchief and dries her eyes.

'You have a read, sweetheart.'

Billy reads attentively. Absorbed in the words.

'Do all mothers like talk to their babies before they're born? Before they even meet them?'

'Yes, Billy. As soon as you feel that special little soul growing inside you, you begin to love them like nothing else you have ever loved.' Rosie softly smiles, stirring her tea.

'Did my mum talk to me?'

'Yes, bloody oath, she did.' Rosie sips her tea. Studies Billy's face. 'I heard her talk to you and read to you, even sing to you. I never saw anyone more beautiful than your mother when she was pregnant.'

'So she wanted me?' Billy rotates an envelope in his hands.

'Yes, of course she did.' Rosie pauses. Hesitates.

How much should I say?

'Your dad was different when Lottie was here. You know, after Will died, we were all a mess. Your father, he loved Lottie and he loved you but he wasn't a good man, not like he is now. He drank too much and he worked all the time. He did anything he could to try to run away from the pain.'

'Did Lottie leave because Dad was an arsehole?' Tears fill Billy's eyes.

'I don't know exactly, but it was never because she didn't love you.' Tapping on the table, Rosie motions towards the final envelope. 'What does your last letter say, Billy?'

'It says …' Billy coughs and clears his throat. '*I regret to say this will be my final …*' Billy pauses. 'What's this word here, Nanny?' Billy shows Rosie the letter.

'Correspondence.'

'*I regret to say this will be my final correspondence. My husband has requested that I do not make any further contact with you. From one loving mother to another, our boy is well. Our boy is loved.*'

I wonder how Daisy felt reading that. What is it like to be separated from your child? Is it the same pain I feel for Will?

'Why did her husband tell her to stop writing?' Billy asks. 'Who made him the boss?'

'Well, sweetheart, in those days, a woman's husband was the bloody boss. Women didn't have the rights they have now.' Rosie drinks the remainder of her tea.

'What does your last letter say, Nanny?'

'This one has a different address. It's from Australia. This is from someone else,' Rosie says as she opens it up. 'There's a tax invoice, that's strange. Oh look there's a little note hidden inside it. It doesn't say a lot.' Rosie checks the back. 'There's no name. It says, *My love. I am working and saving some money. It won't be long now and I'll be back. I have a house in mind. There will be plenty of room for our new family. Sending you love.* Rosie pauses, looking at the note. 'This must be from my father to Daisy. He was going to come back for her.'

'Why didn't he put his name on there?' Billy asks.

'Well, it was a secret. My grandparents didn't approve. As I keep saying, Billy boy, they were different times.' Rosie sighs.

'Would my mum have stayed if it was that time? If Dad told her to?'

'I don't think it is quite that simple. I know this may not make sense but I think your mum left because she loved you. She wanted the best for you. The life she was living here, with your dad, was not making her happy.'

'Like I kind of get it. I sometimes just wish I knew her.'

Where has my sweet, little innocent boy gone? He sounds so grown up. Should I show him the black box? No, I need to talk to Tom. It's not my place, not yet. I better talk to Tom.

'Look, honey, all I can tell you is that your mother loved you more than anything else in this world. She felt that leaving you here with Dad and me was the best for you. She loved you that much and I can promise you that.'

A little blue wren dances on the windowsill. Billy turns to see it. He smiles. It flies away.

WORDS FAIL

Rosie is filled with nerves and excitement, knowing Ainsley is due to arrive any minute.

I can just hear her judgement.

Rosie frantically cleans the house, desperately trying to make it presentable, imagining Ainsley looking around her old farmhouse with condemnation and critical eyes. Rosie envisages her manicured nails, make-up and blow dried, dyed-blonde hair. Dragging on her expensive cigarettes and sipping champagne.

We have grown apart. Worlds apart. I remember reaching out to her after the birth of Anne. Feeling lost and lonely. She was still travelling and partying. She couldn't understand my life. My deep sadness. I have felt betrayal several times. Especially when tragedy has struck. I wonder why I've remained tied to her all these years. I guess we shared our childhood. We shared a lot. I should let it go. Stop the judgement. Stop being a hypocrite. It's so hard. I'm always on edge when she comes. I'm always prepared for when Ainsley arrives, for when she complains. Her negativity. A friend that lets me down. Changes plans. Is unreliable. Wants more. Wants better. Never satisfied. I really wonder why we've remained friends, all these years.

Wiping the table, she cleans with extra care. Noticing the marks on the chair, Rosie dips the cloth in the hot, soapy water in the sink and begins cleaning them.

Something ties me to her. I guess it is our childhood. The time overseas.

I can't abandon her. We've shared too much. I'm still compelled to contact her. To share my story. I guess it is the memory of our connection that I still hold on to. I remember her power during primary school. I always wanted to please her. Impress her. Be good enough to be her friend. I feel so embarrassed to think of me being like that. Being so clingy and needy as a child. I so desperately wanted a friend. A best friend. Ainsley was never that. Not even Polly, the easygoing one I cherish now. It was Mary Jayne. My MJ. The loud and boisterous one. It was like MJ choose me. Mumma loved MJ; they were always close. Mumma never liked Ainsley; it was like she could see this side of her, even at a young age. She could read people, Mumma. Insightful, like a sixth sense. See right through their bullshit.

Hearing the gate, Rosie's heart jumps into her throat. Stopping, she listens to Ainsley's footsteps along the veranda. She quickly puts the chairs back in place as she catches sight of Ainsley through the window.

Opening the door, she holds her breath. As Ainsley enters, her presence infiltrates the energy in the room. Time and space evaporate as they hug. A feeling of home and familiarity washes over her. Rosie's energy lifts. Ainsley is excited, her face is warm and soft. Glowing. Rosie is pleasantly surprised. Ainsley exudes happiness. The image of an Ainsley she remembers from childhood.

'I can't believe you're here,' Rosie finally verbalises.

'Look at you. So bloody youthful.' Ainsley holds Rosie back at arm's length and looks her up and down. 'God, I've missed you,' Ainsley says with tears welling in her eyes.

They hug again. There is love. Memories. Joy that only an old friend can evoke.

They move to Ainsley's favourite spot in Rosie's garden to sit for hours in the shade of the afternoon. Rosie drinking tea. Ainsley drinking wine.

There's a change in Ainsley but I can't seem to put my finger on it.

Looking out across the valley, Rosie soaks in the sun.

'I've met someone,' Ainsley blurts out.

Rosie is lost for words. There is an awkward silence; the words hang in the air.

'What? What do you mean? You're married!' Rosie responds before she can think or comprehend what Ainsley has said, making no attempt to hide her complete shock.

'Darling, we have been unhappily married, forever. You know he's had women on the side. For years. I've always just turned a blind eye. I didn't know what I'd do on my own. With no money. No house. Raising a son. This time, I have found something. A little tenderness in my life.' Ainsley looks off into the distance, shrugging her shoulders as though she is filled with warmth at the mention of it.

'Who is he?' Rosie asks, still in shock.

'No, darling, it's a she.' Ainsley pauses, giving this new information an opportunity to sink in. 'She's an artist and it's been the most amazing time of my life. You just wouldn't believe it.' Ainsley's face lights up as she lets her hands dance with her words. Birds chit-chat in the background as Rosie's mind swirls.

'How did you meet her?' Rosie asks. 'I never thought you were into, like, women?'

'Well, I wasn't, until I met her,' Ainsley says. 'You'd love her. Oh Laney, she is amazing. Like I said, she's an artist. Stunning. Tall. Dark hair. She's fifteen years younger than me.' Her eyes drift off as Rosie senses the deep love and intimacy Ainsley has felt. 'We just started out as friends. I tried to deny the attraction for so long but then it just happened. It all felt right. Shayna explains it that we fall in love with the person and not their gender. You see, she has been bisexual her whole life. We are going to Spain together, when I get back from Australia.'

'Does Rory know?'

'He might. I doubt it. He wouldn't care anyway. To be honest, I couldn't care less,' Ainsley says, sipping her wine.

They talk into the night, moving inside when it gets cold.

'Do you remember the day MJ died?' Rosie asks.

'Yeah, of course I do, like it was yesterday,' Ainsley says. 'She was my friend too, Laney.'

'Well, I can't. Well, I can, but not all of it. There's big chunks missing. I've been afraid to ask. But can you tell me what happened?'

'We were in the caravan. Playing cards. I'm sure I was winning, you were always hopeless at cards.'

Rosie rolls her eyes. 'That sounds about right.'

'Polly came to the door. She was a mess, we knew something had happened. We came out of the caravan. Then she said MJ had been killed in a plane accident. You fell to the ground in a ball. I hugged Polly. Mumma came out the back gate. She was screaming your name. She scooped you up. Carried you inside. Wrapped you in a blanket. We all cried. Pa took Polly and me home. We came back the next day. You were never the same, Laney.'

Ainsley reaches her hand across and places it on top of Rosie's.

'It was like some lights were switched off inside of you. You seemed fine, but Polly and I knew.'

'Did I cry?'

'Not really. It was like you didn't believe it for a long time.'

'I don't remember crying. Why didn't I cry? I feel so guilty. So much pain that I never cried. I just felt like I lost all control. I was juggling balls and then I dropped them. They fell to the ground. I just couldn't pick them up again. I can't remember.' Rosie sobs into her hands. Ainsley places her hands on her back.

'Of course you can't, honey. It was a tragedy. We were in trauma. We have experienced so much tragedy.'

They hold each other. Crying. Rocking. Slowly healing. Mad women rocking.

Words Fail

Sometimes words fail
Tears aren't enough
Pain chokes you
Nothing can soothe the pain

Sometimes words fail
Sorry is too late
Anger eats your flesh
Nothing can ease the pain

Sometimes words fail
Good bye is too late
Sadness drowns you
Nothing can heal the pain

KEY

New Love

> *Deep new love*
> *Wrapped in arms*
> *Of hope and excitement*
> *Not made weary*
> *Yet*
>
> *Deep new love*
> *Soaring on tender lips*
> *Whispered secrets*
> *Thrusting hips*
> *Not made weary*
> *Yet*
>
> *Deep new love*
> *Laughter and song*
> *Not made weary yet*
> *By age or regret*

Pushing the wisteria hanging over the path, draping down from the archway, out of her way, Rosie makes her way through the gate and out into the front garden. She walks past the big bed of bulbs—

freesias, ranunculus, tulips and daffodils—admiring the new blooms. Marvelling at the splendid sight.

Look at the eclectic mix of colour. The fragrant smells. Different shapes.

Rosie bends down and removes some unwanted weeds detracting from the splendour of the flowers.

The beautiful sights and smells; a reward for my hard work. Determination. Perseverance. All these years, caring for my garden. A joy I'm endlessly fulfilled by.

Strolling to the edge of the hill, Rosie reaches over the fence and picks some flowers hanging from the acacia trees. The smell is pungent, like an expensive perfume. Hearing the buzzing of the bees, she feels the force of life surging through her garden. Rosie remembers her children running, playing and digging in the sandpit. Birds feast in the trees. Foraging. Singing sweet songs. Calling loudly. Flying high into the trees to nest. Galahs and lorikeets fly past, partying in the trees in a frenzy of feeding and squawking. The daisies and violets shine their pretty faces, relishing in the warmth and glory of the vibrant sunshine. Cherry blossoms burst into bloom. The trail of a plane flying above, too high to hear, draws a mark across the sky.

I can't believe it's my birthday tomorrow; seventy years old. MJ will remain forever young, always eighteen years old. I miss her, even after all these years. I wish she was here. To hold my hand. Walk beside me in my garden. She will forever be beautiful. No wrinkles. Not burdened by aches and pains. Forever missed. Forever loved.

Rosie passes the tomatoes; basil and marigolds surround them.

A trusted, guaranteed combination. There are so many things in my life I've experienced that MJ never did. Marriage, love, children, loss and travel. I must be grateful for all the blessings in my life. For the precious eighteen years we had together. My soul sister. I imagine her in heaven.

Oh God, I hope she is proud of me. A life I've tried to live twice. Once for MJ. Once for myself. Will it be enough?

As she walks onto the lawn, feeling the texture of the grass, she has a clear image of Anne as a little girl, with her teddy-bear picnic on the front lawn. Surrounded by daisy chains. She feels grateful for the joy her children have brought her.

All unique in their gifts and blessings. All with a special bond. I imagine God must have had big plans for MJ. With all her energy. Her intense love. What a big heart. I'd give anything for a warm hug. I'd love to just sit and chat. Gossip about nothing.

Rosie closes her eyes, picturing MJ bathed in warm golden light.

Retreating to the shade, she picks up her book; she is reading *The Alchemist*. Rosie is loving the story and understands why Anne insisted she read it. Rosie reads the passage several times.

These powerful words, they resonate so strongly with me. I feel compelled. Inspired. I know I need to uncover my treasure. I know I have not yet completed my journey. What would MJ say? She would laugh. 'Just get on with it. Stop fucking around.' *She'd wrap her arm around me.* 'Tell our story, Laney. You have it there in front of you.' *The crack in time, that's where it began. The crack in time.*

As she closes her eyes, the image of an old woman under the expanse of a tree fills her mind. The old woman opens a box. Holding a key. Looking deep into Rosie's eyes, she says, *Find your treasure chest.*

'I know, I know,' Rosie mutters to herself.

A pain surges through her hip. An ache in her lower back. Opening her eyes, she is reminded she needs to go to Tilly's today.

Hopefully she can help me with this bloody pain. God it's hard getting old.

Rosie struggles to get up from the shade-drenched chair. Holding her side, she moans as she gets to her feet. She takes her book inside and places it beside her bed, then grabs her bag and a collection of books to lend Tilly and Ash.

The door bangs behind her. Rosie puts her sunglasses over her eyes. The sweet smell of jasmine catches her nostrils as she walks through the gate and out into her ute.

As she travels along the road, the green hills set against the bright blue backdrop of the spring sky are a comfort and inspiration to her.

What a beautiful time of the year it is.

As she turns up the track to Tilly and Ash's place, she winds down the window and feels the fresh breeze on her face. Birds dart in and out of the trees. Angus cows, feasting on fresh grass, feed their new calves.

Pulling up in front of the old house, she admires the vegetable garden that is overflowing with produce. She takes the bag from the passenger seat and goes inside, hearing loud music filling the house. Tilly is singing and dancing.

It sounds familiar. Roxette, of course.

Tilly turns around, her arms covered in soap from the kitchen sink. She yells, 'Sorry, Laney! I'll turn it down, just getting these fucking dishes done—it never fucking ends, does it!'

Placing the bag of books on the kitchen table, Rosie sits down carefully on an old wooden chair covered in crocheted blankets. The music quietens. Tilly returns, face brimming with happiness. Laughter in her eyes.

'Oh bloody hell, you look like you're in pain,' Tilly says. 'Let's get ya on the table straight away, no fucking around.'

Tilly wipes her hands and arms with a towel. Flicking her head, Tilly directs Rosie to her treatment room.

'Oh, darling,' Rosie says, 'I'm a silly old fool. Don't know what the fuck I've done. I'm not good, that's for sure.' Rosie shuffles down the hallway holding her side.

They move into Tilly's massage room. Tilly helps her onto the bed and she lies facedown. Rosie is reminded of many times Tilly had to put her to bed, after Will died. Drunk.

God bless this girl. She's put up with a lot from me over the years.

Tilly rubs oils into her skin.

It feels like heaven. I love the smell.

There is a warm breeze blowing. Rosie has struggled to walk for days. She thinks of things she's done. Then she remembers moving the hose out the front garden, twisting in an awkward way.

'I've got pain all up this left side, you know,' Rosie says. 'I've always had problems with this side, since I broke my leg.'

'What happened?' Tilly asks.

'I was thirteen; there were six of us. You know, in and on the back of the old ute. You know, the one with flat tyres down the back of the shed.'

'Oh yeah, I know the one you're talking about. It's got a heap of shit stacked on the back.'

'Yeah that's it. MJ was driving, her cousin Izzy and Ainsley in the front. Blake, his mate Nick and I on the back. I was sitting down, staring across the paddock. Polly was on the motorbike. The gears got stuck and MJ and Izzy were trying to move it and they weren't watching the road. They drove off the edge, right above where the culvert is. You know, across from that row of trees on the lane. Ahhh that's the spot, Til. Bloody hell it is hard getting old.' Rosie breathes in deeply as the pain surges up her side. 'Yeah, so, Blake and Nick jumped off and I didn't have time. The tray squashed my leg. Polly raced to get Pa. Ainsley knelt beside me. MJ held my hand. We sang songs. She could brighten me up, even when I was in excruciating pain. Bit like you, Til. I spent six months in plaster. You know, it was just before Christmas. The middle of bloody summer.'

Tilly massages a place in Rosie's back. 'Ash had an accident when she was younger that still gives her grief, up on her shoulder.'

'Really, what happened?'

'Ash only spoke about it once, but yeah, it was pretty brutal. Beaten by a group of girls.'

'Fucking hell, why?'

'She never gave me a lot of details but she was about fifteen at the time. They were at this party. She was talking to this girl. I guess it looked like she was flirting. This group cornered her in the toilets. Called her a fucking dyke whore, dirty lesbian, you know, that kind of thing. You know she's always been strong. She could fight, but they outnumbered her. Grabbed her from behind. Held her down and kicked the shit out of her. She had broken ribs, a fractured jaw. They must have pulled her shoulder out of place and she never went to the hospital or the police. I still remember the night she told me. Ash cried like a baby, Laney. She was so vulnerable. I held her. Rocking. I was so mad. I was sad. I felt so fucking helpless. I wanted to grab that pack of ignorant cunts and smash their fucking faces in, but all I could do was hold her. A mad woman rocking. Hold her. Hear her story. You know I fell in love with Ash. That Ash. That scared and hurt and bloody beautiful girl. I'd die for her. I'm bloody missing her … it feels like she's been gone for fucking ever.'

It's nice to see this side of Tilly. Tender and soft. Losing the bravado.

'How's she going?' Rosie asks.

'She's good, sorting out the kids.' Tilly pauses for a moment, her voice drops.

Looking towards the window, Rosie admires the patterns in the white dreamcatchers rocking side to side.

'You were right, Laney.'

'Well, there's a first time for everything,' she responds with a chuckle.

'I know. It's a turn up for the books, isn't it? Nah, you were right. I need to support her. Ash told me some things. About her mother being an alco. Growing up around it. Her dad running off. She loves her brother. He was all she had growing up.'

'Darling, when we love people, we love all of them, even the ugly parts. Their scars, their past and their family. As inconvenient as they may be.'

'Roll over now, I'll attack it from this angle,' Tilly instructs her as she wipes her hands on a towel. Rubbing Rosie's feet, Tilly applies pressure in a rhythmic and deliberate way. Closing her eyes, Rosie relaxes, taking deep breaths, enjoying Tilly's soothing touch.

'Ash said the worst thing was their laughing. The humiliation. That feeling of being weak and powerless.'

Sounds like poor Mumma. I should have never let her be put in there.

'I was the only person apart from her brother who she ever told. She left school after that, started training horses.'

'Is that where you first met?'

'Yeah, kind of. Remember I went off with Kenny and worked on that station up north. Remember Will was going to come up with us? But he wouldn't leave Stella and she was finishing school.'

'Ah, yeah, I remember that.' Rosie momentarily opens her eyes.

'Well, I went up on a station and Ash was working nearby training racehorses. A massive property. These cunts had fucking ridiculous coin—like, you should've seen it. Anyway, we met at a party. You know up there, neither of us had mentioned to anyone we were gay. It's sometimes just easier to let people assume but not have that awkward conversation and give cunts a reason to fucking hate you. I still remember our eyes meeting across the room. It was like electricity. Or deja vu. Our souls had met before.'

'What did you say to her?'

Tilly laughs as she massages Rosie's leg, each stroke careful and methodical. Rosie can hear Tilly's guineafowl outside. A wind chime singing in the light breeze. 'Probably the dumbest thing. I said, "Um, so … you ride horses for… um, what's it called?" She looked me straight in the eyes—you know her dark eyes—and goes, "Yes, I ride for Black Rock Station. I train the thoroughbreds. I'm Ash." She put her hand out so confidently. "You must be Matilda, the new Jillaroo from next door." I was fucking shitting myself. She was drop-dead gorgeous. So direct and she fucking called me Matilda. I thought I was called into the principal's office, for fuck sake. I was stammering and stuttering like a fucking idiot. Oh God, ya should've seen it, Laney. I'd never felt that kind of energy before; I didn't know how to handle it. Anyway, we didn't see each other for a while after that. I couldn't think of anything else. I got drunk one night and snuck into her room. Got out of there before sunrise. We snuck around like that for about six months. A few people clued on and we decided to get out of there. We bought an old van in the nearest town. Mind you, that was a few hundred kilometres away. We travelled down the west coast. It was the best time of my life. Then we ran low on money and we got a job over the border on a dairy farm. We were there about two years until the old bloke died and his mongrel kids fucking came in and sold the lot.'

'You know, I never even knew all this,' Rosie says. 'I guess I never really asked. I was pretty fucked up when you came home.'

'Well, it was a long time, Laney, before any of us could see through the fog of grief after Will died. I'm going to do some clearing work now, so just make it your intention to release the negative energy and embrace the healing.'

As Rosie rests there, she can sense Tilly's hands moving above her. With her eyes firmly closed, the image of Ash and Tilly first meeting, locking eyes, enters her mind. She's reminded of Ainsley and her new lover. Envisages her parents and their forbidden love. For a brief moment, she feels a longing for love; young, wild love. Tilly's voice breaks through her thoughts.

'I'm tonguing for a cuppa. Ya want one before you go?'

'Oh yes, darling, I'd love one,' Rosie replies as she gently gets off the table.

Driving home, Rosie can't stop thinking about Ash. Noticing an echidna that has been run over by a car—it laying lifeless on its back, on the side of the road—she gasps.

Oh shit, that's a rare sight; you don't see that very often. The poor thing.

Turning a corner, she thinks of MJ.

The one fight we had. It must have been summer holidays, cause Izzy was visiting. MJ was always annoyed when she visited. They were all the same age and MJ's mum always insisted Izzy came to stay with them, to give her sister a break. Izzy's mum had heaps of kids and her husband was a shearer, a hard worker. She was always cooking or cleaning, grabbing him a beer from the fridge.

Izzy had arrived. MJ's mum dropped them off at the ramp and they were walking down the lane. I could see that they were arguing. MJ was running ahead and by the time she reached me, she was out of breath and Izzy was crying and trying to keep up. I can hear MJ as clear as day—'Let's go, quick, get away from her'—as I turned my head around to see how close Izzy was. I must have said something like, 'We can't do that.

Wait for her.' Instinctively, I had walked towards Izzy. I can still see her matted hair. Dirty clothes. The tears running down her cheeks. A pang of empathy beat in my chest. MJ ran off annoyed, muttering under her breath. I wasn't trying to take sides; I was just trying to do the right thing.

Bloody MJ cracked the shits and went home, walked the whole bloody way. Stubborn as a bull. She didn't talk to me for two whole days. I was so lonely. Sad without my best friend. Regretful. I just moped in my room.

Then they returned, her mum driving them to the door. MJ's eyes cast down as she mumbled an apology. She could be so stubborn sometimes. I didn't care; I wrapped my arms around her. MJ stood there like a stiff board. I forgave her in an instant.

How did I lose her forever? Those two days were nothing compared to that moment. That moment I realised she was lost. Gone. Dead. Forever. The world turned a shade of grey. It's so final. Forever is a long time. I feel the weight of forever. Endless days without you.

She pulls up the ute under the shade of a tree and turns the engine off. Sitting in the silence. Lost in memories. Her eyes look across the green, flourishing valley.

Write it down, Laney. Write it down. You know that is the key.

HEART

The sun peers over the horizon, slowly making its presence known. Waking with excitement.

It's strange to be so excited about a birthday at this age.

The house is filled with quiet; no one has woken yet. Rosie slips out of bed to wrap herself in layers. She sneaks out the front door, making sure she doesn't wake anyone. The morning is still; darkness cocoons the valley. Shrugging her shoulders against the briskness of the morning, she walks along the path, through the gate and into the front garden. The horizon has lightened from the calling of the sun. Rosie breathes in the fresh morning air as she wanders in the garden, admiring the plants and flowers. The lawn is drenched in dew; her slippers soak in the moisture like a sponge.

Today I am carefree. Surrounded by my family, comforted by their presence. I'm glad that Ainsley has come and gone. As much as I love her, I don't need this pressure today.

The clouds begin to shift, turning shades of pink and purple. Sitting on the hill, looking over the valley, she watches the sun rise. The sky painted in a spectacle of colour.

God has created a beauty for my birthday this morning.

Rosie soaks it in, enjoying the moment. Enjoying the garden and the valley. A light breeze blows. The horses feed, their coats beginning to shine in the soft light of dawn. Rosie admires the wisteria, dogwood and the bearded irises. There's humidity in the air, suggesting eminent rain.

A rooster crows. Frogs croak. Rosie is cloaked in tranquillity. A longing for her husband's loving arms is strong this morning.

I want to go back to a time when we were first in love. Melting into each other; desire, exhilarating passion, consuming every thought. If only, for just one day, I could go back to that time, with Blake. The two of us. Lost in each other.

Lost in her thoughts, she hears the screech of the gate as Anne walks through, carrying tea; her heart is filled with happiness at this sight. Anne hands her the tea, wishes Rosie a happy birthday and kisses her cheek. Sitting beside her, Anne doesn't speak but sighs contentedly as she turns her gaze to the sunrise. Rosie enjoys the morning glory, Anne's company and the warm embrace of silence. Kookaburras sing in unison; they see them perched on a branch of the tree above.

'Do you have any regrets, Mum, in seventy years?'

'Well, lots really, but none too important. I wish I'd spent more time with you kids when you were growing up.'

'Were you and Dad always happy?'

'Mostly, but not always. Our marriage wasn't perfect. No one's is. We fought. I remember one time—you were very young—your dad lost his temper and threw something across the room. I was going on like a dog with a bone. He was such a patient man. Full of grace. I've had far too many blessings to be getting caught up on regrets. I do want to do something before I die though.'

'You're only seventy, Mum. You're not dying yet.'

'We are all going to die.'

'Of course, but not for a long time.' Anne grabs her arm and holds her, resting her head on Rosie's shoulder. Rosie reaches a hand across to her.

It's not like Anne to be so affectionate.

'Is everything alright, darling?'

'Yeah. So what do you want to do before you die?'

'Write my book.'

'Bloody hell, I've been telling you this forever. Just get on with it, already.'

The sun breaks through the clouds, announcing the new day. Thick rays of golden light spread out in beacons, lighting up the valley.

'I just need to get started,' Rosie says. 'I've been going through my journals and my poetry. I don't really know how to put it in order. There's parts I can't remember.'

'Start from the beginning, when you were born and early childhood, and then just go through the different time frames.'

'Hopefully I've got like twenty years to get it sorted out, before I kick the bucket.'

'At least twenty. I better get inside and check on the kids.'

'Alright, sweetheart. I'm going to sit here a little longer.'

The day unfolds as a time of family, love and celebration. They spend time in the garden, playing cricket, soaking in the sunshine. Tim sits in a chair, behind dark sunglasses, not speaking. Rosie sits down beside him. Tom is bowling and Anne is batting.

'She's got a mean swing on her, Tim.'

'Tell me about it.'

'She could always out-bat both her brothers. You going to get out there and give it a crack?'

'Nah, I'm making the most of having a break. I worked seventy hours last week.'

'So Anne and the kids wouldn't have seen you much, then.'

'I make these sacrifices for my family. To give them the best of everything. The best house, schools.'

'There's more to life than money, my friend.'

'That's easy for you to say when you've inherited two farms.'

'Yes, I was blessed. You know, it came with a lot of hard work and responsibility.'

Anne hits the ball on the edge of the bat. The ball rolls off to the side. Olivia runs to get it, her foot catches something and she falls, rolling on her side. Yelling out, Anne drops the bat. Rosie rises from her seat to run to their aid. As she approaches, she glances over her shoulder. She sees Tim slink away, through the gate and inside, like a snake retreating from a shovel.

The afternoon is quiet. Rosie's guests rest in the house. Sitting by the caravan, she sips her tea.

I love the family surrounding me. The laughter and relaxing together. Poor little Liv, glad her fall didn't cause her any major damage.

As she breathes in, a light breeze rustles through the trees.

I better go inside soon and begin preparing dinner. A big roast lamb, my favourite; may as well get spoilt. I only turn seventy once. I'm actually excited for my friends and family to be coming. I normally avoid attention or people making a fuss over me but today feels special. I'm just going to embrace this time of celebration. I know many who have been denied the privilege of reaching this age. I miss them. I wish they were here.

The wind dances through the leaves, making music.

I know they still are.

They begin preparing dinner.

What a day it has been. Just perfect. A time of family, love and celebration. Spending time in the garden, playing cricket, soaking in the sunshine.

As the dinner is cooking, the sun is setting; the guests are about to arrive.

I better put some wood on the fire. I want the house to be warm enough for everyone.

Kneeling down, she loads the fireplace with red gum. Tom and Billy come through the back door. Billy can't contain his excitement as he yells, 'Nanny, come look, quick!' Rosie walks into the kitchen to see Tom, his face filled with a large grin. Tears fill her eyes as she sees a bundle of black of white. The tiniest, fluffiest little puppy she has ever seen. Billy shouts with glee, 'Happy Birthday, Nanny! Look, it's a puppy. It's a girl.'

Rosie greets Tom with a kiss. 'Thank you, darling,' she says. Tom places the puppy in her arms. Billy jumps up and down. Olivia and Lachie run to join all the excitement. Rosie's grandchildren crowd around her. She bends down so they can all pat the new addition to the family. Looking into the pup's eyes, one blue and one brown, she feels it's wet nose.

What will we call you, precious little one?

As the guests arrive, the kids and the new pup keep each other entertained in the lounge room. When they sit down to dinner, Rosie looks around at her small group of friends and family sitting at the table, filling the house with noise and warmth.

This is a select group. I've never been one to have lots of friends but they are all close. Precious friends. Family I hold close to my heart.

As she sees her new pup chewing on the bottom of Tom's trousers, her full heart begins to overflow with love and gratitude.

I love this poem by Beau Taplin. What's it called? Oh yeah, 'Déjà vu'. I understand why Anne gave me this amazing book for my birthday. She knows me so well. This poem. I feel transported back to that time when Blake and I were so young. He looked so gorgeous. The evening sun cast on his face as he rode his beautiful old palomino across the paddock to meet me. Blake's blue eyes sparkled. Electricity ran through me. His long legs stretching out to climb down from the horse. I can still see him tying her up, his loving hands stroking her white blaze. How he loved that big old horse, his faithful companion.

There I was, trying to play it cool; perched on a rock, waiting by the creek. My legs crossed under my long skirt, my red curls pinned back. I always tried to make an effort without looking like I had made any effort. He would amble over. So casual. Sit down beside me. I can still hear him now. 'Nice night for it.' We would chat, talk about the farms, the weather, until the sunset and darkness would descend. Then we'd finally gain the courage to kiss each other goodbye. I just wanted to melt into this big beautiful man. A kiss goodbye and a promise to meet the following night.

I'll have to lend this to Stella when I've read it. She'll love it.

Closing the book, Rosie relishes in the silence as her family sleep soundly. Closing her eyes, Rosie drifts off into restful sleep, reflecting on a perfect day.

MAD WOMAN ROCKING

Setting sun; dark grey, luminescent purples with strewn pale pinks. The new puppy nests in a ball, sleeping soundly in the corner. Birds are chirping, saying their farewell. Half-moon. Fire burns vibrantly. The smoke fills her nostrils.

Captivating, mesmerising, the glow. The flicker of the flames.

Rosie takes in the scene from the side of the hill. She burns a pile of branches and sticks, collecting random, scattered sticks.

Cleaning, cleansing. Satisfied another day is done.

Light fades, fire is dancing and sending warmth to surround Rosie and her new puppy; comforting and fulfilling. Gum leaves sway in the evening breeze.

Venturing inside to paint, she carries the bundle of fur with her, then gently places her in her soft bed beside her desk. Rosie turns on the music; she begins listening to Dan Sultan's 'It Belongs to Us'.

Anne introduced me to this. She uses it in the classroom. She is so creative and clever.

Rosie thinks about the symbol of fire; the power to destroy, to keep warm, to crack open seeds, to kill, to clean and rejuvenate the land. Embodying the possibility of good and evil.

Like men and women; in my lifetime, we've always walked a fine line. The threatening bushfire the summer Will was born. My fear. Blake away fighting. No grandfather. Mumma here, keeping the ship afloat, as always. Breastfeeding, filled with anxiety. The fear inducing terror, constantly waiting for news. Our smoke-filled valley.

Rosie thinks about the time she was in hospital, curled up in the foetal position; she freezes the image in her mind. Moving the paint-drenched paintbrush, she creates large black swirls. Moulding white elongated eyes, cast down. Mixing white and black. Stirring red and blue to create a dark purple. A woman lying trapped under dark, tumultuous swirls. Trying to capture trauma, distress, turmoil … trying to convey the image in her mind. Rosie layers the paint; it is like a dance of strokes, a big, thick canvas board.

It is raw, messy and I love it. I love to paint in a chaotic, hypnotic trance, losing track of time. Lost in my creation. In pursuit of showing my message, my past. My story. I am one with God. My soul soaring to great heights, free and wild.

The moment transports her to another realm, where time and space dissolve. Once Rosie has finished, she is transported back to the present, awoken by the shutting of the back door. She wipes her hands and tilts her head, assessing the work, before going into the kitchen to greet her visitor.

A smile creeps across her face at the sight of Aunt Phoebe, bringing her gifts.

A surrogate mother all these years despite being so close in age. At times, we were more like sisters. Her husband died young. I worry she gets lonely.

Rosie makes a cup of tea while Aunt Phoebe begins jabbering on about the town's latest gossip. They sit and eat the scones she has brought.

Her specialty. She makes them just like Mumma.

Looking at Aunt Phoebe's dark, wavy, short hair, Rosie notices the grey hair creeping through at the base.

I remember when she had long, dark hair reaching down to her waist.

Aunt Phoebe's blue eyeliner makes her dark eyes stand out. The new puppy darts in and out of her floral dress.

Aunt Phoebe skates her glasses up along her large nose as she appears to notice the paint on Rosie's fingers. 'You doing some painting, lovey?'

'Yeah, just playing around,' Rosie replies.

'I wish I had the talent. I guess cooking is my creative outlet.' Aunt Phoebe offers a polite smile as she sips her tea.

'Do you regret not having children?' As the words come tumbling out of her mouth with little thought, Rosie wishes she could pick them up one by one and stuff them back in her mouth and chew them into pulp until they disappear. Aunt Phoebe doesn't seem to flinch at Rosie's bluntness.

'I don't, darling. I never wanted children and Harry didn't either. I know people have a deep, burning desire or they do it out of obligation, but I just never wanted to give that much of myself.'

'Did I put you off having children, caring for me as I grew up?' Rosie asks, now she realises Aunt Phoebe is happy to talk about it.

'In some ways, yes, but not really. In a way, I knew the reality of children from helping raise you, but I also loved you like a daughter.' Aunt Phoebe reaches her hand across the table. 'I just never wanted to share my time, my space or my husband. Then I had to have a hysterectomy when I had the cancer and I was relieved because the decision was then made for me. I have no regrets and regrets are pointless anyway.' Aunty Phoebe shakes her head, pauses for a moment, takes a sip of her tea and continues. 'Well, that's not completely true. I do have one regret.'

'What's that?' Rosie asks with intrigue, squinting her eyes and drinking her tea, trying to imagine any possible thing Aunt Phoebe could regret.

A person who is so orderly. Aunt Phoebe's house is like a show home.

'I had an affair, years ago.' The words hang in the air like a foul stench.

Rosie feels this unexpected anger swirl in her stomach.

Is there anything or anyone in this life that is pure?

Digesting this revelation, tears well in her eyes.

Even Aunt Phoebe has scars, battle wounds from life. No one escapes walking that fine line.

'What! I never knew about this,' Rosie says in shock, not believing what she's hearing. 'How did Mumma never say anything? Who with?'

'You know Harvey, who lived across the river?'

'He's got a wife and children, Aunt Phoebe. I can't believe it. When did this happen? How did it happen?' Rosie tries to contain the judgement in her voice but fails.

'It was years ago; I think Anne must have been a baby, that's why you never knew. It wasn't public knowledge. I think it was the only thing that Mumma ever kept to herself in all her life.' Aunt Phoebe sips her tea; sadness sweeps over her face as her eyes are cast into the corner of the room. 'You know, I loved him. It was wild and passionate. We were both married; he had children, responsibilities. It all started when he came to school. He was making a delivery of mulch, for the gardens. The parents had organised a working bee. You know his eldest was in year 7 at the time. He came into the office to let me know. I was working late and no one was there. There was a spark from the moment our eyes met; this is something I'd never felt with Harry. It started relatively innocently, but this attraction I couldn't control. We had a wild love affair, then we were found out. Harry knew and he confronted me. I had to come clean. Then it ended. Harvey and his family moved away. That was the end of it.' A single tear rolls down her cheek. Aunt Phoebe stares out the window and off into the distance. Rosie reaches her hand over the table and with tenderness places it on top of Aunt Phoebe's, feeling her pain, her loss, losing the love of her life.

'I can't believe it makes me so emotional after all these years. It feels good to talk about it. It has been buried for a long time.' Aunt Phoebe finishes her cup of tea and within an instant seems to snap back into her normal self. 'Well, I'm grateful, my dear. I had a life. I had one wild love affair in my life and that has made it complete. As much as I said it was a regret, it really isn't. It was selfish and wrong—I admit that—but I wanted it more than anything at the time. Anyway, enough about me. What's been going on with you, with the family?'

Rosie's head is still swirling after this massive revelation and she answers without much thought or consideration. 'Well, you know, it's the same old really; the grandkids are growing too fast. Anne and Tom work too hard.' Rosie picks up their empty cups and puts them on the sink.

'Do you have your statement for me?'

'I do.' Rosie grabs the papers from the bench and hands them over to Aunt Phoebe, who takes them in her hands and begins to read.

Last Week of Life

My grandmother has died.

There is a huge void. This palpable emptiness as a familiar part of home, I'd always known, is gone. Gone forever. My mind struggles with this reality, my heart grapples for meaning and my soul aches for clarity. What has made the death of my grandmother—a powerful life and figure—more painful, more difficult to accept and embrace, is her last week of life.

Though she was old and I logically knew she would one day die, her death came as a dreadful shock. A shock and pain that stabs you in the guts. Disbelief at how she could go. How could she possibly go so quietly and without warning, just unexpectedly. It has been revealed that that was not necessarily the case. After the dust settled and my family returned to the normality of life, my aunty was questioning what had happened, what her last week of life had been like. And the findings were heartbreaking, to say the least. The bandage was removed and underneath was a festering wound. A devastating discovery.

My grandmother spent her last week of life in the care of, what her family had thought, were professionals that could, that were, providing her with constant necessary care. My aunty has met with them and read the records. I know there have been some exceptional people who cared for her with so much love and diligence. I know they gave her time and made a fuss of her. Despite that, it is clear there have been some breaches of professional conduct. I have this image of my grandmother lying there helpless. Unable to move. Unassisted. Waiting for someone to come and no one coming. I envisage her lying there incapacitated, feeling scared, lonely and frustrated. I feel her anxiety. Her pain. Her distress, and I ache. I ache to the core of my being. It makes me think of my children when they were born. Helpless bundles that each night I needed to feed and change and console. How tiring and what a difficult task. My grandmother needed that kind of careful care at the end of her precious life, just like my children at the start of their lives. She deserved it. She had earned it. She was not just a patient to us, like she was to some of the heartless people that denied her care and dignity. She was our mother. Our grandmother, our great-grandmother. A woman who had endured childbirth six times, raised seven children, lost two of her children in all her years. Mumma had been a widow for twenty-two years. She worked hard as a dairy farmer and had lived a rich life full of family and love.

This woman was not dumped in this facility to get her out of the way. She was placed there because her large family thought that she would get the best possible care. Before this, she had lived at home in her large farmhouse, cared for by her family and the support of nurses who came to wash her daily. She was kept happy, healthy and cared for. She called when she needed something and her family always answered the call. She was independent and financially self-sufficient. This is a woman who paid taxes her whole life and was never a burden on the taxpayer. Then to think, she was left alone at night. The call for help with no answer. She was denied independence, control, dignity and respect, for the first time in her life, through systematic abuse and neglect.

You see, she did not die quietly, as we have discovered— for she was not a subservient woman who was afraid to speak her mind—but was silenced. In her final week of life, she was abused and silenced. What compels me to write this is that my grandmother's last week will not be left unnoticed, forgotten, covered over by pathetic apologies and excuses. My grandmother's last week of life was significant and the truth will be made known. When someone goes to abuse another poor, innocent, frail elderly person, I hope the name Pearl Lane rings in their ears. Haunts them at night when they are trying to sleep instead of caring for their patients.

It was revealed that after a night of not being attended to, she made a complaint. They were spoken to about this and instead of acting in a professional manner, they 'had a go at her about it,' as Mumma described to a family member. My aunty has a recording of my distressed grandmother crying, saying they were trying to kill her.

As I heard the report with all these instances of abuse, I kept thinking, if they couldn't look after her properly, why didn't they tell us? Why didn't they talk to her family? We would have helped, taken her home. We would have fixed this.

I was told this as my family arrived home for Christmas to spend time with me. I had to explain to my daughter—the most difficult part of it all for me—she died on Saturday morning, unexpectedly. On the Friday, she was shaking due to her extremely low sugar levels and could not press the buttons to use the phone. Mumma spoke to someone and said, 'I want to call Rosie and get her to bring her swag up here and doss down here for the night.' I burst into tears when I told her this. For they never made that call. I never packed up my swag to be beside my dying grandmother, because they ignored, denied the request of a dying woman. If I had known, I would have been there beside her to hold her hand to comfort her in her time of fear and pain. All of my family, if they had known, would have stopped everything and come to her side. Instead, she was left to be alone. She was allowed to be treated like she was an inconvenience. She was neglected, abused and belittled.

I have a sadness and a rage in my gut that wants to make someone pay retribution for the mistreatment of my beloved grandmother. I am disgusted. Distraught that such negligence, unprofessional conduct, appalling behaviour and lack of care is allowed to occur.

When my aunty, who was grieving the loss of her loved one, uncovered these atrocities and questioned them, she was given excuses, promises of procedural changes and an apology and was offered counselling.

Incompetent people are allowed to continue working. The systemic abuse and neglect of the elderly can quite easily continue. My grandmother, who wrote a long story with many years of tales, had to finish her final story with a week of neglect. A week denied of what she wished to be her final chapter. I'm grateful for the ones with her in those last moments but it doesn't erase the other tragic acts. This is not how I had imagined her last week, never would I ever have wished this to be the ending.

She once said to me that she wanted to die in her garden. When I close my eyes, I have this beautiful image of her in peace, slipping away, surrounded by her glorious garden. Unfortunately there is another harsh reality.

As I long for change, retribution and punishment, I feel such deeply rooted sadness knowing the damage has been done. We can never get back that last precious week of our beautiful grandmother's life.

Aunt Phoebe's face is a flood of tears and distress. 'I couldn't have said it better myself, Laney. Thank you. I better go. My heart is breaking all over again. I won't let these bastards get away with this. I won't.' Aunt Phoebe gets up from her chair, clutching her chest, wiping her face with a hanky. As she gathers her things, their eyes meet for a moment. They are connected through grief, sadness and the pain. The deep pain of loss.

I know I was going to talk to her about Lottie and Phillip but it's too much. It's not the right time. She's too upset. I'm still dumbfounded by her bloody revelation. I didn't see that coming. It will be too much for her right now. It can wait.

As she farewells Aunt Phoebe with a long, loving embrace, she thinks about her.

How would I capture her in a story? Her big personality. Loud. Always cooking. Banging and throwing orders. Dark hair cut short and brown eyes. Wearing an apron. Sometimes selfish, narrow minded and stubborn. She always wanted to be a famous actress. Always ran the school plays. Made all the costumes. Her house and office are immaculate. Made Anne's wedding dress and wedding cake. She is organised but also can be very spontaneous.

Late one night, she put us girls in the car. MJ and I wanted to drive, but she didn't let us. Listening to music, we went to a lookout; I saw a different, more adventurous side to her that night. She could be fun.

Other times she'd tell us off, tell one to stand in one corner and one in the other, facing the wall.

There was that time Phoebe and Jassie had a fight. I had stolen some biscuits. Mumma and Pa were out. Jassie walked in through the back door as Phoebe was belting me. I was crying. Jassie took the belt out of her hands and started screaming—the only time I saw her lose her temper. She screamed, 'What are you doing! She's an innocent child. You have no right!' Phoebe responded with, 'She's not your daughter, her mother's dead. She's just a spoilt brat who needs a good floggin'.' Jassie's face was filled with rage and contempt, disgust, a seething anger. She picked me up and carried me away, saying, 'I may not be her mother but I'm not an animal like you.' Stroking the back of my head, she took me into my room, sat with me in her arms, rocking me. A mad woman rocking.

BLESSINGS

Rosie enjoys the days stretching out; more sunlight, more warmth.

I have more energy, more opportunities to get into the garden; the garden comes to life, bursting with flowers and colour.

She admires the old bathtub, sitting comfortably in the centre of the garden bed. She casts her eyes through the bulbs emerging, ready to flower. Her bearded irises are a picture. She thinks about Mumma's love of the garden. Her love of the flowers. How she described them and admired them. The creeper, akebia, smells pungent, like chocolate; cascading, a mass of flowers wafting its sweet smell through the garden. Light filtering through the leaves of the dogwood creates a spectacle; the pink shade of the leaves is highlighted and she admires its beauty and grace. As the flowers grow, so do the weeds. Rosie decides to tackle the corner of the garden, near the old pump shed.

This beautiful old building was my studio for a long time, when the kids were young. Now I have plenty of room in the house. I love the old building, its cement walls. Old wooden door, peeling paint revealing a light pink colour.

Firstly, she prunes the unruly rose along the fence, containing its sprawling arms reaching out in every direction. The ground is soft, so it's easy to pull the weeds out. Shaking the dirt from their roots, she uncovers worms wriggling for cover in the protective earth.

After filling the wheelbarrow, she wheels it to the compost heaps.

Rosie fills the one on the far left, the most vacant. She picks up the pitchfork and stirs the one on the right, digging and aerating it. It is nearly ready for the garden. She loves the process. Rosie rotates the three bays using the natural cycle; her garden provides its own nutrients and nourishment.

With some dry manure, this will be brilliant out the front under the roses.

After wheeling the empty wheelbarrow back to the corner of the garden, she continues to weed, clearing the dead leaves of the plants. It is a cathartic experience, watching the space transform. Clearing, tidying; fulfilling the garden's splendour and glory.

Once all the weeds are removed, Rosie fills her wheelbarrow with woodchips from the large pile on the side of the hill. Near the compost bays. Rosie wheels the barrow to the garden, empties it into a bare spot, then scatters and spreads the woodchips to create a lovely layer of mulch.

The garden becomes neat and tidy; she stops and admires her work. As the woodchips eventually fill all the bare spots and the corner garden is finished, she brings the hose and waters the plants, now free, no longer competing for space and water from the weeds. Protected by a layer of mulch.

This will serve them well in the summer months ahead.

Watching the water soak into the garden, darkening the woodchips and washing the leaves of the plants, she decides to take a break.

It's lunchtime already. The time seems to evaporate when I'm gardening. Engrossed in the task, no schedule, no pressure. Sometimes I worry I've forgotten something.

Washing her hands in the laundry, lathering her hands in the soap, she smells it—a beautiful creation of Tilly and Ash's. Rosie wipes her hands and saunters inside. She piles a plate with salad she prepared yesterday, and carries it and her water bottle outside.

Sitting near the corner garden, she admires her morning's work and enjoys eating her lunch in the sun. Closing her eyes, she breathes in deeply, listening as the birds sing. A cow in a distant paddock bellows. She considers what she will do next.

Tom pulls up out the front gate; she hears the gate swing open, his long strides as he walks around the garden.

'What's happening?' Tom asks as he approaches.

'Just takin' a break, what are you up to?'

'I've got to move some cows and calves from the bull paddock down to the corner paddock. You want to give us a hand?'

'Yeah, I'll put some boots on.'

'I don't need you to do much, just go on the road in the ute and block them from going the wrong way.'

They make their way out the front gate. Tom jumps into the buggy and drives down the lane. Rosie gets in the ute and follows him.

As she glances across the valley, there are faint remnants of snow still on the mountains. The sun is bright and warm; she winds down the window and hangs her elbow out, welcoming the breeze blowing in her face.

Putting her hazard lights on, she pulls to the side of the road, watching Tom round up the small mob and head them towards the open gate. They move slowly and wander out onto the side of the road; she moves closer to block them and head them in the right direction. Checking in the rear-view mirror, she notices a white ute coming over the hill and down the road. Rosie roars past the cattle and down to the other gate, turns around and blocks them from going past the opened gate.

Waiting patiently, she takes in the view. Waving as the white ute goes past, she sees a fox jump up through the long, dry grass and turn its head suspiciously before running across the road, through the neighbour's paddocks and out of sight.

It looked quite young, that fox. It's not the one from up on the flat I've seen.

The mob of cows and calves rush fervently down the side of the road. Rosie moves forward to block them; they are directed into the paddock. Tom gets off the buggy and shuts the gate.

'That's a job done,' he says as he leans against the passenger window.

'They're a healthy-looking mob,' Rosie responds.

'They're in good condition, the mongrels. Those calves kept getting through the fence up there. I'll have to strain it. Well, I better go, got to fix that leaking trough over near my place before I get Billy from the bus.'

'Righto.'

'Thanks for that.'

'Anytime, darling. Send Billy up with a container of milk.'

'Yep, will do. I'll see ya.'

Tom taps on the roof of the ute as Rosie checks the mirror before driving out on the road. Appreciating the splendour of spring. The vibrant blue sky. Driving along the road home, surrounded by the blessings of beauty.

As the sun begins to set—clouds covering the west, blanketing the mountain range—she walks eagerly to the orchard with her basket in her arms. A cool breeze whistles through the trees; she feels warmth in the air. Rosie feels summer approaching. A sign of hope and inspiration. Inspecting each tree and picking the ripe fruit, she considers the need to cover the trees with nets.

Before the birds are able to destroy the ripe fruit … I might be too late.

Rosie takes her basket filled with oranges, peaches, plums and apples. She walks slowly up the incline, the worn path, stopping to watch the setting sun and admire the colours of the clouds: shades of purple, streaks of faint pink. She opens the side gate, which screeches then bangs shut. Walking inside, she places the basket full of fruit at the end of the long white table. After making a cup of tea, Rosie takes her full cup and goes outside to enjoy it amongst the sunset.

Relishing in the moment, she sits and sips, letting her thoughts come and drift away. Rosie is relaxed, peaceful and lost in the moment, feeling content with her day's activities and feeling excited about the following day. Thanking God for the blessings of her life, she leans back in her old wooden chair.

I wish my old dog was still beside me but I'm grateful for all the years he was. That reminds me, I better go and check on that new little one. I haven't even given her a name yet. I remember Polly took six weeks to name one of her kids, can't remember which one now. I was bloody horrified. I need to write to Jassie, to send in the post tomorrow. I better do that now, before it gets too late.

Entering the room, she sees the bundle of fur is curled up, asleep. Rosie bends down and strokes her fur, careful not to disturb her. Lying beside the bed are the remnants of a chewed toy. Rosie sits down at her desk, retrieves her writing paper and her favourite pen, and begins to write. The words fall on the paper like fresh flowing water.

MOTHER

Rosie walks down the steps; it is dark and damp. It has a stench like smelly socks. The walls are lined with fruit in jars, preserved.

Look at these boxes of junk, stuff Mumma and Pa stored away years ago. This seems like such an overwhelming job. Where do I even start?

Rosie begins by removing the cobwebs; she gets another light, a small lamp. Rosie lights a scented candle—for light and to remove the smell as well. Moving boxes up the stairs, she watches her feet. She moves them outside into the daylight. Many things have been destroyed by water, or time has caused rot and decay. Rosie puts the piles of stained papers in the compost bin. Finding boxes of empty jars, she puts them inside to be cleaned.

I know Stella will love these.

Sweeping the floor, she thinks about Mumma, sitting in her chair, drinking her cup of tea. Rosie remembers Mumma's warmth, her feeling of being home.

I miss her. I imagine heaven with all my loved ones. Even my mother, someone I never had the chance to know. I wonder what she was like. What will it be like meeting her in heaven? Daisy must know Will. It makes my head swirl.

Rosie leans down and pulls out a pile of canvases stacked in behind some boxes. Leaning them against the wall, she brings the lamp closer so she can inspect them. Picking one of the old paintings up, she studies it.

Look at the mountains, horses in the foreground. I'm surprised how good this is. It's definitely not mine. Let me try and read the signature.

Leaning in closer, Rosie slides her glasses down. She feels shock. An intrigue, and a swell of emotion as she finally realises it is signed, *Daisy 48.*

The year I was born. She must have painted this while she was pregnant with me.

Rosie looks through the others, discovering something she never knew.

I wonder why my grandparents never told me that Daisy painted. I guess this explains why they were so encouraging of me painting. It couldn't have been easy; I certainly made some mistakes with Billy. I really empathise with the tough job they had in raising me. A little girl without a mother.

An image of Aunt Jassie comes into her mind. Jassie is young, she is pale, small, very petite, her sandy light-brown hair neatly tied back. Her pretty face covered with glasses. Sitting up in her bed with a book.

Jassie was obsessed with reading. Always happy to sit in the shade and read while I swam or played. Her small bedroom had books stacked everywhere. Obsessively neat and tidy. She taught me to read with an abundance of patience. Endless kindness. Quiet encouragement. What would I have done without Jassie? All those precious times watching The Wizard of Oz *together.*

After stacking some empty crates on the shelf, Rosie pulls a box out; it has old frames covered in dust. It gets up her nose, making her sneeze. Shuffling through them, she pulls one out; it has a photo in it. She recognises it as Mumma's familiar face stares back at her. The black-and-white photograph conveys a tall woman, stern, frowning—always with her hands on her hips, framing her large waist. Rosie admires her short, curly hair and dark eyes. Staring, she appreciates Mumma's physical stature and strength.

She had a hard life. Had to grow up quick. Worked hard all her life. So quick to judge, loud, opinionated, always complaining. How she hated drinking. Set high expectations. So rough around the edges.

She smiles as she thinks of Mumma, the photograph reminding her of a woman she so deeply loved and admired.

Mumma really wanted to see the farm, her garden and her family prosper. Such simple needs and desires. Also so generous and kind. Give any poor bastard the shirt off her back. Charitable and thoughtful. It reminds me of the poem I wrote when she died.

Rosie goes inside to find it, taking the photograph.

I might put them together; something I can give to Anne.

Took Some Killin'

You never left us guessing what was on your mind, you always let us know
Your family, farm and garden were your joy and you loved to watch them grow
Give anyone the shirt off your back
No time to be around you and be slack
A list of jobs for any poor bastard that walked through the door
Some news, a cup of tea, a chat you'd applaud
Love of canasta only when you could win
Throw it down the hill, bypass the bin
If only I could shoot, you'd say
We were all very grateful to this day that was never the case
First to make comment on your weight
Always on the phone

You were the epitome of home
Honesty
Generosity
Didn't care what people thought
So many valuable things we were taught

Such an intelligent mind
No one like you we will ever find
Spot a cow in calf a mile away
Always a dairy farmer up at the dawn of day
A great memory for dates and names
Complained about your knees and all the pain
A great love of animals, food, flowers and the latest gossip
Never meet anyone as honest
Loved a nap in the chair, a cup of tea, leave the tea bag in and
two tablets please
The simple things in life you loved
A tough life with amazing things you did, you took in your
stride, with ease

A beautiful combination of contradictions, like day and night
Like black and white
So harsh yet so soft
Subservient you were not
So loud but also so quiet
Couldn't keep a secret
Filled with such confidence
Yet, endless humility
So many blessings and endured much tragedy
Patient to wait for when a baby's born or crochet a big

beautiful blanket
Impatient and wouldn't want to wait a minute for a cup of tea
Show as much excitement for a freshly born foal as a newly
born great-grandchild
What you thought we were always told
Didn't like to hang around after a feed
She'd help anyone that was in need
She treated everyone the same, didn't matter about titles or
fancy names
So many sayings we always loved, like wouldn't that root your
boot, plaiting his legs, watering that paddock makes my blood
boil—a way with words
A way to always make us laugh, always honest
Your thoughts we always heard

She didn't like housework or exercise, didn't like falseness,
turning down the TV or animals in the garden
Wholesome, raw and real, down to earth is an understatement
People loved her for her brutal honesty and gave pardon

We are all so blessed to have had so many years
A big empty void with many tears
Many stories left to tell
A life lived well
I think God kept her away for as long as he could cause he
knew she'd be taking charge, throwing orders and having a
good word with them
I look forward to when my grandchildren ask, what was
Mumma like? And I'll tell them about a woman that was one
of a kind, there'll be lots to explain

Many stories and sayings, plenty to describe
Her life like a garden at the mercy of the seasons
She enjoyed the flowers of the spring
Many weeds
Harsh frosts of winter
Now she's on her way to her last and final garden
As she arrives I think she'll be saying
I took some killin'

As she quietly sits at her desk—the newly discovered paintings stacked in the corner—her pup comes and jumps up on her leg, begging for attention. Picking her up, she tenderly strokes her fur. 'Hey, little girl, what are we going to call you? You can't go without a name for much longer.'

Looking over at the paintings, she considers sorting them out.

I don't want to study them right now. I feel too shocked by them still. I feel weary from a morning of painting, gardening and cleaning out the cellar. Discovering things packed away. What else could I possibly discover? Why now? What is the universe trying to tell me? Is it conspiring?

Rosie closes her eyes and an image fills the space, like a dream. She visualises a woman and a little girl with her back against a big old elm tree, book and pen in her hands. Rosie then sees the woman and the little girl making daisy chains, bathed in warm light, sitting on the edge of the hill. Another image creeps in of a woman hugging a little girl, taking her hand and walking with her past the dam, towards the water.

Rosie begins crying, rocking the tiny pup in her arms. She rocks in her chair, an old lady now, still holding the little girl inside of her who misses a mother she never knew.

I need to push through this block. I can't make excuses. I must try and fail. I need to know I have exhausted all possibilities. I know the answer. I need to give this a shot, in case I do succeed. I could fulfil this wild dream. My mind constantly trying to hold me back. This judge telling me I'm not good enough, I'm being stupid, even considering it. I have one life, one chance.

The pen flows across the paper, her wild dreams dancing around her.

I thought I knew who I was
For all these years
Now I know
I have a brother
Another part of myself
An unknown part
Foreign part
Not knowing what words to say
I must let them fall out
Scatter on the table
Confusion in my son's blue eyes
Preparing him for the image of his dead brother's face
To stare back at him
To waltz into our lives
A haunting ghost
From a foreign land
A cousin he never knew he had
Silent response speaks loudly

Anne will be different
No surprise
Plethora of questions
Excitement and curiosity

Delving into the emotion

Drama

Like this is a reality TV show

Hear her brain ticking across the phone line

This is life

Blood

History

Skeletons uncovered in the closet

Fresh wounds uncovered

My mother's child

Firstborn child

Taken

My parent's love

Denied

Paintings buried

Truth buried

Deceit and lies

Hurt resides

Stella is always the hardest

To tell

To explain

Her precious heart has already been

Beaten

Broken

Hardened

By life's tragedy

Telling her of a face that looks like her lost love

A newfound family

Stella is always the hardest
To endure the sadness
Pain in her eyes

Stella is always the hardest
Feel her pain
Powerless to take it away

    Placing the pen on the desk, Rosie closes her eyes and strokes the fur of her pup. As she rocks in her chair, her dreams dance above her like butterflies fluttering. Tears roll down her face. She feels fearful of the truth.

    'I know what I'll call you, little one.' She looks down at the content pup snuggled into her lap.

    'I'll call you Grace.'

Rocking, Rosie closes her eyes.

A mad woman rocking.

PART FOUR

You've always had the power my dear,
you just had to learn it for yourself.

— Glinda the Good Witch, *The Wizard of Oz*

Burning Desire

The fire burnt with ferocity, it spoke of destruction,
passion, death and desire.

ANGELS

Reading one of her old journals, Rosie desperately searches for inspiration.

I just need a beginning, an ending, a plot. I know my story, of course I do, for Christ's sake. It's my bloody story. I am also filled with so much fear and doubt.

Grace plays with her toy at Rosie's feet, her black-and-white head shaking as she wrestles its lifeless body. Flicking through the pages, Rosie comes to a story she wrote a long time ago.

This must have been after the birth of Anne.

Rosie reads it, thinking about the sunflowers in her vegetable garden. Transported to that time and place.

The feelings of uncertainty as a mother. This tiny, precious little gift in my arms. Solely dependent on me. I was born at that same time; I became a mother. Nothing was the same again. Through the challenges, transformations, trials and tribulations, it was all so worth it.

Birth of the Mother

She gently planted the seed beneath the warm, protective earth, an earth full of nourishment and life. Planting it with purpose and love. A heart full of hope. She spoke many prayers. In that moment she made a silent promise to always care for the seed.

Each morning, as the scorching summer sun was rising, painting a masterpiece of pinks and blues across the sky— reminiscent of God's magic—she would go to the spot in her garden. She had cleared a space there, created a home, and she would diligently water her seed. As the water flowed from the watering can in a cascading stream, gently moistening the ground, she would pray that this little seed would survive. Would eventually sprout. A promise of life and beauty. She dreamed of days ahead, where she could enjoy the fruits of her labour. For now, she watered each morning and waited with eager anticipation.

As the sun was going down each day, she crept to her special spot in the garden. Her little seed she would check and watch, hoping to catch sight of it sprouting its first stem through the crust of the earth. How she longed to see her beloved seed sprouting into life. The warm wind blew around her and she knew she must be patient and wait. Wait for the time. Give it time to grow. Slowly grow.

As the leaves were changing colour and the heat of the summer sun subsided, she knew it was time. Any day now. How this scared her. Was she ready now, after watering and caring for this little seed, to see it? Could she care for it? Despite her fears and trepidation, she was overcome with a love. A new love she had never felt before. A foreign love, one that made her shudder with its force. An innate love that ran through her like the pulsating blood in her veins.

The leaves crunched below her feet and she walked along the now-beaten track to the spot. She had now made more room for the seed to grow, to let more sunlight in. Though the sun was going down, the soft light was enough to illuminate the magical sight. The seed had finally sprouted. The precious seed had broken through the earth and was clearly there. A new life, born into the world; a new life full of promise and possibility. Waves of emotions swept over her. An inundation of an extraordinary mixture of wonder, amazement, apprehension and elation. She saw her seed that had become a seedling, for the very first time. She was filled with hope, nervousness, excitement and relief; it was still alive. Still slowly but surely growing. Then a powerful resolve took over her. I must care for this little seedling. Protect it with my life. Give it all that I have. For I am its mother. It will not survive or thrive without me.

In the morning, after a restless night of tossing and turning, she went to her seedling. Feeling a chill in the fresh morning breeze, she smelt the autumn leaves covered in dew carpeting her path. Her seedling was beautiful, but so tiny and fragile. So she built a cover, a nest to protect her seed from the imminent winter. She gave it fertiliser, knowing with time and patience her seedling would grow. Prosper. Be something beautiful one day. Throughout the autumn and the cold winter days, through thunderstorms, dreary days of fog and harsh nights of frost, she cared for her seedling. With determination. Through exhaustion, but always with love. In prayer and honour of this gift God had given her, she relentlessly cared for her seedling.

The welcomed spring arrived with its sunshine and soul-quenching warmth to feed the new mother and her seedling. Now the seedling had grown into a plant. An immense, towering, very sturdy, robust plant that could stand on its own. Marvelling at it each day, she realised she had achieved something so miraculous. She had brought life into this world. Helping it grow, keeping it alive to watch it thrive. Seeing that this little plant had so much promise, she knew that one day it was going to bloom. As she sat in the shade of the gum tree in her garden, she dreamt of all her plant could be, even a red rose or white dahlia, and she hoped that it would light up the world with the beauty of its flower, whatever it might be. As she listened to the birds chirping in the tree, singing songs of hope, she felt a pain in her chest—the love she felt that pulsated through her heart with ferocity. A wild love, not of this world. This was the greatest gift she had ever received. It filled her with a joy she never knew existed, so powerful. A power beyond words.

The mother did her ritual walk along her worn path, down to her garden where her strong plant was growing. The summer breeze swept through her hair; she took a deep breath, remembering a simpler time before this little seed was planted in her garden. Missing that time but simultaneously she could not imagine her world without her plant. How would she survive without the joy of watching it grow? Unable to contemplate not caring for this precious gift. As she felt her feet firmly on the path with each purposeful step, she reached her garden. Blood of love running through her veins. With renewed strength and the dreaded winter behind her, she was left speechless as she looked up and saw for the first time. The setting sun casts a spotlight on an amazing creation. A huge. Gorgeous. Golden sunflower. Blooming; lighting up the world.

Rising early, Rosie hears the birds sing outside her window. She throws on her shorts and faded t-shirt, and wraps her headband around her red curly hair.

I'll need a haircut soon.

Yawning and rubbing her face, she puts on her well-worn thongs. She steps outside; the sun is bright. She can feel the heat in the air already.

I think it's going to be a hot one.

She ventures out into the garden to turn on the sprinklers.

I better get the garden watered before it gets too hot.

Taking her water bottle in her basket, she heads off to collect some stones down by the creek. Hearing soft pit pats behind her, she turns to see Grace following faithfully. 'Stay here, little girl,' Rosie says, leading the pup back inside. 'You're too wild for a walk. Don't want you to get run over.'

Passing the dairy, Rosie notices Billy washing the yard and Tom cleaning the dairy plant out. The cattle dogs greet her as she walks on. Rosie notices the chooks are still locked up. She goes over the ramp and along the laneway. Opening the gate, she untangles the wire that is tightly twisted. The gatepost is leaning and worn. The earth beneath her feet is dry, moulded into the crisscross shape of the tractor tyres. Walking through the gate, she turns and admires the splendour of the mountain.

Always there. Standing proud and strong; the backdrop of my life.

Closing the gate behind her, she ties the wire back up.

I better make sure it's shut properly. That's the last thing Tom needs is cows getting out.

She walks on the dry grass through the paddock, towards the creek. The dry white cow bones parched by the sun, lying in the gully, catch her sight. Rosie sees the pile of ash from the big fire they had last school holidays when Anne and the kids were here. Tom had the tractor and loaded it with big logs; Billy collected small pieces with the buggy, with Olivia and Lachie helping. She visualises it, the flames, the glow and power.

I love that job. One of my favourites on the farm. No fires this time of year. Bushfire season.

Walking over to the ridge, down the track, making sure not to tread on the rocks, she can hear the creek flowing. A breeze sweeps past her. Once at the bottom, she walks on the gravel and then through the creek. The water is cool and refreshing; it cleanses her skin as it glides past her. She walks slowly to make sure her feet are stable and avoid losing her thongs on the slippery stones.

This reminds me of riding my beloved, old pony, Trixie, through the creek. After school in the summer, we would cross the creek and then I'd take her into the open paddock. I would give her a kick in the guts and get her to race across the clear paddock, at full-speed cantering. The wind in my hair. Such a feeling of freedom and strength. Trixie's powerful legs rushing underneath me. Just the earth, the horse and reins. Like I was flying. Then there was the bloody shock of her shying, heading up a bank, under a low branch; me falling off with a sudden thud. The earth suddenly hitting me within a second.

Filling her basket with round stones, she carefully selects ones with unique shapes and colours. Rosie carries them in her arms as she walks on the bank. Needing a rest, Rosie sits by the creek in his fishing spot, just above where the cows cross. Rosie drinks from her water bottle and sadness comes over her.

This place always does this ... evokes the memory of spreading his ashes here. The family gathered. Our heartbroken Stella. How the hot wind blew. Our heads down. Blake looked so old. His face so pale and grey. He was never the same again. A broken man. A shell; he never recovered. I'd give anything to see Will's beautiful brown eyes. His cheeky grin. That distinctive laugh and his beautiful red curly hair; just like mine.

She gets lost in her thoughts. Dragonflies dance above the gentle, glowing creek.

He was nothing like Tom; he was short and strong, wild like blazing fire. I wish my memories were stronger. Vivid enough so I could reach out and touch him. I always wondered where the red hair came from. I still remember when Mumma told me. I must have only been very young. She was so blunt when she said it. 'We suspect that your father was the farrier that had passed through town. He had your red curly hair.' Your mother was only sixteen; her hair was brown and thin like Mumma's.

I've never really missed my mother. I never knew her. She died as I was being born. As I entered the world, she left the world. I never felt like an orphan, either. I just saw Mumma and Pa as my parents. I didn't know any better. It was all I knew and all I loved. I wonder how Robert felt. Did he know we existed? I guess he must have at some point. He had planned to come looking for us. Did he know our mother had died?

Will got the mysterious red hair and he was wild to go with it. Tom and Will were like chalk and cheese their whole lives. Tom the most placid and content baby. Will did not rest. Or sleep. He rolled early, crawled early and did not walk, he ran. He never had any money. He lived for the moment, for the party. A daredevil. Always injuring himself, causing me so much stress and anxiety during his short life. The most charismatic child, he was cheeky and funny. Will was everyone's favourite in the family. He was the glue. Anne adored him; quiet Tom protected him and took him to do things. They were very close. Then we all had to find a way to live without him.

A tear rolls gently down her cheek. The agony and grief are raw, like a fresh wound.

So quickly I'm transported back to that time, feeling like it has just happened. These intense memories hold such power and strength. I can feel the hot wind blowing the morning after he was gone. The world changing permanently. The dark clouds in the sky, his wild spirit swirling in the atmosphere. See the dark room, time disintegrating; night and day morphed. His lips—his beautiful big lips—turning blue as they turned the machines off.

The birds sing a mournful song. Rosie listens to the creek flowing. Tears escape her eyes like a dam wall breaking.

I would love a strong glass of whisky. I know that path. I know that path all too well. Since giving up the drink, I know I can feel this pain. I know there is courage and light within me.

She sits there, marinating in the memories and turmoil.

Oh God, I'll never forget picking up the phone. A police officer telling me, 'There has been an accident. Your son was in an accident. He is being airlifted. He is in a critical condition. You need to get there as soon as you can.' I can picture myself running around like a madwoman. Screaming. Grabbing things and rushing to the car to get to my boy. Everyone getting in the car in shock and disbelief. Driving for hours to get to the hospital.

Entering the hospital and seeing him, thinking, There's my boy. My
strong, healthy boy. *It is cemented in my memory. Will, my precious boy,
lying there with machines attached. They were keeping him alive. There
was internal damage. I just wanted him to wake up and for the craziness to
end. That following day, the doctor came with the news. 'Unfortunately,
there's nothing more we can do; he has had a stroke, a severe bleed in the
brain. He cannot recover from this.' The machines needed to be turned
off. He could not be saved. Our small world was shattered. The pain cut
through us. Severed us. Tom wailed like a little boy. Anne held his hand.
Stella was beside me. Blake and I stood on either side as they pulled out
the tubes. My boy took a breath and coughed. Then the remaining life
drained from him. His wild spirit flew away. It was surreal, like a dream.
Words, they just aren't enough to describe the excruciating pain. The loss.
The grief. Endless suffering.*

As Rosie listens to the creek flowing past, a bird in the tree whistles.
She is lost in her memories. The serenity softly drapes around her.

*Then life went back to 'normal'. When everyone continued on with
their lives. That was when it was the hardest. Lying in bed. Crying.
Screaming. Unable to go to work. Unable to function. Crying in pain. A
brutal agony. Physically feeling as though my heart was broken.*

Sitting there on the cold, hard stones, Rosie is immersed in her grief.

*MJ was different. That time. The sadness. How strong and heavy it
was; a weight that stopped me from crying. Crying would bring relief,
but this was a deep pain. It just weighed me down. The shock. Losing my
breath at the news. The fear surging through me. Panic. Disbelief. The
world falling apart. Crumbling in my hands. Like walking through the
confusion of a dream, with no understanding or control over what was
happening or where I was going or how I was acting. Outside of my body.
Not feeling. Not connecting. Unable to grasp the enormity of the pain.
The grief. The loss. To lose my best friend. The worst possible pain I could*

imagine anyone feeling. It was the same pain. It was different, though. I was so young when I lost MJ. You don't ever think something like that would happen to you. It always happens to other people.

A willie wagtail bounces on a dead willow branch. Looking up, Rosie sees a white streak cast across the sky.

That long night before they turned the machines off, I tried so hard to bargain with God. Change things. Praying, Please, take me—spare him. If you save him, I will do anything. *The longest night of my life. Waiting. Sitting beside Will. Praying, over and over. Please, God, don't take him. Please, God, don't take my boy. Sitting beside him, rocking. Praying. Rocking back and forward, like a madwoman. Crazy with fear and longing. Desperate pleas. Rosary beads threaded through my fingers. Tears streaming down my face. Like when he was a baby, checking him to see if he was breathing. I did the same thing that night. I knew the machines were keeping him alive and breathing, but I had to check and see. I looked at his red curly hair. What a beautiful boy he was. I was constantly longing for his eyes to open. To see the big brown eyes look at me. Just let me know everything in the world is all right again. Rocking beside him throughout the night; dozing and waking to check him, to hold his hand throughout the night until the sun rose again. A mad woman rocking.*

Knowing she can't sit in this pain for too long, Rosie whispers a quiet prayer, then picks up her basket of stones and water bottle. Crossing the creek, she pauses, then reaches down to splash her face with the cleansing water. It is fresh and washes away the tears. Rosie decides to walk along the dry, dusty cow track that leads to the dairy. As she wanders, she notices a patch of green grass.

I remember sun baking with MJ there, when we were kids, after swimming in the creek. Towels laid out. Lying on our backs, trying to make shapes with the clouds. Life was perfect. Just the two of us. I was never alone. We were always together.

It makes her smile. The land holds her memories, her joy and sadness. The sun is warm. She flicks some flies out of her face, breathing in the fresh air, taking her time. Trekking up the steep bank, she feels her muscles tense.

I have strength in my legs still. There's still life in this old girl.

Rosie climbs under the fence; it is electrified, so she is extra cautious. Walking past the arbour, she sees the large cactus in the front yard; its flowers are closed. She walks through the gate, then reaches down and turns on a sprinkler at the corner of the house.

I might pick some flowers from the garden today.

Rosie goes in the house through the back, hearing the familiar groan of the door. As she places the basket of stones on the long white table, Grace races to greet her. Rosie reaches down to pat her, a bundle of fur and excitement. 'Good girl. Now let's check to see what you've managed to destroy while I've been gone.'

She hears footsteps around the veranda as she inspects the lounge room. Billy comes tramping into the kitchen; he has milk and eggs for her. Rosie smiles with warmth at the blonde-haired boy. 'These are fine-looking specimens,' she comments as she places them in the fridge. 'Do ya want a milo?'

He smiles with pride. 'Yeah, thanks, Nanny. Those eggs are from the little black hen. She's just started layin',' Billy says with gusto in his voice as he takes a seat at the table in his usual spot. Grace starts chewing his sock.

'What do you call her?' Rosie asks.

'Martha,' he replies as he sits up at the table and makes himself comfortable. He pats and wrestles Grace.

Rosie gets his milo ready, knowing exactly how he has it. 'What's Dad doin'?' she inquires.

'Aw, ya know, doin' some jobs.'

Rosie chuckles to herself. 'I know your dad; he's always doin' some jobs. No rest for the wicked, I guess.' Rosie places the milo in front of him, with a big spoon. She sits opposite him, watching as he spoons the drink into his mouth with delight.

He has his mother's brown eyes. Tom's blonde hair. The same gap in his front teeth as his mother.

Rosie sits comfortably, enjoying the silence. A moment to be with him. Watch him. Leaning under the table, Rosie says, 'Gracie, you can leave him alone, you little pest.'

'Nanny ...' he says in a drawn-out way, like it's a question.

'Yeah, Billy?' she responds.

'Do you believe in God?'

'Yeah, I do actually. Why's that?'

He pauses as he shovels the milo into his mouth. 'Um, well, what do you think he looks like?'

'Well, that's a good question.' She takes her time to consider the question and her answer, then explains. 'Well, ya know, I don't know, but sometimes I think it's an old guy. You know, with a big beard. You know, like Santa Claus. But I also hope when I get to heaven and meet God, they are actually a woman. I imagine she's short, little, and is wearing a pretty dress. She's smiling and dancing.'

Billy listens intently as he sips the last of his milo. Rosie gets two plates out of the cupboard and some freshly made banana bread from the fridge and slices it. After spreading butter on the bread, she places a slice on each plate. Rosie puts Billy's plate in front of him and begins to eat hers.

'Nanny ...' he says in the same way as before.

'Yeah, Billy?'

I wonder what else he might ask. Hopefully something a little more simple.

'Is Uncle Will with God?'

'Yes, I really believe he is,' Rosie responds.

'When I get to heaven, will he know who I am?'

'Of course he will,' she says adamantly.

'How will he know who I am, if he's been in heaven ever since I was born?'

'Well, you know he watches you, 'cause he gets like a pass from God to visit us sometimes. You know, as a spirit. It could be a bird, a butterfly or a chicken. The breeze, even. He watches us and protects us, like an angel.'

He nods as though he is satisfied with the answer.

He probes further. 'Can you see a spirit?'

'Well, that's a tough one. It's more like you sense it, or you feel it, or you are reminded of them, when you see something beautiful or breathtaking.'

'Nanny, is my mum in heaven?'

'I don't think so, Billy. We think she's on an adventure. Well, that's what I like to think.'

'Where is she?' Billy asks.

'I don't know, dear. You know, she decided when you were a little tiny boy, before you can remember, that she needed to go. Even though she loved you more than anything. She decided that your dad and I needed to look after you. She went searching for something. We are not sure where, but I know she definitely loves you.'

I hope I'm saying the right thing. I hate lying. I hate lying to him but I can't tell him the truth until I speak to Tom first.

'Will she ever come back? If she knew Dad wasn't like he was back then. If she knew he was different now.'

'I don't know, but I just pray that she is happy.'

Rosie thinks about the person Tom was then. She wants to tell Billy the whole truth but she knows it's not her place.

It is hard to imagine that Tom was ever like that. Drunken and violent. Tom's inconsolable, uncontrollable grief. Sadness does unthinkable things to people sometimes. It was never an excuse. Lottie needed to leave. I feel sad for Billy. I know that feeling of growing up without a mother.

She watches as Billy eats the last crumbs of the banana bread, picking them up with his fingers.

I vividly remember the night Lottie left. It was a storm-filled night, with thunder. Lightning and pelting rain. Lottie bursting through the door with Billy wrapped up in her arms. She and Tom had been fighting. Tom had been drinking. Lottie's lip was cut. She smelt of whisky. Billy was screaming and Lottie placed him in my arms. Lottie was soaking wet, from rain, from tears. Lottie screamed, 'I can't fucking do this anymore! We can't do it!' Tears streamed down her face. 'Look after my boy. Please look after him.' Placing a dummy in Billy's mouth, I rocked him. Lottie kissed his head, saying, 'I love you forever. I love you, my sweet boy.' I gave her a reassuring nod, grabbed Lottie's arm, looked into her eyes. There was nothing to say but we both knew it was goodbye. I cried, sitting on the floor. I was so mad. So disappointed in Tom, for fucking it all up. So mad at Will. For leaving us all in this fucking mess. Mad at Blake for going too soon. Mad at God for taking them too young, too soon. Sitting on the floor, I rocked Billy to sleep. I sat there praying. I promised to protect this precious boy for as long as I lived. A mad woman rocking.

Rosie smiles, but senses that Billy notices her sadness. He changes the subject. 'Dad reckons we'll get some more chickens after harvest. I've already thought of some names.'

'Oh yeah, and what have you come up with?' she asks while placing the empty cup and plates on the sink. 'Wanna go pick some flowers for the table with me?' She feels a desperate need to move. Run from the memories.

'Yeah,' he says, as he gets up to go and put his gumboots on. She quickly grabs her scissors and a basket.

'Can Gracie come?' Billy asks.

'Yeah, she can,' Rosie says. 'We just need to watch her.'

'I am thinking Betty, Daisy, Penny, and Bob for a rooster,' he says with delight, counting them on his fingers.

'They're awesome names. How do you think of these things?' Rosie asks as they walk out into the garden, Gracie prancing and bouncing after them.

'Well, Dad reckons chickens should have old ladies' names, like old-fashioned ones. He tells me a heap and then I get to pick which ones they'll get. He said after harvest we will get a surprise.'

'Oh, did he,' Rosie responds, wondering what trick Tom has up his sleeve.

Billy chats away as they walk through the garden, picking flowers.

Thank you, God, for Lottie leaving me this bundle of joy to love. Thank you, God, for Tom's wake-up call. The best thing she ever did was driving down the road and never coming back. Please let me live a long, healthy life to continue to protect this angel sent to me.

STELLA

Tentatively looking in the mirror, her dark eyes staring back at her, Rosie carefully puts eyeliner on. She puts each earring in the hole, thinking about the time she had them pierced with MJ.

We were so excited; we thought we were so cool. I hardly ever wear them now but I figure I'll make a little effort to go out for the day and visit Stella.

Rosie looks at her wrinkles reflected back at her.

I've earned these; some people don't have the privilege of growing old, of getting wrinkles. Imagine what MJ would look like in her seventies; I didn't even get to see her in her twenties or thirties. She'd be beautiful and wise. A lifetime of missing you, my dear friend.

Rosie inspects her crooked, stained teeth.

I have often entertained the thought of getting them fixed but I could never justify spending the money. I'm too old for that nonsense now.

Rosie puts on a dress; it is light and comfortable, cream and pale pink. Slipping on her sandals, she feels excitement. Rosie notices the stack of paintings resting together beside her desk. She begins to flick through them. She pulls out one. It's dark. A bleeding heart in the centre. Waves at the bottom, with dark, formidable clouds and rain.

I remember painting this after Will died. I remember the ache, intense pain. Weeping. Sobbing. Wishing the paint would take it all away. I knew it had a part to play in my journey. There was a time when all the tears dried but there was anger and disbelief. Questioning. Trying to numb the pain with pills and alcohol. I know that had a part too, in my journey.

Loading up the back of the ute, Rosie ties the crates on. She pulls the rope tight, then shakes the crates to make sure they are sturdy. A collection of empty jars she has cleaned and wrapped in newspaper to stop them breaking and potted plants fills them.

Random things from my garden. Hopefully Stella likes them. Japanese anemones, polyanthus, begonias. Some bearded iris I have pulled out while weeding.

Lifting the bonnet, she props it with a stick. She checks the water and oil. Rosie starts up the ute, warming it up; the white Ford Courier.

I'm surprised it still runs. I remember when we first bought it. A gift from Blake. Something practical to cart plants and canvases. I have loved it ever since.

She packs her camera and water bottle, then places the eclectic bunch of stones on the passenger seat.

I know how much Stella loves them.

Reversing out, she still expects to see her faithful dog waiting at the gate. There is an empty place.

Little Gracie is inside instead. Hopefully not destroying anything.

The gears crunch and the clutch is stiff.

I remember the times it would get stuck in third gear or when it lost fourth gear altogether. I better be gentle with the old girl; she gets me from A to B still.

After swinging out of the garage and onto the front lawn, she heads down the hill, past the dairy. Dogs bark. She drives slowly, watching out for any chickens passing by. Reverberation of the ramp shakes her in her seat. She heads down the home road, looking each side at rolling hills and cows grazing. It is a glorious sunny day. Warmed by the sun through the glass, Rosie turns on the radio. Like a strange message from the past, she hears her wedding song, 'We've Only Just Begun'.

The lyrics hold so much meaning even after all those years.

Rosie sings along. Nostalgia, sadness and happy memories wrap around her. She imagines standing in front of the arbour. An empty place beside her.

If only that girl knew then what lay before her. She was so naive, innocent and blinded by love. If only I could go back, for just a moment.

Rosie turns onto the main road and heads around the back way to Stella's place. She thinks about Will and Stella and the music they should have danced to on their wedding day. A moment of sadness stings her eyes. Listening to the song on the radio, she wonders what song it is; the lyrics are poignant and appropriate.

What an amazing song. That's what it is called, 'Weathered'. I imagine Stella and Will dancing to it on their wedding night. So many broken dreams.

As she drives around the back road, Rosie remembers the first time she laid eyes on Stella.

She was a young, tiny, little thing. Covered in jewellery. Stella had a beautiful sparkle; a burning fire in her green eyes. Long, beautiful, thick, brown hair. A creative spirit. Adventurous and fun, just like Will. They were intertwined. Kindred spirits. I knew my Will had found his girl.

Rosie looks in the rear-view mirror and all the snow has melted on the mountain range. The white lines flicker underneath the Ford Courier and the white posts fade past in a blur. She notices a kookaburra sitting on the fence post as she turns the corner. She looks up on the hill, at the edge of the property; a fox scurries up the hillside and out of sight.

Rosie drives along the bitumen road over a bridge and turns left up the dirt road.

I better slow down. There's often cows on the road.

Rosie checks the fuel gauge and temperature.

About half a tank, plenty to get home.

Some colourful rainbow lorikeets dart past her and into the bush. Rosie ponders how Stella's life has unfolded.

She has had some fleeting affairs. I wonder if she's lonely. Unmarried, with no children. I still long for the granddaughter I always imagined Stella and Will would have had. A little girl with red curly hair. Big, beautiful brown eyes. I know that it is futile to continue to dream. They are all frivolous fantasies. Stella is so talented. A gardener. A poet and sculptor. I can't believe the things she makes out of all that junk. Such a talented welder. I wonder where that poem is she wrote. That one she gave me; I'll have to look for it when I get home. The pain that poor girl has endured. I can't blame her for how much she drinks and smokes. To go on without him. I imagine she must be lonely. I know she's never recovered but you'd barely know it if you met her. So strong and resilient. It's a shame she hides up here from the world, but I guess this is what she needs. This is what she loves.

At the gate, she climbs out of the ute and swings it open; she takes her camera out and takes a shot looking down the valley, towards the river. A sight to behold. Driving down the dirt track, she admires the gum trees lining the driveway. A little stream runs; she drives over the bridge, through the gate and into the house yard. Stella's two staffies run to the car to greet her. They are shiny black, very round. Friendly and energetic. Rosie notices Stella in the distance, at the bottom of the garden—her hair tied up in a messy bun on top of her head. A cloth headband. She's wearing a flowing, colourful skirt and long earrings made with feathers. Stella's top is lopsided, exposing one shoulder. It glistens in the sun. She's draped in jewellery; a nose ring, her big, bold rings.

Her eyes don't sparkle like they used to; age has wearied them. Life has hardened her. But look at her, barefooted. A beautiful soul. Petite and still as beautiful as the day Will brought her home to meet us.

Rosie drives around the back, passing her home.

A humble place she built herself. A simple shed with all the basics she needs.

Rosie parks under the dappled shade of a Japanese maple, and gets out to greet Stella. The dogs greet her with zest.

I love these dogs, look at them.

Rosie bends down to pat them with a loving greeting. Stella walks over to the ute, smiling and inspecting the gifts on the back. Rosie takes the basket of stones from the front seat. Handing them to Stella, as she gives her a loving embrace. 'Hello, darling. How are you?'

'Yeah, good,' Stella responds. 'You look great. Your hair is getting long. You want a cuppa?'

'I'd love one,' Rosie answers. 'The place is looking lush and green.'

Stella leads the way, carrying the basket of stones as they go inside. Rosie sits down at the long wooden table, admiring the large bowl of stones interspersed with crystals. Picking up a pink one, she moves it in her hand, feeling its surface before placing it back in its place. As Stella fills the kettle and lights the stove, Rosie looks to the cross on the wall. A picture of Will. There are beads hanging in the doorway and books stacked in piles.

I always love to come and observe all the treasures Stella has. It's always so interesting. I always notice something different. I love the sweet smell of her house, lavender and maybe gardenia. I love its rustic look. The mixture of corrugated iron, brick and wood.

As Stella's bare feet move about the paved bricks that make up her floor, Rosie admires her toe rings and anklets.

Stella loves decoration.

'Did you get much rain down here last week, lovey?' Rosie asks.

'Oh, bugger all, really,' Stella replies as she swirls the teaspoon in a cup. 'I think five mil, barely enough to wet the ground.'

'We got about the same. They predict more next week. So hopefully we get a good soaking then. How's your artwork going?'

'I think I've finished the big one I've been working on. Maybe needs a little touch-up. I'll take you up and show you.'

Stella brings the cups of tea over; she hands one to Rosie. Stella leads the way as Rosie follows her outside. A quiet hangs in the air. They sometimes say something without speaking. They take the tea outside to sit in the sun. Stella rolls herself a smoke; she licks the paper and spins it in her fingers, lighting it. Stella takes a deep drag and exhales it as a thick cloud forms. They sip their tea.

'Let's have a walk around the garden,' Stella says. 'You can show me where to plant all the new treasures you brought me. Then I'll show you my new masterpiece.'

They begin to stroll slowly, stopping to admire the garden. Tall gum trees stand strong.

'How's Anne and the kids?' Stella asks.

'Yeah, good. Spoke to her the other night. She's still working too hard and juggling everything. You know what she's like. She just recently started sewing, so that's been good for her. She did some course or something. Got any plans for Christmas this year?'

'No, I haven't. Haven't even thought that far ahead.'

'Why don't you come to our joint for lunch? You know I always cook too much.' Rosie smiles warmly.

'Yeah, I will. Thanks, that'd be good. Good to see everyone.'

Stella points out changes. Flowering plants. Her vegie garden. Sprawling orchard. Elaborate compost piles. They walk and talk.

Stella opens the shed door, putting on some boots sitting by the door.

'Watch where you walk, Laney. There's always bits of sharp metal lying around. Well, here it is. My latest project.'

Rosie inspects the eagle with large wings; it stands as tall as them.

It looks strong. Determined. Fierce. Ready to take flight. Look at this collection of rusted metals. It is so beautiful.

It makes Rosie pause. She's in awe admiring it. Her eyes feast on the sight. Rosie circles the large construction.

'How do you do this? Where does your inspiration come from?' Rosie queries.

'It's just magic. Big magic.' Stella leans on a wooden seat, grinning. Admiring her creation. 'I've been seeing these two large wedgies for a long time, circling up on the ridge. I've tried to capture their enormity. Their grace. Their power.'

Arching her head up, Rosie says, 'Well, you've certainly done that. I could admire it all day but we better go and unpack all those goodies in the back of the ute.'

As they walk down to the ute, colourful birds fly in and out of the trees. The staffies weave around them, making sure they are not missing out on anything.

Unloading the plants, they stack them against the corrugated iron, in the shade of the veranda.

'Where will I put all these?' Stella asks.

'There's no rush, just keep them watered. These Japanese anemones need a shady spot.'

'I actually have a good spot for them in the top garden near the shed; I might put them in this afternoon. Ya gonna stay for lunch, Laney?' Stella asks, admiring the plants. Her hands on her hips.

'I better go, thanks, lovey. I have some raking to do for Tom. He has nearly finished harvest. You know he doesn't let me help much these days so I jump at the chance when I can.' Rosie grins, giving Stella a quick wink.

'I know what he's like. But you don't need to overdo it, either.' Stella smiles, looking at two kookaburras resting on the fence.

'I take things very slowly these days. Don't worry, honey. Give us a hug. My beautiful girl.' Rosie hugs Stella goodbye and their shared grief is palpable. An unspoken connection.

Should I talk to her about Lottie, about Phillip? No. Not now.

'You smell so good,' Rosie says.

Stella laughs. 'New shampoo from Tilly. Need to get onto it, Laney.' Rosie breaks their embrace. Holding Stella at arm's length, she looks into her eyes.

'Take care, my girl.'

'Always, Laney. Always.' Stella's smile doesn't quite reach her eyes.

Jumping into the seat, Rosie waves goodbye, yelling out the window, 'Love ya!'

'Love ya, leave the gate open.' Stella waves and reaches down to pat her two fat, black staffies.

Looking in the rear-view mirror, Rosie takes a deep breath.

Stella has been a blessing of my loss; a friendship. A support. A shared pain; a circle of severe pain.

Rosie closes the gate behind her. Spotting Tom's vehicle in the far paddock, she heads in his direction. The sunlight is bright, glaring through the windscreen. Pulling up, she climbs out, watching a bale being spat from the back of the baler and rolling into place. As she walks over to meet him, Tom stops the tractor and climbs down, looking weary.

'How's Stella?' Tom asks.

'You know, the same old. She said she'll come over for Christmas lunch. Getting a few bales off this paddock?' Rosie thrusts her head in the direction of the scattered hay bales.

'Yeah, it's come up alright.' Tom casts his eyes over the expanse of hay bales, scattered across the paddock like marbles spilt across the floor.

'Ya wanna get us started on the paddock?' Rosie asks Tom.

'Yeah, nah. You'll be right. It's all ready to go, just be careful on the first lap. There's a bit of wire in that top corner over there. You got plenty of water? It's going to be hot today.' Tom wipes the sweat from his brow.

'I've got my bottle in the car. I'll grab it.'

'Righto. I'll leave ya to it. I wanna get this paddock finished, hopefully before milking.'

'Ok, darling. Catch ya.' Rosie swats a fly from her face.

As she walks to the tractor, the smell of cut grass makes her heart sing.

A good season. A time of hope. I'm looking forward to spending the afternoon on the tractor. The hours I've spent daydreaming, lost in my thoughts, driving a tractor. I love doing this job. It's good to feel useful. I'd love to paint an eagle, like Stella's big construction. I've got that blank canvas in my old studio I should use.

Watching the rows, Rosie makes sure the wheel lines up with the edge of the pile of cut grass. Checking the rake behind her, she makes sure it is spinning properly. Admiring the vast, blue sky, she looks to the mountain.

It is so grand. Strong. Permanent. It is home. I might give Anne a call tonight.

I remember when I got back from overseas; I must have spent a hundred hours on a tractor that season. It wasn't a nice tractor like this beauty, with a cabin and air conditioning. It was that old beast. The old Fordson. It seems like such a crazy adventure now. Going overseas for a whole year. Living in London and travelling around Europe. The gorgeous children I looked after. I wonder what they must be like now. Those times I'd take the family's dog for a walk through the park. The big, beautiful oak trees with their big arms reaching out. How wild and adventurous I was then. Going out partying. Our time in Amsterdam, riding around the city on a bike. The canals. The churches. The beautiful artwork. I can see myself dancing on the dance floor. I feel that same feeling of being free. Wild. Crazy and youthful. The gardens. The tulips. What a sight. What an experience. Then there was the anxiety and fear of travelling; how stressful and daunting it was. Getting lost in the streets of Venice. Seeing The Last Supper *in Milan. Getting up really early to find the small, insignificant church to get tickets; I got lost and an old Italian man stopped and gave me a lift, barely deciphering my English and strong Australian accent. MJ would have loved it. That was all that was missing. The empty place beside me. I have a longing to travel but my desire to stay at home is stronger. I fear something could happen and I hate to leave my garden.*

The sun through the glass of the tractor is hot and strong. Rosie puts on the fan.

I much prefer the heat to the cold. I might go for a swim in the creek when I'm done.

The sound of the rake is hypnotic. Swinging her head, she checks to see if the rows are remaining straight. The bright sun illuminates the valley. She remembers time spent in hospital. Her mind drifts.

I'm not sure if it was days, weeks or even months that had passed. There was the news. The crack in time. Then there is a blur. Fragments of

memory I can't quite piece together. The fog was thick and dark. Mumma
came into my room asking what was wrong. I was lying on the bed, in the
foetal position. I was rocking. Eyes closed. I was cold. Extremely thin, not
being able to eat. Pa picked my tiny frame up and carried me in beside
the fire. Mumma wrapped a blanket around me. I was sick with grief
and loss. I was fearful of going to hospital. Terrified of being carted away
from them. Being sedated. Highly dependent and trapped. Monitored.
Medicated. Naked, lying on the floor of the shower. I only have patches.
Little islands of memories.

I'm sorry Mary Jayne. I'm sorry I wasn't strong. I'm sorry I couldn't
hold it together. Guilt stricken. I never said goodbye. I never told you how
much I loved you. It was too late. Rocking. Mad. Crazy. A mad woman
rocking.

Looking into the skies, Rosie notices two planes chasing each other
across the sky, leaving long white streaks.

A lifetime ago now, how did I ever survive that? Then recovering
in hospital. Finding sanity. Walking around the tiny courtyard. Meeting
many people. Hearing their stories. Returning home. Not able to go back
to work. Returning to the farm and the garden. Painting and writing
poetry. Lonely. So lonely. Desperately missing my best friend.

She pulls the tractor to a stop after the last run. Time evaporated
while she was lost in her thoughts. Climbing down, she watches a
breeze catch a pile of hay, lift it and spin it in the air, making it dance
before resting it down. Rosie strides over the runs of raked hay, towards
the creek. Rosie ventures up to the deep swimming hole to swim. The
water washes over her.

Cleansing. Fresh. The first time I kissed Blake was on the bank of
this creek. My friend. My neighbour. We had become something more, in
that moment. His blue eyes, sparkling. Electricity, running through my
body, feeling his gentle touch. It took me so long to realise he thought of

me in that way. He was home working on the farm. I had returned from overseas. Most of our friends had moved away. Gone to the city. Our friendship blossomed into something more. I always felt he was too good for me. Too handsome. Too sensible and kind. It took me a long time to accept that I deserved that happiness.

Rosie swims. The cool water washes over her body. Diving under, her body immersed in the water. Standing up to feel the sun's warmth on her skin, she is transported to a time of youth and innocence.

Holding Blake's hand. Talking about nothing. No children then. No farm to run. That letter he wrote to me. What a beautiful, precious boy, my man.

Pangs of sadness hit her chest.

It's been over ten years without him. What we could be doing. What we could have shared. What I put that man through. The shame and regret I feel. All those times when I fell apart. He had to pick me up. Losing Will. Postnatal depression. The dreaded drinking. No wonder the poor bastard died young. As he always said, 'Anything for a quiet life.'

Rosie walks to the bank and wipes her face with the bottom of her shirt. Sitting on the bank, she watches the water run past.

Like time, like life, it continues. Uninterrupted. Don't try to swim against the current. Flow with the river.

I will never forget the day Blake died. A stormy night. The clouds gathering thick and strong. Driving home alone from the hospital. Alone. The pelting rain. The wind raging. Tears flowing. I just let it all drown me, like the water. I knew this grief. An old friend. Back to visit me. I drove through the hills. Watching the setting sun cast a spotlight on the gum trees lining the road. I thought of my children's pain. Another fracture to our little family. The pressure placed on Tom's shoulders. The grandchildren missing out on a time to know, to grow with their grandfather. I drove through the pelting rain until it cleared. I drove over the hill, into the valley. The sun setting. The rain clearing. An abundant rainbow shining; its vibrant colours glowing. Framing the valley. Through the sadness and grief, I marvelled at this wonder. This spectacle. I felt like Blake's spirit was there, in that moment. A final kiss goodbye. I knew I would survive. I know this is the price to pay for growing old, watching the ones we love go before us.

Her thoughts are broken by the sounds of the ute. Barking dogs about to round up the cows.

I better get back to the house to water the garden.

Rosie walks back over to the Courier and drives home. She pulls up into the garage; the gears crunch as she puts it into neutral and puts on the handbrake. She ties up her wet hair and hangs her towel on the fence to dry. Looking down to the vegie garden, she stops and admires the sunflowers.

They stand tall. Large yellow, orange faces. Proud and strong. A creation of God.

Rosie watches the cows walking up to the dairy. She listens to the hum of the dairy; a light breeze rustles the leaves of the trees. Soaking in the warmth of the sun, she brushes a fly from her eyes. She turns on the sprinklers. It is stinking hot and she is thirsty. Rosie goes inside and drinks some cold water from the fridge. She pats Gracie, who is sprawled out under the fan, sleeping contently. Rosie sits at her desk; she searches for Stella's poem.

I know it was in a plastic pocket.

Rosie opens up another box. Flicking through; she finds it and begins to read it.

In the Grip of Death and Desire

*If only, I could escape the memory of that intense pleasure we
shared*
Then maybe I could escape this pain
I bask in the sun of desire
Simultaneously becoming its slave
Ruled once by your tower
Now by God
Trying to construct the monument you desire
Reinventing myself in your image
You filled the hole
I endlessly pursue to fill
Hoping He will
You were in my grip
But now no longer
I'm searching for you incessantly
To walk down the aisle of heaven
To wed you for eternity
The tower was once my life
Now God's life
A writer's life
Pencil and penance
Loving you was once my life
Now I'm God's wife
Writing to heal
To conceal
Imagination
Spirituality
Satisfying you

While feasting on your flesh
Was once all I had
Now no more
Now I live for more
Now I come knocking on God's door
Filled the empty vessel
Once with your love
Now only memories
Thoughts of you above
Our life in the heavens will be golden
Devoid of the worries of money
Of commitments
Our love with flourish
What I've lost in this city will be regained in the next

I'm within the grip of death and desire
Imprisoned by their power
The tower of your love
At the centre of this city
Has been destroyed
Burnt to the ground
All that remains is an urn, full of dust
Remnants of what it once was
The memories of the ascent of the tower haunt my weary
nights
As I wait to be transported to the next
I dream of the new eternal tower built in its image
In the city to come
I worship the God of my cities
As I wait to find you once again

Writing is my freedom
My futile cry for help
My vain attempt to escape
The grip of death and desire

Your yellow eyes bore into my soul
The day before we released you from the machines
That played the vital role of your organs
In my dreams I see the city
You are there
My lover
My friend
Each night I venture to the city of desire
To escape the empty streets this city of death possesses
But as I wake I'm thrust back
Wake amid the corpses of a life once filled with love
I wallow in the repetitive days of routine
Obligation at the mercy of money
Trying to mix some meaning into the assortment of fiscal
pursuits
Of employment
Qualifications
Accommodation
Liberty in my pencil
As I dream of days
Basking in the sun
Getting stoned and making love
I try to live up to expectations so high
The unattainable pursuit of pleasing
Daydreaming I go to a world where the two cities meet

Become one
Borders cease to exist
Day and night dissolve
Life is filled with warmth and love
But as I daydream
The harsh reality is
That these cities
Are immutably separate
As consciousness can never know the unconscious
The city of death can never truly know the city of desire
Without crossing the border forever

Oh God, this girl. Her words.

Rosie holds the pieces of paper against her chest. Looking through the pile, she finds another piece of paper.

This must be something else Stella wrote; it's her handwriting, I don't remember this one.

Message to Heaven

Watching you die was like watching a sunset slowly fade from the sky. Such beauty, slowly disappearing. Holding on and simultaneously letting go. Vibrancy. Energy evaporating. Then only darkness. The cold harsh reality; you are gone forever.

You lay there, the shell. I saw you like this so many times; sound asleep, like a sweet baby. You were the best sleeper I'd ever known. The machines were there but all I could see was your beauty. The boy. The young beautiful man I loved with such intensity. You were so close but so far.

I arrived at the hospital. I remember it so vividly. I was met by Anne. She was visibly upset. She said you had a stroke but I didn't really understand.

I wrote you a letter; I guess a part of me knew. This was it. I read it to you. A final goodbye; asking how I was going to do this. Live my life without you.

We all stood in the room. It was dark. Tom wailed. I can still hear his cries. He wailed like a little boy whose precious heart was broken. I remember how I cried the same, in months to come, when the house was empty. I cried the other night like that. It's as though you are suffocating; you are aching as it is tearing you apart. Tom was opposite me. Anne beside me. I guess at the time I didn't allow myself to feel too much; I was insignificant to the family, to the enormity of their pain. Your lips turned blue. You choked; your last breath, drowning. Fighting to stay; the most horrific thing I have ever endured. Death. The harsh reality. There was nothing poetic or beautiful; it was just harsh. Raw. I wish I had better words. Words truly fail. It was like nothing I have seen before.

Sometimes I really wish I could remember you better. Your lips. Your laugh. Voice. Your gentle hands. I seem to remember you best in the end. These images so easily, quickly return. The happiest memories are the hardest.

The worst to remember, as I just drown in sorrow. Like the time we stood in front of the mirror. Your big, beautiful, strong arms around me. A picture of youth. Naked. Wholesome. Vibrantly intoxicated by our love. I asked if we look good together. You smiled. Kissed me. Held me. We were so gorgeous. Young and happy. I guess I feel old and bitter remembering. Our bodies were one. Our hearts in sync. Priceless moments I cling to like a life raft in this massive ocean of emotion and disappointment. The severe reality of life continuing without you.

Do you remember when you broke your leg and I looked after you? Snuggling into your presence. Sometimes I close my eyes and try to imagine doing this once again, as if nothing has changed. You were in pain and I tried to comfort and care for you but no number of hugs could help. I had nursed you through all those times of injuries. Falling off the skateboard. When I first met you, you had hurt your arm. Nine lives, you had. But they ran out. I loved that time, caring for you, of keeping the fire stoked, our little retreat.

I remember making love, your big, strong arms lifting me up and carrying me to the bedroom. How we yearned for each other. How we loved each other. So young; I was so in love with you. My mind thought of nothing else. My body ached for you.

Sitting beside you. Kissing you. The most beautiful kiss ever, so soft. I would give anything to experience that, one last time. To make love with vigour and passion; soft, calm and sweet. I guess I hold on to these because all the guilt and questioning are futile. It just makes me so angry. In some ways, I am just filling in time; waiting for heaven, doing the best I can. I have had other relationships since. There have been glimpses of passion, lust at best. But Will, no one has my heart, it is yours for eternity. No one has looked at me the way you did. I have not loved anyone like you. I loved you with an intensity that consumed me. I will always love you. I will be moving on with my life though. Please forgive me. I may fall in love, get married, have babies; I may devote my life to a family. If this happens it will not touch the part of me that is yours. My one and only, true, first love. I will keep you in my heart. Remember you. Dream of you. Always yearn for our life lost. Our baby girl we should have had. Please be at peace. Wait for me in heaven. Hear my prayers. Watch over me. Never doubt my eternal love and devotion.

Stella's words shock Rosie. She wipes tears from her eyes as she rocks in her chair. She slams her hand on the desk. Grace lifts her head in surprise at the sudden noise.

It cuts deep. I feel such an intense pain and longing. I feel so robbed that Stella and Will couldn't live this dream life they had ahead of them. Stella is so talented; I'd love to be able to write like that. I'd love to be able to capture the feelings, the emotion.

Rosie takes a deep breath, watching Gracie as she stretches and rolls over. Putting a CD in the CD player, she reads the cover to find the right song.

I love the Counting Crows, this song, 'A Long December'. Stella and I have listened to it so many times over the years. Especially after Will died. The lyrics. The melody. They somehow speak the words I don't have, to describe this pain.

OLD SOUL

Rosie puts the book of poetry down, resting it in her lap. Taking her glasses off, she rubs her tired eyes. She places the book carefully back on the pile beside her and retrieves her journal. She opens the blank page, pen in hand, and prepares to write. Frustration creeps through her, with a loud voice of doubt and fear.

This is ridiculous. You're too old and stupid. How could you ever be a Plath? How could I ever be something or someone? I've been defined by others my whole life. The granddaughter of. The wife of. The mother of. I have these silly, wild fantasies of being someone in my own right. I've always wanted to write a book. Why is it so bloody hard to trust myself? I always grapple with this; the fear seems to win. Time and time again.

Rosie puts the pen down and decides to go out into the garden. She collects some boxes and scissors out of the garage. She wanders, selecting the best blooms to fill a box. Captured by the colour and scent.

My garden is like a buffet, so much to choose from. A delight for the senses.

Rosie places the full box on the long white table. Slowly, she arranges the flowers in bouquets, selecting their spot and arrangement, placing colours that go together in a thoughtful selection. Billy's footsteps running along the veranda break into her thoughts.

'What are you doing, Nanny?' Billy asks, his hands on his hips, puffing loudly.

'Just picking some flowers. I was thinking of taking them into the cemetery today. What are you up to?'

'Dad's gone into town to get some stuff. I was just gonna stay with you until he gets back.'

'Alright, well make yourself useful and take that full box to the garage. Make sure you're careful and don't spill them out.' Rosie watches as he carefully carries the box through the gate and into the garage, his golden hair glistening in the summer sun.

Always eager to be involved. So eager to please.

Billy and Rosie load up the back of the ute with the boxes of flowers.

'Can I come with you, Nanny?'

'Yeah of course, Dad will be a while I reckon. Jump in.'

On the drive into town, the sun is warm as it shines through the glass. Rosie glances across at Billy, who sings to himself as he taps on the armrest.

I'm amazed by Billy's enthusiasm. Everything makes him joyous and excited.

Rosie smiles seeing his tanned skin glistening, his mind ticking over as he gazes out the window. They park under the shade of a tree; the old ute splutters as Rosie turns the ignition off. They climb out and unpack the boxes.

It is our first visit to the cemetery to put flowers on all our graves for a long time. This is something we have done many times over the years together.

Billy asks where Will's grave is; she explains he was cremated. Answers a plethora of questions that follow. Rosie looks at Stella's mother's grave; as she places some gum leaves on it, she reads all the names.

There's Stella's name. One of nine.

Sadness descends on her.

Oh God. Stella's mother died when she was so young. Raised by a stepmother. No wonder Stella left home early. I actually loved when she lived with us. Just a baby, at the age of seventeen. Now she's so independent. Buying her own property. Building her own place. My special girl. Precious soul.

As they place flowers on graves, Rosie explains who they are, and Billy reads the headstones. They come to her mother's grave.

'Whose grave is this, Nanny?' Billy queries.

'This is my mum's grave. So, your great-grandmother's grave. Can you read what it says?'

'Yeah. *Daisy Lane. Be-lov-ed.*' Billy sounds out the word.

'Good, keep going.'

'*Daughter of Pearl and William Lane, sister to* ... what does that say?'

'Phoebe, you know Aunty Phoebe. Keep going.' Rosie says with encouragement.

'*Jasmine, Percy, Rex and Paxton. Forever cherished mother of Rosie.* Is that you, Nanny?'

'Yes, darling, and her dad, William, is who you are named after.'

'I thought I was named after Uncle Will?'

'Well, yes you were, but Uncle Will was named William after his great-grandfather.'

No mention of Robert. He was just erased. Erased from her story. My story. Hidden. Lost in lies.

'Nanny, is my mum's grave here?' Billy asks, an innocence in his questioning.

'No, she's not. Why would you think that, honey?' Rosie asks.

Billy explains, 'A woman comes to me in my dreams. Sometimes when I walk down to the compost pile and the wind blows out of nowhere, I see a little blue wren.'

'You know, it's funny you say that. Blue was your mum's favourite colour. Wherever she is, God is looking after her. God is always with her. Are you sad without your mum, Billy?' Rosie asks. Placing her arm around him, she looks at the flowers in his hands.

'Sometimes, 'cause the other kids have a mum, but I have you and Dad. I sometimes wish I had a brother,' he responds maturely. A big grin on his face. Escaping her embrace, he runs along the edge of the graves.

He seems so old and wise. The little boy I love is growing up into a teenager. An old soul. He has walked this earth before.

She watches him with wonder and awe as he runs around the cemetery.

Rosie continues walking and comes to MJ's grave. Bending down, she wipes the headstone with her hand, removing any dust. Billy runs back to her side.

'Whose grave is this one?'

'This is my best friend's grave, sweetheart.'

'You have a lot of friends in the cemetery, Nanny,' Billy says nonchalantly as he does a handstand, attempting to walk on his hands, before falling on the dry grass.

'That's right. That's what happens when you get old, like me.'

'What was she like, Nanny, your best friend?'

Lying down, Billy looks up at the sky. Rosie lies down beside him. They watch big, fluffy, white clouds drift by. A big white streak breaks the sky in half as a plane flies above.

'Well, darling. She had long dark hair and the best laugh you've ever heard. She'd laugh with her whole body. She was so happy. Full of life, like you when you get excited.' Rosie tickles his side and he laughs loudly.

'Every school holidays, we were inseparable.' Sitting up, she dusts herself off. 'Can you pass me those flowers, please?'

Billy passes her the bunch of flowers scattered amongst gum leaves.

She arranges them, then places them in the jar at the top of the grave.

'MJ was my best friend and her mum and my mum were best friends. I knew her my whole life, since we were babies. We would sit up late at night talking. Discussing boys we liked at the time. Then when we were teenagers we'd go to dances. She always said "Love ya", every time we said goodbye. There was one time we didn't. The last time I saw her before she left on her trip. I didn't want her to go. I was being selfish. I wanted to stay and go to the dance. Blake, your grandfather, was going to be there. I stormed off and all I said was "See ya". I regret it every day. Guilt is a horrible thing.'

'Talked about boys. What? That's weird.'

Rosie laughs. 'You'll understand why, soon enough.'

They collect their things and wander back to the car hand in hand, arms swinging rhythmically. Rosie's red curls dance in the warm breeze.

'Why did she die so young, Nanny?'

'I wish I knew that, honey. I really do. Something Uncle Will used to say was, "Only the good die young".'

Driving back through town, Rosie looks to a house and a memory of picking Will and Stella up from there flashes through her mind. Thinking of a poem she found of Stella's recently, she tries to remember the name, but it evades her. Rosie drops Billy off at the dairy to meet Tom.

'Thanks for your help, lovey.'

Billy grins, cheekiness spread across his face. 'Love ya, Nanny.'

'Love ya.' Rosie sits for a moment, watching him bound out of sight. As she drives into the garage, the name comes to her.

'Forever', that's what it's called.

The heat of the day hits her as she gets out of the car. Retreating to the cool of her study, she picks up a book from the pile and begins to read. Staring across at the red bricks, she marvels at their individuality.

Their age. Their strength. If the walls could talk. I should get up and do something.

For a moment, Rosie watches the fan on the stand as it swings back and forth. The lace curtain sway. The hot, scorching sun can be seen beyond the shade of the veranda.

My days have been flowing to a consistent rhythm. Up at 5 am, before the sun, to turn on the pump to fill the tank and water the garden. Do my jobs before the heat of the day sets in. Then it's time for lunch and then back to my study or bed to rest. I've found myself lost in a book, napping, until the sound of the dogs barking and the dairy starting reminds me of the time. Wrestling with myself before I get out of bed, or Billy comes calling. We walk down the hill to the pump. He swims. I move my legs in the water while Billy tries to do handstands on the bottom of the creek. As the sun sets, we water the vegetable garden. Tom feeds his pigs. Billy locks up his chooks, talking to them like a teacher talking to their students.

I love this time of year. The slow pace. I feel so blessed. Life is easy. Life is good. I don't want to ruin this time. Why can't the skeletons stay in the closet? Billy needs to know. I need to stop putting it off. He seems to make that assumption anyway. I still haven't told them about Phillip or Robert. Anyway, there'll be a time. It will all unfold as it should.

As Rosie closes her eyes, rocking in her chair, she considers drifting off to sleep. She hears the clang of the back door, accompanied by a call. 'Nanny, where are you! Nanny, want to go to the creek for a swim?'

Opening her eyes, Rosie smirks.

Forever

I remember it all
The tears
The tantrums, it all

Mostly the love and passion
A world away
Like a dream
Just memories
A web of pain
Drives me insane
Fill my brain
With knots
Of love lost

I remember it all
Your lips
The look you gave me, from across the room
When I came home
Love in your eyes
Waiting for you, all night
Waiting for the clang of the bike
The old rusty gate

I remember it all
The first night
Look across the room
Our last kiss
The night you told me you loved me
As we made love

I remember it all
Knocking on the door
Walking in the gate at a party
Falling into your lap

The clang of the bike
The old rusty gate

I'm scared I will forget
Scared that is all I get

Would trade it all
For one more
Summer day, basking in the sun
Immersed in your love

Miss your voice and your laugh
Miss our nicknames
Loved you that much
Drove me insane

Give it up
Throw it all away
Just for one more day

Riding on the bus
Skipping school adventures
Just the two of us
Living each day as our last
All a distant past

I remember it all
Your last breath
The heartbreaking pain
The screams of lonely nights

Excruciating loss
Your death
What a mess
The blame
What we became

Heaven must need you
I'd give anything
Just one last time
To tell you I love you
To hear the clang of the bike
The old rusty gate

You said, only the good die young
Forever
Will be our love
Forever
I will remember it all

BAGS TO CARRY

Dear Laney,

I'm on the floor, writing this. Days in my dressing gown. I can't stop the tears. The ache. She's gone. The love affair is over. I want home. Home with her. Home with you, in our valley. I'm angry with myself. For fucking everything up. She told me a few home truths. I kept thinking of you. So, it's confession time. I wish I was a better friend. I was jealous of how close you and MJ were. I was so cruel to Polly. I see now how I've always been so selfish and self-absorbed. I have had this hurt I've carried. I'm not making excuses. I'm just saying, I'm sorry. This dreaded guilt and sorrow is like a festering wound.

I've had to go back on medication; I've been to my psychologist. She is teaching me so much. I wish I learnt this as a wild teenager. I am trying to find myself, to fill this void from within instead of seeking it externally. Maybe MJ was right; maybe I've always been a selfish attention seeker. I wish our last conversation wasn't so angry and harsh, filled with venom. What is that saying of Maya Angelou's? When you know better, do better.

I've just stopped drinking. Six days sober. I'm riddled with anxiety. I'm sweating, my mind racing. It feels like my heart is just going to beat right out of my chest. In the doctor's waiting room I was fidgeting, biting my nails. I haven't done that in years. I just wanted to vomit. Laney, I don't want to leave the house. I feel nervous and sick all the time. My hair is a mess. You should see me. I'm a mess. I just cry, in a pool of worthlessness, drowning. I feel ashamed and embarrassed to even write to you describing this pathetic state I'm in. My heart is broken. Shattered. I'm completely lost.

The rain is falling outside; I watch the drops weave tracks down the windowpane. I think of home. The precious gift rain is at home. I think of the darkness. The metaphorical and real darkness surrounding me. Remember that year there were those bushfires, which burnt all the surrounding mountain ranges. The valley was filled with smoke for months, an ever-present haze. That's how I feel now, a haze of remorse. Sorrow. Pain seeps through the cracks, a stench that drowns everything. I don't know if I can survive this. I feel this may be too much. I'm thinking of coming home. Home for good.

How did you ever survive the trauma in your life?

Here are some poems for you.

I miss you and you are always in my thoughts.

Ainsley B. Porter

Festering Wound

I was crying out for help
No one could hear me
Only seeing the behaviour
Never acknowledging the pain
Buried
Festering wound
Oozing filthy puss
All I wanted was healing
All I wanted was escape
Called me a drunken whore
Left me in the filth of the gutter
To lick my festering wound

Wild Love

No one wants the half-eaten fruit
Placed back on the shelf
To slowly wither and rot

Scars across my body
Like tattoos telling
Stories of trauma,
Grief

Yearning for wild love
Connecting
Eyes lock into eyes

Unspoken words
Touch speaking passion
Reciprocating desire
Melting into lost moments
Wanting to stop time
To stay forever
Wrapped in sweaty arms
Moist lips
Tangled in hearts beating in time

Untamed
Free
Wild love
Dancing with abandonment

Clutching the papers against her chest, Rosie closes her eyes and lets the tears fall.

Oh fuck, Ainsley! My girl. When will you be free? Free of this shit. These heavy bags of guilt. The shame you keep dragging around. Life's too short for this, especially at our age.

She picks up the pen and places the pages on the side of her desk.

Dear Ainsley,

Some journeys are not meant to be straight and easy. Your choices all had a purpose. You have achieved great things in your life. Don't forget that. I know that's hard to see through the darkness you're in. You have always been a good friend, not a perfect one, but a good one. MJ loved you. Remember, she was honest. Harsh with her words.

Perhaps a little self-righteous. We are all fallible. We must accept the reality of our actions. Our choices. Don't waste precious time on regret. I forgive you. I love you for all that makes you you. Your faults. Your failings. The darkness that plagues you.

As I get older I see the trauma in my life in a different way. I see that there are many blessings from the loss I have had to endure. I have gained so much strength. An appreciation for all the gifts life has given me. I make the most of the moment; I appreciate little things. The sweet sound of a bird singing. The cool breeze. The glow of the morning sun. Though you are in this haze and I know this haze you speak of, you will see sunshine again. Let yourself grieve. Let yourself feel this loss, this pain. The awful price of love is the risk of losing it all.

I love your poetry, I always have. We can be honest with each other. We can be raw. Let go of the shame and guilt you hold on to. I carry shame and guilt too. I feel its weight. Life is short. We were blessed with more than most. Let yourself be free.

Sending you love, my dear friend. Across oceans. From our mountains. Know that my love is eternal. You are broken right now but you can mend with time.

Be kind to yourself.

Rosie M. Lane

Placing the pen down, Rosie licks the edge of the envelope, then gently folds the letter and slides it inside.

I'll post this today, express post, don't put it off. Oh God, the things I am putting off. That big black box torments me. I need to stop grappling with this decision to tell Tom and just do it. Life is short. I need to take my own advice. I'm afraid to open the letters, to read them. I'm scared of what I might find. I fear I don't have the strength to handle it.

Bending down, she pulls the black box out from under the bed. Leaning against the bed, her legs spread open on the floor, she opens the box. Skimming through them, checking the dates, she notices the familiar date and the consecutive years.

One for each birthday.

Picking at random, she reads one with trepidation.

Dear Billy,

Happy 4th Birthday, my beautiful boy. How I miss you! I think about you every day. I imagine how big you are. I bet you are just like your Dad. I miss your sweet smile.

I'm so sorry for leaving. I regret it every day. I think about you and wonder what you look like at four; you must be a clever boy now. Nanny has probably taught you to read by now. I miss you. I wish I knew how to return to you but know your Mummy loves you. I always have. I always will. I know your Nanny will be taking good care of you; she loves you as much as me.

The last two sentences are scribbled out. Rosie manages to decipher them.

I'm lost my dear boy, wrapped in shame; guilt. I don't feel worthy. I hope to get my shit together and get back to you.

Face filled with tears, Rosie reads no more, placing the letters back in the box.

A voice from the dead. Haunting and raw.

Moaning in a heartbreaking wail, Rosie lets herself be engulfed by this wave of grief. Guilt. Shame.

I want to fix it. I want to fix all the fuck-ups. It's all too late.

Rosie hugs her knees in tight, drenching her hands in tears. Feeling Lottie's sadness. Knowing how it feels to miss your boy. Her mind drifts to an image of what Billy was like at four; a sweet boy full of mischief. Reminded of the cuddles and laughing at his funny observations of the world. His playfulness and delight in everything. Knowing all that Lottie missed out on and she received, a dagger of guilt stabs Rosie in the guts. As she holds her head in her hands, Lottie's smile fills her mind; she is lost in the moment remembering Lottie when she first came to town with her boyfriend, and got a job at the pub.

How her boyfriend soon left, then she met Tom. A wild girl who loved to party, she straightened out when she was pregnant. Gave up drinking and smoking. After Billy was born, they were both drinking. I should have got involved then. I could have stopped all this. Oh, darling Lottie, what a life. Tough life. Abused. Left home when you were just a baby. Nowhere to go. She found us and I let her go. I let her drive out into the night. I can't keep carrying these bags of guilt. Dragging this shame around.

The tears stream down her face. Rosie sits in the pain. Deciding to put the letters away for when Billy is older, she places them under the spare bed with resolve.

I want to preserve his innocence a little longer. I'll talk to Tom, he can decide. This is the right thing to do.

A bird sings outside. She unstraps a bag full of emotions from her back and leaves them there as she walks on through the day.

There is the sound of the screeching gate. Rosie lifts her hands from the bubbles of the sink to wipe them dry.

Someone must be here.

Gazing out the kitchen window, she sees Tilly's blonde hair. Filling the kettle with water, she turns to see her cheeky grin.

'Hey, darl, got a few goodies for ya,' Tilly says as she lifts up a cloth bag.

'You sayin' I stink, Tilly, my girl?'

'I've smelt worse, trust me. You got any of those Anzac bikkies of yours kicking round?' Tilly searches the table.

'In the cupboard, top shelf.'

Tilly finds the tin, brings them with her as she makes herself comfortable at the table.

'You been keeping out of trouble, my girl?' Rosie asks.

'You know me, Laney, always causing a bit of fuss,' Tilly says. 'I had words with my neighbour. That fucking dog of his, I told 'im he better keep it chained up otherwise it's gettin' a bullet.'

Placing the cups of tea on the table with care, Rosie sits in her seat opposite Tilly.

'You can't shoot, Tilly.' They begin to laugh in unison.

'Yeah, I know, but that fucking wanker doesn't know that, does he?' Tilly's eyes sparkle.

She has an energy that is infectious. An energy that makes me feel excited.

'How's Tom getting on?' Tilly is serious, sipping on her tea as she grabs another biscuit.

'I worry about that boy, to be honest, Tilly. He just works all the bloody time. It's like he's paying some kind of penance. I don't know if it's still about Lottie or what.'

'I think it's about Will.' Tilly eats her Anzac biscuit, admiring it as she takes each bite.

'Will?' confusion spreads across Rosie's face.

'You know he blames himself. He was meant to go in the car with him that weekend. Tom pulled out at the last minute. Tom must think if he'd gone, the accident wouldn't have happened or it would have been him.'

Rosie shakes her head in disbelief. 'I never knew that.' Pausing and looking out the window, in a quiet voice she says, 'He never said. He never mentioned anything about it. I thought Will had always planned to go on his own.' She takes a sip from her tea as the new information swims around her head. She rubs her forehead with her hand. 'How'd you know this?'

'I had a dream, a real weird one about Tom—like Will was sending me a message—then I asked Stella. It all sort of made sense then.' Tilly stands up and goes to her bag. 'I've made up this remedy. I want you to spray it everywhere. I'm hoping it will help.' Tilly holds up a blue spray bottle.

'It's amazing these magic potions you come up with.' Rosie smiles.

'Well, Laney, use it.' Tilly's eyes fixate on Rosie, drilling into her. 'If there's something you're not telling Tom, it's time to tell him, Laney. Get it off your chest.'

'You're right. Just waiting for the right time.' Rosie looks into her cup of tea, avoiding eye contact. 'Have you been reading my mind again, Till?'

Tilly smirks. 'I just know when something's bothering you.' She flashes a quick wink as she grabs the door handle.

'Well, I better go. Ash will be at home cracking the whip.' Tilly moves with excitement and anticipation. Hesitating, she reaches back over to the tin to grab some more biscuits. 'Better take a couple of these bad boys for the trip home. They're the fucking best.'

'You'll give yourself a gut ache. Come give us a hug before you go.' Rosie remains in her seat, feeling weary. Tilly moves to the other side of the table, hugs her and gives her a kiss on the head.

'Love ya,' Tilly says.

'Love ya, my girl,' Rosie responds. 'Stay out of trouble.'

'Always.' A cheeky grin fills her face; Tilly winks, closes the door and walks around the veranda with an audible spring in her step.

Making her way back to the sink of dishes, Rosie submerges her hands in the warmth and bubbles. Rosie ruminates about what Tilly has just revealed.

Tom feels responsible for Will's death. It's like Cain and Abel. Romulus and Remus. The killing of the brother. He was meant to be in the car with him. I was meant to be on that plane. I should have been with her. He thinks if he was there with Will to protect him, like he always had ... He really blames himself. How can he seriously blame himself? How can he carry this around? I know how he does. What am I going to do with this boy? Those bags of guilt. The shame he is carrying must be so bloody heavy. Those bags are too heavy for us to carry.

MOUNTAIN

Rosie rises early. There is quiet outside. Golden rays are melting across the horizon.

My old body clock is set from years of milking cows early each morning. Raising children who did not allow sleep-ins. Some mornings the sunrises are plain, a disappointment, but I still love to see the sun rise, to catch the spectacular ones. Each single day, each single one, different, unique. God's creation; a perfect surprise. Combination of light and cloud; I imagine there is a wonderful science to it all. I love the mystery and the magic I rise each day to enjoy.

Walking around her garden, she drinks her warm, thirst-quenching tea. Placing her empty cup on the windowsill, she picks up her secateurs and moves to the side of the house. Rosie begins pruning the hydrangeas, selecting each branch, a new bud to cut to—throwing the cut branches on the ground in a pile. Admiring the pruned bushes, she finds satisfaction in giving them a new lease on life. From the corner of her eye, she sees Tom come around the corner and out into the garden.

Nearly a spitting image of his father. I'm surprised to see him. I'm surprised he is not working.

Rosie continues cutting, then squeezes the secateurs together and locks them shut. Rosie senses that Tom wants to talk about something as he takes a seat on the garden edge of the raised bed.

'I am thinking about going on a holiday. Taking Billy somewhere, after Christmas time. Turning most of the cows out,' Tom says.

'That's a great idea, darling. What's brought this on?' Rosie frowns, searching his face.

'Well, I don't know. I figure Billy deserves to have a holiday away, like normal kids.'

'I don't think Billy's one to worry too much about being normal,' Rosie insists, wiping her hands on her pants.

'I just feel bad for him, being on his own with no mother or brother or sister. I was thinking of asking Anne and the kids to come, but then I thought you might like to come and I was worried about no one being here, except Uncle Puck.' Tom begins to ramble with nerves and anxiety.

'I wouldn't worry about me; you know I love to stay home, if I can.' Rosie's voice drops with what she hopes is comforting reassurance. 'I can ask Ash if she can milk the cows. Anne would love to spend some time with you, Billy and the kids.' She takes a seat beside him.

Tom's arms are crossed as he rests on his long legs. He seems hesitant to speak.

There's something on his mind.

'Mum, have you heard from Lottie?'

Rosie is stunned at first to hear him speak her name; she hasn't heard it pass his lips since she left. Hesitant to respond, she knows she cannot lie.

I know I have to tell him.

A knot forms in her throat.

'Well, it's funny you ask that. I do actually have news of Lottie but it is not great,' Rosie says, unsure how to phrase it to make it sound less tragic.

Tom looks down. A broken man. 'I need to know.'

'When I went to Anne's a while back, back in the winter, I visited Aunty Jassie, as you know. I found out that Jassie had crossed paths with Lottie.' Pausing for a moment, she lets her words sink in. 'Lottie wasn't in a good way. Aunty Jassie helped her as best she could but she couldn't save her.' Rosie holds back tears.

'Is she gone?' Tom asks.

'Yeah, sweetheart. A suspected overdose.' Looking at the ground, Rosie feels the weight of the words as they hang in the air like thick smoke. Tom clutches his head in his hands; his torrent of tears wet the ground below. Wrapping an arm around him, Rosie continues as she scratches the ground with her feet. 'Aunty Jassie gave me a box, with some letters and some jewellery for Billy. All Lottie had.'

Tom grips his forehead as he cries old tears; the sun sneaking through the trees illuminates his head resting in his hands. Looking up momentarily, Rosie sees a blue wren dart about the tree, dancing on the branches, and then flutter away. Tom cries out. Rosie soothingly rubs his back, like she did when he was a little boy. 'It's all my fault,' he says through endless sobs. 'I should have never done it. I was just a fuck-up. I should have chased her, stopped her. I should have run after her. What the fuck was I thinking?'

'Darling, we all wish we could go back and save her.' Rosie tries to comfort him.

Sometimes there are no words adequate. Sometimes, words fail.

Sitting beside him, Rosie holds him. Her little boy, now a broken man; she rocks him back and forth, tears running races on her cheeks. The garden sings songs of sorrow.

I'm so mad. Mad that life has been so cruel to this foolish, precious boy.

Rosie slowly rocks him.

A mad woman rocking.

BIRTH

There's noise and excitement when Rosie wakes. She races out of bed.

I've slept in. The kids are already up and opening their presents.

Wrapping her dressing-gown around her, she goes out into the lounge room to see Lachlan and Olivia surrounded by gifts. The tree has piles of wrapped presents underneath it.

Anne yells from the kitchen, 'Merry Christmas, Nanny!'

'Merry Christmas!' Rosie responds.

Bending down, Rosie affectionately kisses the kids on the head as the chorus 'Merry Christmas!' rings in her ears. 'Look what Santa gave us,' Olivia says.

'You are very lucky. Wow. Look at it all.' Striding into the kitchen, she passes Tim, who she kisses on the cheek and wishes a merry Christmas. He quietly sips his coffee and watches the kids.

Sitting down, she thinks of many gifts given and received at Christmas.

Anne loved to read, always, as a child, a teenager, and a young adult; always advanced for her age. There's so many authors and books. So many years, sharing our love of reading. We shared a special interest and bond and introduced each other to amazing texts, like Jeanette Winterson's books, Jennifer Strauss's poetry and To Kill a Mockingbird. *Christmas always evokes memories. The memory of Will getting his first fishing rod, catching a fish. How proud he was to show it to Blake. Their faces said it all. As a child, opening up a gift, paints, canvas and an easel. I was so grateful and excited. I painted all summer holidays. Making the old pump shed my studio. Moving pots and cleaning it. Mumma had saved up for it all year.*

A smile crosses her face as she remembers the simple paintings of parrots, hills and landscapes she created with such passion and joy.

The sound of the children splashing, playing and laughing fills the air. The adults are sitting by the bank. Rosie is drinking some sparkling mineral water, but everyone else is drinking cold beers from the esky.

I could not think of a better way to enjoy celebrating the birth of our saviour.

Rosie watches Stella as she splashes her feet in the creek, her hair tied up high on her head, wrapped in a colourful headband. The water glistens at her feet, reflecting light, making small waves. Her long floral shirt sits in the water and she looks lost in the movement of the water.

It's good to have Uncle Puck here.

Rosie watches him as he sits there beside Tom, talking about the farm, cattle prices, predicted weather, saying, 'There's no public holidays for dairy farmers.' She thinks about all the Christmas mornings she spent in the dairy. Her mind fills again with the memory of the year they bought Will his first fishing rod.

How he ran up to the dairy to show his father. A big trout. His father was feeding calves, a quiet man who didn't say anything. I still remember

the look on Blake's face as Will showed him the fish he caught. He was
proud. He was proud of his boy. A precious memory, stored away. A good
season that year. We could afford to spoil the kids. The pile of books Anne
received. Tom had the new chook pen that Billy is still using now.

Her thoughts are broken by Billy's voice. 'Nanny!' he calls out.
'Watch this.'

Rosie looks up and watches him as he propels himself off a rock
protruding from the water and catapults himself into the depths of the
deep waterhole. Rosie laughs and claps, thinking of Will climbing the
trees along the banks of the creek and jumping in from great heights.
Never afraid of heights or injuries.

The afternoon fills her with endless joy and happiness. A time
of relaxation, fun and enjoying the fresh flowing water. Holding the
precious moments, she wishes it could last longer.

Maybe this is the right time? When will I have everyone here to tell
them all at once?

As they gather on the bank, drying themselves, Rosie decides she'll
tell them.

'So there's something I want to tell everyone,' Rosie says in her
loudest voice possible.

'Oh no, is everything alright, Mum?' Anne asks.

'Yes. Yes, everything is alright. I have someone coming to visit next
week.'

'Do you have a boyfriend, Nanny?' Billy asks.

Everyone laughs.

'No, honey. Oh God no. I have a nephew. A nephew called Phillip.
He is bringing his family to visit.'

'What do you mean, a nephew?' Tom asks, frowning as he leans
forward in his chair.

'A young man found me and I discovered I had a brother. An older brother who was adopted. Phillip is his son.'

A cocky squawks as everyone sits in silence. The news seeps in slowly.

'This is a bit of a shock,' Anne says. 'It's a bit out of the blue.' She continues to dry herself and dress the kids.

'Well there's a bit of a bigger shock. That's why I want to tell you while we're all together.' Rosie takes a deep breath. A knot forms in her throat. Her voice cracks. 'Phillip looks identical to Will. He is a spitting image of him.' Rosie looks over at Stella to read her face. Her eyes quiver as she stares at the ground.

'What do you mean, Mum? Like, identical?' Anne probes.

'Yes, I thought he was Will when I first saw him. I just wanted to prepare you all.'

'What day's he coming?' Anne asks.

Tom gets up from his seat and wanders along the bank.

'Next Wednesday,' Rosie answers. 'Before you go back.'

Rosie watches Tom as he stands throwing stones into the creek. Stella follows him.

'How long have you known this? Why didn't you tell us earlier? Give us a bit more time. Especially Stella.' Anne points upstream towards Tom and Stella.

'Well, I don't know.' Rosie tries to defend herself. 'It was a bit to get my head around, Anne.'

'You do this all the time. For fuck sake. Let's get up to the house and get changed.' Anne packs up the kids and storms off. Tim follows, carrying their bags.

Rosie looks to Uncle Puck. 'Well, this is why I don't bring things up. I get a reaction like this.'

'She'll be right, love,' Uncle Puck says, swigging from his beer bottle.

Billy runs back quickly. Giving her a hug, he says, 'Love ya, Nanny.'

'Love ya, sweetheart.' Tears form in her eyes.

Glancing upstream, she sees Tom put his arm around Stella as the water flows past.

After dinner, they sit up into the night. Drinking, laughing and reminiscing. Everyone goes home or goes to bed. Stella and Rosie are the last ones up; Stella has had too much to drink to drive home and reluctantly stays.

'You can go to bed if you like,' Stella says as she takes a sip of red wine from her glass. 'I'm going to stay up a bit longer.'

'Nah, it's alright. I'm not tired.' The moment reminds her of many drunken nights with Stella. Sitting up until all hours drinking, talking and sharing their messy grief.

'I'm sorry I didn't talk to you earlier about Phillip,' Rosie says.

'Don't stress about it, Laney. I know it's hard to bring these things up. I'm fine with it, really. Obviously it will be hard meeting him but you know I'm kind of curious.' Stella smiles.

'Well, it nearly fucking killed me when I saw him. I wasn't prepared. A complete bloody stranger. He's lovely so I think it will be nice for everyone to meet him.' Rosie sighs.

'Did you hear from Tilly today?' Stella asks.

'Nah, I didn't. She's at Ash's brother's place, I'm pretty sure, for Christmas this year.'

'I thought she couldn't stand Ash's brother.'

'She can't, but I think she's making an effort for Ash. She's getting soft in her old age.' She smiles.

Stella raises her eyebrows; her mouth clenches as she expresses her surprise. 'She's full of surprises, our Tilly, isn't she?'

'She's certainly one of a kind, but I can't fault her. She's dragged my arse out of the shit a few times over the years. I'll never forget it.'

'You know, we kind of had a moment once, years ago,' Stella says.

'What do you mean "a moment"?' Rosie asks with intrigue.

'Like we had an awkward moment, where …' Stella pauses for a moment to consider her words, and continues. 'We were both drunk at her place. This is before Ash came along. She kind of went to kiss me. It was so uncomfortable at the time. I didn't realise I was giving off those signals and she felt like that about me. It was weird. We never spoke about it.'

'That doesn't really surprise me really; when you and Will first got together, she was really weird about it, for a long time. I thought she hated you because you got in the way of her friendship with Will but then there was probably a different dimension to that, now that you say that.'

'It's funny to think about it now, like we are good friends now. There's no awkwardness and I love Ash. She's the best thing that has ever happened to Tilly. Let's hope she keeps her head down and bends a little.'

'Yeah, she can be hard work sometimes. Ash has come here a few times to stay when Tilly's hit the piss and started her shit. She's lucky Ash is so forgiving.'

'We can all be dickheads with drink, can't we?'

'I know that better than anyone, darling, and on that note, I think we better get to bed.'

'I'll just finish this last glass.' She swirls the remaining wine in the bottle.

'All right, sweetheart,' Rosie says as she stands up and kisses Stella on the forehead. Stella wraps her arms around her waist in a loving embrace.

'Night, sleep well,' Stella says. 'Love ya.'

'Love ya.'

WILD

Looking at the tiger lilies from her garden, she mixes the paint, trying to match the rich reds and deep pinks. She spreads the paint thickly on the canvas, music ringing in her ears. Rosie loses herself in the moment, absorbed in the shapes, the tones, texture; trying to replicate the beauty of God's creation. The light comes streaming through the window, weaving its way through the lace curtains. She hears the front door.

It's unusual for someone to come in that way.

Tom appears in the doorway and makes his way to the corner of the bed and sits down. Rosie can tell he has questions; it always takes him a lot of time to process things. Knowing instinctively that for many days now he has been digesting the news like she had, Rosie continues to paint.

I know Tom well; I know this doesn't come easy to him. To talk. To ask. Always stoic, hardworking. So much like his father.

Once he begins, the questions spill out uncontrollably. 'Should we tell Billy? Do you think he has a right to know? Have you read the letters?'

Rosie paints for a while, pondering all his questions, breathing deeply.

I know I need to be strong for Tom; it's time for me to guide him.

'I don't think we should tell Billy yet, not until he is older, but I think he already suspects she's gone.'

'Fuck, Mum, he's so young. How do you tell a little kid a mother they can't remember is dead? Now we've got this whole new family. Some dude who looks like his dead uncle.' Tom leans back on his hands, shaking his head.

'Well, fucked if I know, darling. I don't have the heart to take his innocence away. Not just yet. Ultimately, it is up to you. You're his father. If you think that is the right thing to do. I'll support your decision.'

'I don't want to lie to the kid but I don't know if he needs to be told right now.'

'I have only read through one of the letters. It was a beautiful letter to Billy for his fourth birthday. Looking at all the dates, there must be one for each birthday. I think when he's older they will be a great comfort. But he is your son, Tom, and these are your decisions to make. Honestly, I have been a mess since I found out. I don't know exactly what the right thing is to do.' Rosie pauses for a while.

I know I need to tell Tom everything I know.

Taking a seat beside him, she wipes the wet paint on her hands with an old tea towel. 'Lottie was on the streets. Aunty Jassie crossed paths with her while she was in a women's refuge. Apparently, she was doing well for a while. Then the drugs just got a hold of her again.' Rosie moves closer to Tom; he has his head in his hands as he listens. 'This is not what you want to hear but I know you need to hear it. Lottie told Aunty Jassie a lot about her childhood. I'm not sure if you know this, but she was abused by her stepfather and ran away from home. Lottie had demons, Tom, lots of demons. The only time they were at rest was when she was with you. When she was pregnant. When she became a mother. Lottie told Aunty Jassie this. If we can't believe the word of a nun, then who can we believe?'

Rosie puts her arm around Tom as he sobs; she strokes his back like she did when he was a boy. To her, he is always her precious little boy. Rosie remembers when he was inconsolable as a child after his favourite chook, Bucket, died. How she held him. He was devastated.

Such a caring, quiet, sensitive boy. Bloody Blake kept making jokes about poor Bucket kicking the bucket.

Enjoying this moment of connection, she breaks the silence and asks, 'Is there anything I can do?'

Wiping his nose with the sleeve of his shirt, he responds, 'Nah, I think for now we just let sleeping dogs lie. I think you're right. Billy's too young for all this, but if he asks, I think we need to be honest and tell him his mother's in heaven. As for the letters and the rest, we can wait 'til he's older and can handle all that.' His tears soak into the tissue she hands him.

This has been a huge release for him. A painful yet cathartic revelation. I'm grateful to share his vulnerability.

'Time for a cuppa, I'd say,' Tom says as his tears dry, wiping his nose on his sleeve.

'Yeah, I'd say, I'll put the jug on.'

They both go into the kitchen, without speaking. Rosie fills the kettle, puts it on, and places two cups on the bench while Tom goes out the back to the outside toilet. Her thoughts are cast to the passage in *The Alchemist.*

Hearing footsteps, Rosie catches a glimpse of Stella as she walks past the window and around the veranda to the back door. Tom follows her in. Rosie fills three cups.

'Hello, darling. This is a nice surprise.'

'I had to come into town to grab a few things; I thought I'd call in on my way home,' Stella says. She turns around. 'Hi, Tom,' she says with a warm smile.

Tom's face has been washed clean. 'Hey, Stell, what's happening?'

'You know, same old, just keeping out of trouble. Did yas get much rain last week?'

'About half an inch, bugger all, really, but better than nothing.'

'I measured twenty mils at my place. It's enough to top up the dam a bit.'

They sit at the table, in their normal places. Stella has her place.

'They predict more rain next week,' Tom says, then sips his tea. Rosie gets the biscuit tin out of the cupboard and hands it to Stella and then Tom.

'You've got some nice-looking calves down there, Tom,' Stella says. 'You still pumping plenty of milk into them?'

'Yeah, bloody oath,' Tom says, dunking his tea bag in his cup. 'You looking for any bull calves? I've got three you can have. I shouldn't even bloody have them this time of the year but that bloody angus bull got in. The old sow had thirteen piglets last week, she rolled on one but the other twelve have survived.'

'You should see 'em, Stella. Little buggers,' Rosie says as she wipes the bench down. 'They lie out in the sun. They're so quiet. It's surprising the foxes haven't got any.'

'That's 'cause they're so quiet. They're the quietest piglets I've ever come across,' Tom says as he gets up, puts his worn-out cap on. 'I better go get Billy off the bus and round up the cows.' He places his cup on the sink. 'Thanks for the cuppa, Mum. Good to see ya, Stell. Let us know if you want those calves and I'll bring 'em out next week.'

'That'd be good. I've got a fence you can help me strain, while you're there,' Stella says, smiling a cheeky grin.

'Alright, I'll bring the strainer. Catch yas,' Tom says, grinning slightly as he closes the door.

'He's a good boy, our Tom, isn't he, Laney?' Stella says with warmth. She sips her tea and pulls out her tobacco to roll a smoke.

'He is. A heart of gold, that one. Did you make it over to see Tilly for a treatment?'

'Yeah, I did actually,' Stella says as she licks the paper of her cigarette and rolls it in her fingers. 'I'm going to go out for a smoke,' she says as she picks up her cup and the lighter from her bag. Rosie admires Stella, hair wrapped in colourful headbands, her floral skirt moving about her decorated ankles and bare feet. Her singlet reveals her tanned arms.

Olive skin from her Italian grandparents.

They sit outside under the shade of the veranda; there is warmth in the air. A light breeze floats through the trees, making them sway gently.

'So I went and saw her,' Stella says. 'My lower back was killing me. You know the stuff she does … she did all these massage movements. Then I had this intense pain, like heaviness in my right arm. So she goes around and holds my hand. Then after a little bit she says, "Will's here. He has something he needs to share."' Stella pauses, looking out towards the caravan on the side of the hill. '"He wants to tell you that you are soul mates." She then said that he's happy. It's okay to move on, that I taught him so much. "He's so proud of you. You are allowed to let this sadness and grief go. It has no place anymore. He surrounds you all the time. He will for the rest of your life. When your life is over, you will see him again."' Stella drags deeply on her cigarette; tears form in her eyes.

A deep sadness and longing fills Rosie's stomach.

What? My boy, my sweet boy. Why didn't he speak to me? Don't be so selfish. How could you think that? Stella needs this, she deserves to be happy.

'That's amazing. How are you feeling?'

'Yeah, it was pretty intense. Bit freaky at first. She's helped my back; she wants me to go see her once a week for a while. I just don't know if I can ever move on. Have I left it all too late? What about having children? I'm thirty-four. Have I left it all too late?' Stella begins to cry. Puts her cigarette out. 'I'm sorry. I don't mean to get upset.'

'Darling, Will wants us all to move on and be happy. You are allowed to. If that means being with someone else and having children, that's ok. You and Will are forever connected. Your souls are destined to be together. Nothing can change that.'

Rosie wraps her arms around Stella and they stand together, crying, tears rolling down their faces. Stella's voice quivers as she says, 'I wish my memory was stronger. So strong I could still reach out and touch him, taste him and smell him. I hate that my memory fades; time buried him deeper and deeper. Sometimes I just try to forget. To avoid all this pain. I feel so lost with this endless emptiness. Each night I go to bed with a ghost. I can't escape this. At times I've considered ending it all to reach him quicker but then I can't risk not getting to heaven. I pray that God takes me sooner rather than later. I've never been able to connect, to reach anyone else, to feel that love. That is once in a lifetime. My time with him came to an abrupt end.'

Stella's flood of raw emotions has Rosie in tears. Holding Stella's face in her hands, she speaks softly. 'Oh darling, if there were any words to make a difference, I'd speak them, but sometimes words just simply aren't enough.'

As Rosie holds Stella in her arms, they cry in unison. Cry for their boy. Their precious boy. Taken too soon. They rock together. Mad women rocking.

Wild

Beautiful mind
Wild
Runs with wolves; wild and free
Dances on water and I'm beginning to see
She has transfixed me

Wild

A beautiful contradiction
So strong but gentle as the breeze
I'm beginning to see
She has enthralled me
Her touch holds the power of the sea
Conjure the water and wind with ease

Wild

She is something beyond this world
A formidable force, more than a simple girl
She has captivated me
I'm beginning to see
When she looks at me
I'm as captive as she is free
Spontaneous spirit, her touch ecstasy
Her mind sharp and witty
Her heart strong and gritty
She looks deep into my eyes
I can't breathe

Wild

She is wild, as I take her hand
I finally understand
I'm falling
Falling, falling
Wild
I can finally see

RED TAIL

'Phillip, this is my daughter, Anne, and my son Tom.' Rosie watches as their eyes are transfixed on Phillip.

'I'm so pleased to finally meet you.' Phillip puts his hand out. Anne ignores the hand and wraps her arms around Phillip. Tears run down her face.

Pulling away, Anne says, 'Sorry, you just …'

'That's ok. I know. I look like Will. You should have seen your mother's face when I appeared on her doorstep. It was quite a fright for her.' Phillip speaks with compassion in his voice.

Anne wipes her tears. Kookaburras sing loudly in the trees.

'Nice to meet you, mate.' Tom puts out his hand, a tear balancing on the inside of his eye refusing to fall.

Phillip reaches out and shakes his hand. 'You too, Tom.'

'There's no DNA test required, Mum. By golly he's a dead ringer for Will.' Tom glances over at Rosie. Her face is drenched with tears.

Billy bursts through the gate.

'Dad!' he yells. 'Lachie won't let me go first!' Billy pauses as he realises there is a group of people he's never seen standing there on the front lawn.

'Billy, come and meet some cousins of ours,' Tom says. Billy runs to his side. 'Billy, this is my first cousin, Phillip, and his lovely wife, Kylie, was it?'

'Hello, Billy,' Phillip says, a smile across his face.

'Nice to meet you, Billy,' Kylie says as she threads her arm through Phillip's.

New Times

> Two families come together
> Like magic we fit together
> Come with news
> A father's gravestone
> Relief and disappointment
> Cousins meeting
> Children playing
> Laughter
> New connection
> Our family has grown
> Watching with wonderment
> Unexpected happiness
>
> Phillip and Anne talk of teaching
> The noise and activity
> Like old times
> These are new times
>
> A brother
> A father
> A mother
> I wish I knew
> Tom sits quietly
> Billy loves new friends
> Shows his cousins the lay of the land

Like a tourist guide

New times
I marvel at what the future holds

Exploring photo albums
What we share is greater
Than what divides us
Long summer day
Filled with
New memories
New times
To cherish

The words flow. Fall onto the paper. Like magic. Like water. Effortless.

I am content when I can write. A weight has been lifted. I'm so relieved I'm not holding on to these secrets anymore.

Reflecting on the new year and what is to come, Rosie turns the page and continues writing.

Digging in the soft ground, Rosie moves some rocks to extend the garden bed. Big, fat red worms try to race to escape. Gracie lies comfortably in the shade, chewing on her rope. Finding an empty pot, Rosie places the worms in there with some soil.

Billy will love these big suckers for fishing or to add to his worm farm.

Rosie scrapes back a layer of thick mulch created by the fallen leaves rotting; the soil is dark and rich underneath.

Billy arrives, calling out to her. 'Nanny!'

'I'm out in the garden!' she shouts. He runs towards her.

He never walks anywhere. It reminds me of Will at that age.

Rosie stands up straight and stretches her back, wiping the dirt on her trousers.

'What are you doing?' he asks as he bends down to pat Gracie.

'Just fixing up this bed here. Look what I found for ya,' she says as she picks up the pot filled with healthy worms and passes it to him. He runs his hands through the soil to uncover the intertwined worms. Billy looks impressed.

Bloody good find those fat suckers.

'Do you want to take 'em down and throw a line in?' Rosie asks.

'Yeah, my rod's in the shed,' Billy replies with excitement. 'I have to feed the chooks and then collect the eggs first. I'll be back.' He gives her the worms back and then runs off.

Rosie yells out, 'Tell your father what you're up to before you come back! I'll put Gracie inside.' Rosie looks in the old pump shed and finds an old rod of Will's; she dusts it off and checks the hook. Rosie pulls it out and gets ready to go down the creek.

Billy returns with his fishing rod. They walk down the steep bank, through the thick elm suckers; they need to take their time. They decide to make their way to Will's fishing spot.

When they arrive, they clear their spot, placing the rods, worms and net carefully on the bank. They pick up the worm container and their fingers search for the thickest worms. They begin threading the thick worms on the hooks as they wriggle. They are slimy. Casting their lines in, they sit in silence.

It is rare for Billy to be quiet and simultaneously still. He takes fishing seriously. I never really worry about catching fish. I just enjoy the peace and quiet. Hearing the birds, listening to the flowing water. It is a lot to ask Billy to sit and be still for that long.

The silence and tranquillity are broken by Billy's rod bending and flicking with a bite. He rushes to pick up his rod and yanks on it. The excitement quickly ends as it gets off, swimming free. Disappointed, Billy reels the line with the empty hook in.

Trying to cheer him up, she tells him, 'That was a good bite. Wait a bit longer next time. Make sure the fish takes the bait and hook.'

Billy frowns as he listens.

The same way Tom does when he concentrates.

Billy carefully places more worms on the hook. They dance and squirm. Taking care, he casts the line in. Sitting and waiting patiently, he gets a stick and begins to dig a hole in the ground. His rod taps, taps again; he grabs it in anticipation and waits a bit. Then a big bite forces the rod to bend towards the water. Billy hesitates for a second. Lifts the rod up. He begins reeling it in; Rosie grabs the net and moves beside him.

'It feels like a big one,' he says as he keeps reeling it in. They get a glimpse of the big fish as it comes to the surface, rolls and swims upstream.

'Oh, Jesus, Billy. It looks like a whopping cod. Keep going. Give it a chance to tire itself out. You don't want the line to break,' she instructs him as she excitedly waits on the bank with the net.

He persistently reels it in, bearing the weight of the rod; he moves downstream a little to get a better angle. He makes progress. He reels it into the bank. It is massive. Rosie gets the net under the fish, finally securing it, and they bring it onto the bank. Billy is so relieved. Excited. Proud of his catch. Billy carefully removes the hook with the pliers, making sure not to hurt the fish. Billy proudly holds it up, its beautiful flesh glistening in the sun, speckled in shades of gold and green. Its large mouth gasps for air. Rosie takes a photo. They marvel one last time at this beauteous creature. Its wide head. Its colouring. Billy releases it with care back into the creek. It splashes and quickly disappears within the depths of the fresh sparkling water. Happy with the catch, they walk back up to the dairy. Billy can't wait to tell his father. Show him the picture.

Thank God I brought my camera for the trip.

Rosie tries to keep up with Billy as he races to the dairy to tell his father the exciting tale. She hears the dairy being turned off. The familiar dogs barking. Tom meets them on the side of the hill, his overalls splattered in cow shit, legs apart, resting in his worn-out boots.

He reminds me so much of Blake with his hands on his hips.

Looking from under his dirty peaked cap, he calls out, 'How'd youse go!'

Billy runs ahead. Rosie struggles behind, losing her breath as she tries to maintain the pace. She hears Billy telling his father—Tom's arm around him, listening intently to the story. Billy re-enacts the actions of the pull on the fishing rod. He yells out to her, 'Hurry up, Nanny! I want to show Dad the photo!'

Rosie moves quickly to greet them, taking the camera off from around her neck and passing it to Tom to look.

Rosie stands there, enjoying the precious moment. Admiring the grandeur of the gum tree standing tall.

Fed from the run-off of the dairy all these years.

Nesting birds sing sweet songs as they perch on the gum's strong branches. The setting sun showcases the white and grey of its bark.

Tom exclaims, 'Geez, it's bloody massive! You didn't photoshop this, did ya, Nanny?'

They continue to laugh and joke about catching the fish as they walk towards the dairy, before going their separate ways.

As she walks up to the house, she takes a moment to look across the paddocks. She sees a red tail, weaving through the tussocks, as she soaks in the present moment.

I know one day I will miss this. I know all things fade, change. Nothing lasts forever.

Waving to Billy and Tom as they turn around before heading down the laneway, Rosie watches Billy's mouth moving incessantly. Tom's face is filled with pride and joy.

She walks inside and looks through the pile of letters on the end of the table that Tom collected from town. Rosie skims through them and recognises some handwriting. Pulling the letter out, she opens it and begins to read.

To my dearest Rosie,

It is so good to hear from you. I feel doubt and strength in your words.

Sometimes I imagine a different life, a different path but I believe that my purpose was to serve not receive. I've seen the result of people's choices in life. I am happy with my choices. My life is safe, comfortable, and predictable; I'm protected and cared for.

You should be happy with your decisions, your life, your gifts and many blessings. As I have reminded you before, God has a plan for you. A path lies before you that is paved in gold. You are destined for greatness. We all have a path we must walk. It is not always easy but there is a purpose to it all.

In my thoughts and prayers, always.

Jassie

Clutching the letter to her chest, she holds the words like treasure.

I wish she were here. Oh, dear Jassie, she always knows the right thing to say. Thank you, God. Thank you for our Jassie.

'Oh Gracie girl, let's make a cuppa and have a rest. What do you think?' Rosie reaches down and pats her soft fur. Gracie looks up at her with adoring eyes, wagging her tail, her long hair sweeping the floor.

Sipping her tea, Rosie smiles, thinking of the day. Thinking of Billy's joy and excitement.

I'm so grateful for it all. I can't help but wish that Will was there with us today. He probably was, he is probably with us often, as often as he can.

Opening her journal, the image of the red tail fills her mind as the words drip onto the paper.

Spirit

In the darkest days
Through the darkest nights
The spirit lives on

There are many roads we may not walk
Questions left whispered on sorry lips

Forever unanswered

As the sun sets
Birds call their mournful cry
Wild horses gallop
The spirit defiantly lives on

Tears will flow like muddy rivers
Hearts will ache unbearable ache
Beneath impenetrable grey skies
Sadness burnt on ancient mountains
A burning wound festers

In the darkest days
Through our darkest nights
The spirit courageously lives on

Forever scarred

The spirit
The wild storm
Balm to our wounds
Drenching thirsty land

Words fail
Memories swirl
Spirit dances in the wild winds

In the darkest days
Through the longest, darkest nights

A wild spirit gallops
With the wild horses
Forever roaming free

COCOON

There is no greater agony than bearing an untold story inside you.
— Maya Angelou

Tom and Billy come inside for some afternoon tea before milking the cows.

'I was thinking we could go spotlighting tonight, something fun and different to do,' Rosie suggests.

'Oh please, Dad. Can we? Can we, please?' Billy is so excited and enthusiastic from the mention of the idea that Tom can't say no.

Tom rolls his eyes as he glances towards Rosie. 'Yeah, all right. As long as you don't make too much of a racket on the back.'

'I won't, I promise,' Billy says as he hangs off Tom's neck.

They arrive after dinner; Billy is a ball of energy and enthusiasm. They pack the ute. Rosie puts on her striped beanie and thick coat before climbing on the back. This evokes many memories from her childhood spotlighting with Blake and MJ.

Pa took us. Blake was such a good shot even when we were so young.

That's where Tom must get it from. MJ was always on the spotlight. I'm glad it's Friday night so Billy can afford to stay up late.

Rosie feels so much joy watching him there. Standing beside her, grinning. So happy to be going on this exciting adventure. Tom drives them along the road to the side of the mountain, near the thick bush. They crouch down out of the wind as they go around the road. They enter the furthest gate on the farm.

This is the rough country, where the paddocks meet the bush.

Rosie looks up the hill.

I can barely see anything. It's a dark night, best for shooting.

Billy jumps off and opens the gate. Tom drives slowly; Rosie casts the spotlight across the paddocks, along the ridges and the boundary of the bush.

'Stop dancing around, Billy,' Rosie tries to say quietly.

There is a rocky patch where rabbits are usually found. She casts the spotlight over the ground, slowly and smoothly, as she was taught as a young girl. There is a rabbit she spots in the headlights. Tom pulls up. Opens the door. Grabs the gun and leans it on the car door. Rosie darts the spotlight away momentarily, to make sure it's not scared, and then back on the rabbit. He takes aim and pulls the trigger. The rabbit drops to the ground.

Tom is a great shot. He barely ever misses.

Tom puts the gun down in the cabin. Billy jumps down and runs over to collect the rabbit. Rosie shines the spotlight on the lifeless rabbit as they collect it.

They continue along the scattered rocks filled with rabbit burrows in the paddock. They kill a few more rabbits. Billy is equally excited each time. The pile sits on the back of the ute. Blood trickles along the tray.

As they go over the ridge, Rosie shines the spotlight up a gully. It captures a fox stunned by the light. Standing fixated. Rosie puts the spotlight down and then back on the fox again. Their eyes meet, for a moment. Tom stops the ute in anticipation. Rosie darts the light away to give it a chance. It runs off into the night. Rosie chases it with the light. Relieved that it gets away.

Tom says, 'That healthy bugger would've made a good skin.'

'Yeah, he would've. I think I've seen it before.'

I know they are vermin. I know it's best to kill them, but this fox. I recognise its eyes.

Tom starts the ute. They keep going. They do a loop and see a couple of kangaroos that bounce away.

There is a possum in the tree near the gateway. Its bright eyes shine in the branch of the tree. Billy gets down and opens the gate as Rosie admires the possum climbing, clinging to the branches. Billy and Rosie crouch down out of the wind as they drive around the road. Rosie sees an old wombat, the one she thinks must live in the big hole near the culvert. Rosie shines the light and then they leave it alone, heading for home.

They arrive home and Tom parks at the front gate.

'Do you want to come in for a hot drink before you go home?' Rosie asks.

Before Tom can answer, Billy says, 'Yes,' and runs around the side veranda. Tom grins and grabs the rabbits off the back of the ute. He takes them out the back near the woodshed to gut and skin them. Rosie packs the spotlight away and follows Billy inside.

Tom brings the cleaned rabbits inside. He hands them to his mother.

'I'll make a nice stew out of these tomorrow,' Rosie says.

'Do youse wanna come out the back?' Tom asks. 'I want to show yas somethin.'

'What is it?' Billy asks impatiently.

'Well come out the back and have a look and you'll find out,' Tom replies.

The three of them walk outside, Tom leading the way. He leads them to the woodshed, telling them to be quiet. He lifts up a bag to reveal a cat and four kittens. 'Oh, look at the ginger one,' Billy says with excitement in his voice.

Rosie smiles. 'What a surprise, Milly girl. I'd wondered where you'd got to.'

They do not disturb her for long; they cover her over and go back inside. They sit at the table, sipping on their warm drinks. Billy begins making up names for the kittens and going over every detail of the spotlighting. Enjoying every moment, Rosie notices Tom's look of contentment on his face.

He looks in this moment like the young man I used to know. Before tragedy. Before life, the burden of responsibility made him hard. Before all his dreams were lost. Broken.

'Righto, Billy boy. We better get home.' Tom rises from his seat. Billy loudly departs, spreading his excitement along the paths as they walk along the verandah and out the front gate.

Tom is never one to stop and make small talk. Always on the move.

Retreating to bed, Rosie feels tired from the night air.

Sleeping soundly, she has a deep sleep with vivid dreams. Rosie sees the fox. Its penetrating eyes. It running past the swimming hole, wattle in the background. There is Tom reading Billy a letter, cuddled up. A pup races around at their feet, playing. A warm glow surrounds them. Then there is an image of Will as a little boy. He is racing through the bush and he is showing her the way. She follows, trying to catch up with him. They come to a waterfall.

When Rosie wakes in the morning, the dream is at the forefront of her mind. An impetus to search for the story she wrote when Will was around one year old.

I had suffered from postnatal depression and couldn't write anything for such a long time. I had written poetry all my life.

Frustration and panic surge through her body as she struggles to find it.

Surely I didn't throw it out. I never throw anything out. I know I haven't thrown it out.

She discovers it, finally. 'Aw, here it is, finally,' she says to herself. 'I knew it was here somewhere.'

I need to organise all these notes better.

Rosie reads the story with intrigue, as though they aren't her words.

I haven't thought about this in so long. I had forgotten I'd even written it. I guess it was about thirty-something years ago. It seems like yesterday. That vivid dream. I remember when I wrote this. I'd just started to recover. That first year with Will. Losing Pa. It was all so much.

Rosie remembers what it was like to see the sun shine again. For the depression to lift like the fog blanketed across the valley. Rosie reflects on what it felt like to find inspiration and understanding. To emerge from a cocoon, to fly, free. A beautiful, colourful butterfly, roaming; soaring to new heights.

Discovering Big Magic

The pregnant caterpillar was placed in the cocoon of motherhood and after a year of trials, tribulations and searching, she emerged as a beautiful butterfly to discover her big magic.

Her crown was found at the top of the final steep and dreadful climb through thick blackberries. Luckily, all the cuts and bruises came with the nourishment of their berries. The crown was rusted and damaged from the harsh winter weather. The storms of the spring. She picked it up and thought of days when she wore it so proudly, when it glimmered for all to see. She had been someone. She had been important. That seemed like a lifetime ago now. A distant memory of a kingdom she no longer needed.

She was now humbled by this journey into the wilderness. They were both thirsty as the sun beat down on them; she admired his beautiful golden curls as they glistened in the sun. Only for a moment. For now she knew there was work to be done. Work to build a new home at the top of her mountain. The mountain she had loved all her life. That protected her. That was her wilderness. Now she had conquered it; now she was ready to build a new kingdom for her and her prince.

She made a track, cutting away at the thick branches. As they cut her, she wiped the sweat and blood from her brow, knowing over the ridge there was water. Life giving, thirst-quenching water that would soothe her soul. Though fear and inspiration were on either side of her, pushing her to cut away in a fierce determination, she remained strong with resolve, dreaming of the cascading water. His hand was sweaty and all he wanted was to run ahead or behind but she kept her little prince close, comforting him with her words—her words of strength and guidance—as she kept her promise. I will always protect you. As she cut, she discovered a wild goat track below her blistered feet. They were gaining ground along the thin track where wild goats had once roamed. Their hooves leaving marks. Permanent imprints in the land. A sense of relief and excitement washed over them. They heard the roar. The big, powerful roar of the water as it rushed over the rocks, plummeting to a big pool of cool, refreshing water. They moved with greater speed, pushing aside the thick scrub that hung over the little goat track like a crocheted blanket. Her ragged clothes clung to her side and her tarnished crown would fall to the side but remained firmly on her head. The little prince called out with excitement and pointed as they climbed over the top of the ridge, which opened up into a wide-open chest of a valley protected by the arms of the ridges that lay either side. They laid their eyes on the majestic sight for the first time. Devoid of words. Left breathless. A huge. Awe inspiring. Imposing. Beautiful waterfall. It was a torrent of water. A creation. A miracle of soul-soothing creativity. They knew this was it. This was finally what they had searched for. This was big magic.

She held him tight. Rubbed his nose with hers ever so

gently. Looked deep into his big, beautiful brown eyes. They spoke without words. They just knew. It was time.

A warm, wild wind blew around them, not stirring the large gum trees buried in the banks. It circled them. Dancing at their feet. Wrapping around them, pushing them forward. Pushing them to the edge of the strong boulders that firmly sat beneath their tired feet. For a moment, she wanted to retreat to the safety of the kingdom below, but she took a deep breath, smelling the familiar scents of the bush, the smell of home. She felt the warmth of the hot, harsh summer sun on her olive skin and as the wind blew and sun beat down on them, the queen straightened her battered crown and her little prince clung to his strong mumma as they jumped. They propelled off the ledge into the wide-open expanse, feeling the spray from the powerful water rushing over the rocks beside them. They moved through the thick air with grace, like they had butterfly wings, inspiration and fear carrying them off the edge of the large rock face into the life-giving water of the big magic.

Within moments that felt like forever, they were suspended in between the safety of the rocks. Time stood still and the wild wind held them there momentarily before plummeting them into the safety of the deep, crystal-clear water. As they came to the surface, they gasped with the shock of the cold of the water. Taking a deep breath, they knew they had made it to the end of a long and hard journey. As they played, splashing and drinking the fresh, beautiful, clean, life giving, soul-soothing water, they were filled with happiness. They basked in a sense of relief and achievement. They knew their journey had come to an end, whilst feeling this was also just the beginning.

Sitting the story down at her desk, Rosie takes a deep breath. She walks into the kitchen and begins making a tea while wiping sleep from her eyes. She is thirsty, so she drinks the quenching water from the fridge. Taking the tea to her desk, she sits down to write.

How do I begin? What do I say? What do I leave out? I had the blessing of being raised by strong women, not perfect women. Unique in their strengths, flaws, daring to live their lives true to themselves. I want this to be about them. To honour them. For all the mad women rocking I've known and loved and for all to come. I want to tell my story, to leave them something. This is stupid, bloody crazy; I have nothing of value to say. Who would possibly care? Who would read it?

The image of Will running stirs a deep desire in her.

None of that matters. I know that it is time for me to begin. The crack in time. When it all shifted, broke apart.

The roar of a plane flying overhead interrupts her thoughts.

Carrying her fears, Rosie picks up her pen. She carefully opens her new leather-bound journal to the first page. As the ink marks the page, she feels inspiration and purpose flow through her as she writes.

Mad Woman Rocking
By Rosie Lane

For Mary Jayne

The wild wind, dancing through the old elm trees,

spoke of her bravery; it whispered signs of success. A woman who had always bitten off more than she could chew. Striving for brilliance.

Rosie drives along the road. A plane creates a long white streak across the sky. The radio plays.

I love this song.

Rosie turns up the volume.

ENDLESS GRATITUDE

Firstly, I am forever grateful to Natasha Gilmour, who saw potential in my humble manuscript. Who was instrumental in bringing my dream into reality. You have nurtured this dream and supported me throughout the process.

Thank you to the kind press team, especially Georgia for editing and Nada for creating the most perfect book cover.

To Stacey, Kalon, Murray, Grandma, Ger and Grandad, the ones I love in heaven. Thank you for inspiring me and being a guiding presence in my life.

To my sister, Emily, who has shared my journey and inspired me to keep revising and sending my manuscript out into the universe. Please remember, miracles do happen.

My soul sister Gina, who read the very first short story and then the first draft. Thank you for encouraging me to keep telling my story. Thank you for teaching me about the power of creativity. May we share many more stories.

My soul sister Em, who read an early draft. I will be forever grateful for your praise and understanding. You were a shining light who helped manifest these wings. May we never be afraid to dream big.

To my parents, I imagine raising a mad woman has been both a blessing and a curse. May you always know my endless love and gratitude for all you have been as my parents and my friends. I will be forever grateful for all your hard work and sacrifices.

To Alex and Cassie, thank you for being fundamental in building and living my dream on my mountain. Thank you for your love and support.

To Lee-Anne Hunt, thank you for your friendship and for all we have shared. The grief and the love of our Stace. May we always feel her presence.

To Lyn for having the courage to read this story. The story that holds our pain and our reality. Thank you for your support and unconditional love.

To my teachers, who changed my life. Who inspired my love for learning, art, literature and words. Who ignited my desire to write. Jose Miller, Melanie Seabourne, Helen Marshall, Fred Anderson, Richard Crees, Sue O'Neill, Helen Daly, Helen Hughes and Margaret Davis, I thank you.

Sarah and Jonathan, aka Wils and Parky, thank you! I couldn't ask for better friends. You have loved me in my darkest days and I would have been lost, then and now, without you.

My boys, Jake, Knox, Stuart, Gazza and John. I love you. Thank you for letting me always be one of the boys, in my own Fazza kind of way.

Angela, for your healing and guidance. Endless love and gratitude.

Sarah Elijah, who was there for me when I found the strength to write my book. You are a loyal, supportive friend who has walked a parallel path.

Renata, for dinners and lots of late-night chats. You have helped me find my wild woman, strength and courage. Especially assisted me to learn how to eat the chicken and not even feel guilty about it.

My girls-gone-wild crew, Catherine, Sarah, Nadia, Zan and Margie. Returning home, I never expected such an amazing group of women to be in my life. I am so grateful.

My aunties, who have all shown me examples of strong women. To my extended family. You have all had a significant part to play in my life and this I am very grateful for.

To the many families I have been a part of. My Pine Mountain family. Lyn, Jim, Chevy and Luka. Thank you for welcoming me into your family and letting me remain a part of it. The Towong Road family, the Pannach/Supermarket family, the Collins family, Peter, Jodie, Justin and Shannen, my Kew family, Anna, Couttie, Ros, Frances, Jonny and Keyan, the Campbell family, my St Joe's and Valdocco family. My London family, thank you, especially for all the craic with Damien and James.

To the boys of St Joe's and the students of Corryong College. Thank you for giving me a fresh start—a chance to truly discover my potential—and for teaching me so much.

To Father Carey, Lyn and Sister Pat, for nurturing my spiritual journey. Thank you.

Beau, my beloved boy. My wild child, you are an endless source of inspiration. Thank you for changing my life in the most profound ways. This journey would never have been possible without you. Words cannot describe the love and total awe I have for you. May you always see beauty in the world and bravely share your stories.

Lastly, to Elm Hill. While writing *Mad Woman Rocking*, I feared that you may be lost to us. I also dared to dream. A place that holds my stories, memories, my hopes and my dreams. My home. *Mad Woman Rocking* is because of you and for you.

ABOUT THE AUTHOR

Farrah B. Mandala lives in an off-grid eco cabin in the Australian bush, on her family's dairy farm at the foothills of the Snowy Mountains. She is an English teacher and lives with her five-year-old son, the laughter of kookaburras, a friendly willie wagtail and circling wedge-tailed eagles.

Farrah shares her poetry, writing and artwork on her blog at madwomandreaming.blogspot.com, on her website madwomanrocking.com and her Mad Woman Rocking Facebook and Instagram pages. With *Mad Woman Rocking,* she highlights the unique experiences of women in a story that's relevant, inspirational and quintessentially Australian.